Praise for The

"The opioid crisis creeps into every corner of America, so it's only fitting that it spills into the literary world in a chilling and chillingly realistic new book from a Missouri writer. . . . What McHugh does so well is create a realistic slice of life for a sizable part of America struggling with family problems, depression and inertia that stops them from taking charge of their lives. . . . She writes with authority on the unspoken rules and the social strata that are part of every town."

—*St. Louis Post-Dispatch*

"Calling all fans of *Sharp Objects* and the third season of *True Detective:* You need to read Laura McHugh, the literary queen of the emerging Ozark Noir genre."

—*Refinery29*

"Sometimes you pick up a book so beautifully written and resonant that you want to savor every word and swirl it around in your mouth like fine wine. Laura McHugh's third novel, *The Wolf Wants In,* is such a book. The combination of McHugh's lyrical yet vivid writing and her honest, insightful portrayal of grief results in a haunting story."

—*The Big Thrill*

"McHugh . . . delivers a disturbing story of an entire dysfunctional community affected by opioids. Fans of Julia Keller's 'Bell Elkins' books will appreciate this sobering, hard-hitting mystery."

—*Library Journal,* starred review

"In this intelligent thriller set in the opioid-ravaged town of Blackwater, Kans., . . . Sadie Keller and her sister, Becca, are desperate to know why their normally healthy brother, Shane, suddenly died. . . . Across town, 18-year-old Henley Pettit knows she will always be tainted by the 'knotted threads of her family's misdeeds' if she stays in Blackwater. . . . Henley desperately wants to start a new life anywhere else, away from her often-missing opioid-addicted mother and the crimes of her uncles. Elegant plotting, finely honed character studies, and lyrical prose draw the women's lives closer as Sadie and Henley deal with their own small-town ennui. This emotionally resonant tale will also appeal to literary-fiction readers."

—*Publishers Weekly*, starred review

"Laura McHugh's foray into southern gothic is a journey into the depths of rural Kansas, a hotbed of opioid and crime. . . . This atmospheric thriller finds . . . two women grappling with the weight of family history, loyalty, and justice, and is sure to grip anyone looking for a finely drawn, character-driven mystery that delves into the realities of rural America."

—*CrimeReads*, "The Most Anticipated Crime Books of Summer"

"Sadie's and Henley's voices, both marked by world-weary determination, add compelling dimension to this affecting opioid thriller."

—*Booklist*

"In a small, dead-end Kansas community devastated by the opioid epidemic, two young women grapple with dark family secrets. . . . Readers will become invested in the struggles of the well-drawn lead protagonists; the stoic and resourceful Henley will especially remind Daniel Woodrell fans of Ree Dolly, the heroine of *Winter's Bone*. . . . atmospheric grit lit with emotional depth."

—*Kirkus Reviews*

BY LAURA McHUGH

The Weight of Blood
Arrowood
The Wolf Wants In

THE WOLF WANTS IN

RANDOM HOUSE
NEW YORK

THE
WOLF
WANTS
IN

A NOVEL

LAURA
McHUGH

2020 Random House Trade Paperback Edition

Copyright © 2019 by Laura McHugh
Book club guide copyright © 2020 by Penguin Random House LLC

Published in the United States by Random House, an imprint and division of Penguin Random House LLC, New York.

Random House and the House colophon are registered trademarks of Penguin Random House LLC. Random House Book Club and colophon are trademarks of Penguin Random House LLC.

Originally published in hardcover in the United States by Spiegel & Grau, an imprint of Random House, a division of Penguin Random House LLC, in 2019.

"Where the Darkness Comes From" by Laura McHugh reprinted by permission of Powells.com.

Library of Congress Cataloging-in-Publication Data
Names: McHugh, Laura, author.
Title: The wolf wants in: a novel / Laura McHugh.
Description: New York: Spiegel & Grau, an imprint of Random House, a division of Penguin Random House LLC, [2019]
Identifiers: LCCN 2018043805| ISBN 9780399590290 (paperback) | ISBN 9780399590306 (ebook)
Classification: LCC PS3613.C5334 W65 2019 | DDC 813/.6—dc23
LC record available at https://lccn.loc.gov/2018043805

Printed in the United States of America on acid-free paper

randomhousebooks.com
randomhousebookclub.com

1 2 3 4 5 6 7 8 9

Book design by Elizabeth A. D. Eno

For my family, with love

THE WOLF WANTS IN

CHAPTER 1

SADIE

NOVEMBER

A bitter wind sheared through the darkness, biting into my exposed flesh and lashing my hair across my face. I'd stupidly worn flip-flops to take the dog out one last time before bed, and my feet were half numb as I stumbled along the path at the edge of the woods. Gravy had been lured out for a walk fairly easily with a heel of bread but predictably turned sluggish when I tried to maneuver him up the sloping field back toward the house. I couldn't blame him; my place didn't feel like home to him yet, the wood floors too slippery, the stairs too steep for his stubby legs, the furniture not yet sufficiently covered with his fur. I wiggled the leash, begging him to hurry up and pee, knowing full well how futile it was, that the elderly dog would wet himself in his sleep no matter how many times I took him out. The wind receded without warning, pulling me off balance, and in the merciful lull the night was eerily silent, as though all the creatures in the blind depths of the cedars were holding still, waiting out the storm.

My phone buzzed and I nearly dropped it, my frozen fingers skittering across the glowing screen. When I saw that it was Becca, I didn't want to answer, because my sister only called this late if she'd seen something awful on the ten o'clock news or if someone we knew had died. Less than a month ago, she'd called about Shane.

"Do you have the news on?" she asked. She was whispering, as she always did when Jerry and the boys were asleep, and I could barely hear her.

"No, what happened?" I stamped my feet, trying to revive feeling in them. Gravy's pace had slowed from maddeningly snail-like to standstill. He watched the tree line, his tail low, a pale specter in the darkness.

"Hunters found a human skull in the woods outside Blackwater. They're not saying too much, but the lady said it was small . . . like a child's. Maybe Macey Calhoun's."

My gut hollowed out and I bent over, feeling like I might vomit. Macey's absence had mostly faded from my thoughts, the way other people's tragedies tend to do in the face of our own problems. I had brought a chocolate pie over to Hannah Calhoun after her husband had disappeared with their daughter, not knowing how else to help an old friend I'd barely spoken to in years. It had gone as uncomfortably as I expected it would, Hannah accepting my offering and shutting the door without saying a word, consumed by her loss and uninterested in my sympathy.

Macey and Lily had attended preschool together in the basement of Shade Tree Methodist from the time they were babies until Lily left for kindergarten. Hannah and I had been close then, bound by our daughters and the common struggles of new marriage and mother-hood. Hannah had recognized my ineptitude in styling Lily's hair and took pity, teaching me to French-braid and making enormous bows for Lil to match the ones Macey wore every day. Macey would be nine now, almost ten, more than a year behind Lil, who only vaguely re-membered their preschool friendship when the Amber Alert shrieked out of my phone this past spring and I told her that Macey was missing.

The bitterness of the Calhouns' divorce and ensuing custody battle was public knowledge, but I'd assured Lily that Macey was safe with her father, who disappeared with her during a weekend visitation, and I'd believed it. I had lost touch with Hannah before our marriages fell apart, hadn't been there for her in any way until the awkward pie, and I didn't know what to do for her now. I ached for her, what she must be going through, waiting to hear if the skull belonged to her child.

"You still there?" Becca asked.

"Yeah," I said. "I hope it's not her."

"They could be wrong." Becca always held out hope for happy end-ings long after most people gave up, her optimistic gene a fluke in a family of cynics. "Maybe the skull's not even human."

"Maybe," I said, turning my back to the wind, my ears stinging.

"Kendrick might have to cancel your meeting tomorrow."

"Yeah. I'll let you know." So far, Detective Kendrick hadn't been terribly helpful in our effort to make sense of all the unanswered ques-tions surrounding Shane's death. When I first asked to meet with her, she'd told me she had *real* work to do, as if the sudden passing of a thirty-six-year-old didn't warrant even the briefest examination. True, it wasn't unusual for someone to die young in Cutler County—there had been so many overdoses in recent years that an article in *The Kan-sas City Star* bemoaned the decimation of the next generation of farmers—but our brother wasn't an addict. Kendrick had only agreed to meet with me on the condition that I would stop calling, and now she had every reason to blow me off. As much as I wanted to know what had happened to Shane, I couldn't blame her if the sheriff's department focused its limited resources on the discovery in the woods.

"I've got to get inside," I said. "I'm freezing. I'll drop Gravy off in the morning."

Gravy showed no sign that he heard his name, his attention focused on divining scents in the night air. I bent to pick him up, the one thing guaranteed to rile him, and as he squirmed away from me, I was able to shepherd him back up the hill.

It was a relief to get out of the wind, even if it wasn't exactly toasty in the drafty farmhouse. I wedged a few sticks and a thick block of wood into the stove and prodded a ball of newspaper into the embers, my cheeks burning as the radiating heat began to thaw them. Ribbons of flame curled up the kindling, persuading the split edge of the log to ignite.

Shane was the one who had taught me how to make a fire, back when we were kids. We had run away once, when I was six and he was nine, scared that Dad would whip us when he discovered we'd knocked Grandma Keller's angel figurine off the living room shelf and broken its wing. It was cold that day, too, and we only made it as far as the field behind the barn. Shane showed me how to build a fire with dead leaves and a rotten branch and the matches he'd been clever enough to bring along, and when it turned dark, he sang Christmas songs to keep me from crying, promising to take all the lashes himself if Dad caught us, though I knew it was never that easy. Becca came to find us for supper and led us back to the house, where she unearthed an old tube of superglue and reattached the angel's wing before Dad got home.

We had our roles, even then. Becca, duty bound, quietly fixing things; Shane, both troublemaker and protector. I was the baby, desperate to grow up and get out, though in the end, I hadn't gotten much farther than when Shane and I had run away—the other side of Shade Tree from the house we grew up in.

I was on the road by daybreak to meet Detective Kendrick before work, dropping Gravy at Becca's house with a bag of pee pads he refused to lie on and a basket of toys that he hadn't touched since he'd come to stay with me. Becca and her boys liked having him over to visit— having Shane's dog there made it feel like he was still around—but I was secretly grateful Becca's husband was allergic, so I could keep Gravy most of the time. He'd been a welcome addition, the house too empty now that Lily was staying with her dad during the week to attend the suburban middle school that he'd insisted was better than the one in Shade Tree.

As I started down the highway toward Blackwater, I tuned in to the local talk-radio program, hoping to hear more about the skull in the woods, but there was no new information.

The leaden sky lightened a few shades as the sun climbed above the dead fields, the towering silos of Sullivan Grain, where my dad had worked until the day he died, rising in the distance. The highway used to run straight through town, but a new spur bypassed it altogether, crossing the river while the old road wound north through Main Street. Blackwater was the county seat and the anchor of our small constellation of Kansas farming towns beyond the Kansas City suburbs, communities connected through high school sports rivalries and livestock auctions and the shared Walmart out on the highway.

There were no stoplights downtown, only four-way intersections where manners dictated that two drivers arriving at the same time would insist, through a series of patient hand gestures, that the other person go first. Main Street had shriveled as the suburbs expanded their reach and their offerings, but thanks to the grain elevator and the jobs it provided, many local businesses were still thriving, including the Blackwater Diner, the Feed & Supply, and Why Not Donuts, beloved for its old-fashioned cream horns. There were two gas stations on

Main, though Casey's was the only one where you'd dare use the bathroom—it wasn't unheard-of to find someone passed out on the toilet with a needle jammed in a vein at the Conoco—and you couldn't turn your head without seeing a church. It was downright bustling compared to Shade Tree's lifeless town square. If I turned off on a gravel road north of Casey's and followed it past Pettit Brothers Auto Body & Salvage, I would end up at Shane's house, where he had died. Instead, I parked in front of the Cutler County courthouse and headed into the police station to meet Detective Kendrick.

I was sent back to her office, where I caught her with her hand on the knob. "Hi," I said. "Detective Kendrick? I'm Sadie Keller." The nameplate on the door revealed that her first name was Lacey, and the look of exasperation on her face, as well as an audible groan, made it clear that she'd forgotten about our meeting.

"Not a good time," she said, her voice sharp but slightly less nasal in person.

She didn't look at all like I'd imagined her over the phone. She was petite and wiry and wholesomely pretty, like a scrappy Girl Scout, her lithe frame bundled in a puffy down coat, auburn hair swirled around her shoulders like she'd just come in from the wind.

"Five minutes? I know you're busy."

She pulled a tube of Carmex from her coat pocket and swiped it across her lips, the sting of menthol scenting the air.

"Please?"

She groaned again, shoving open the door like she was storming a crack den and motioning for me to sit in a chair with a duct-taped armrest. There was nothing remotely personal among the neat stacks of papers and files on her desk, no family pictures, no knickknacks. A medal from the Kansas City Marathon hung from a coat hook on the wall.

"All right," she said, sitting down but keeping her coat on. "Clock's ticking. What is it you think I can help you with?"

"We just want to know what happened the day Shane died. We haven't been able to get any information. If you could tell us what you know, whatever details you might have, that'd be a huge help."

"You've talked to his wife, right? She could probably tell you more than what's in the report."

"We tried," I said. "That's the problem. She hasn't been terribly . . . communicative since he passed." My eyes filled at the word "passed," as they still did sometimes, and I blinked to keep any tears from spilling out.

Kendrick breathed heavily through her nose, her nostrils flaring. "All right." She unearthed a folder and opened it, reading in a brisk monotone. "He went to work that morning as usual. Reported to his supervisor that he wasn't feeling well, and left early. When his wife arrived home that evening, she found him unresponsive. She declined to perform CPR, per the 911 dispatcher, claiming he was already cold. Prescriptions for high blood pressure and high cholesterol were found in the home, indicative of heart disease. Wife indicated that deceased's father had also died of a heart attack. She declined an autopsy, and the coroner ruled natural causes." She looked up. "That's all I've got."

"So he didn't for sure have a heart attack? It was just assumed? Why would she decline an autopsy?" Crystle, Shane's wife of one year, hadn't said anything about it.

Kendrick tossed the folder onto the desk. "Autopsies aren't cheap. County sure as hell can't afford it, so it would've come out of her pocket. I'd be shocked if somebody *did* ask for one. Especially when it appears to be a natural death."

"So they decided natural causes based on prescriptions they found? Are they sure they were his?" Shane had never had any health problems, to our knowledge, aside from a bad back.

Kendrick checked her watch. "I don't have that information," she said. "You'd have to get his wife's permission to see his records. Look, I've got to get back to work." There was a flicker of weariness on her face, her eyes darting away, and I wondered if it had something to do with the skull, if she already knew more than was shared on the news. When she spoke again, her voice softened slightly. "I'm sorry for your loss. I know it's difficult, not having the answers you want, not knowing every little detail. But you've got a body. You had a funeral. That's more than some people get."

It was dark when I left work. Spending all day in a windowless office at the health department left me starved for daylight, and it would only get worse as November wore on and the morning commute turned dark, too. I loved my job, or at least the idea of it—social work was highly rewarding, though it was depressing at times, the terrible things you'd see, the knowledge that no matter how hard you tried, you couldn't fix everything. The fallout from the drug epidemic had introduced new problems and compounded existing ones. Older people who would normally turn to their families for help now had children or grandchildren stealing their money and pills, and when those kids overdosed or went to rehab or prison, they left behind babies the grandparents were ill-equipped to raise.

On the way home, I called Lily to ask about her day. She spoke in run-on sentences, her voice squeaking with anxiety as she detailed a difficult social studies assignment and recounted, word for word, an incident in the school cafeteria where someone she thought was a friend had made fun of her lunchbox. I smashed down the maternal desire to turn my car toward the city and go get her and wondered for the thousandth time whether it had been the right decision to let her switch schools.

I heard Greg in the background, cajoling the baby to swallow her rice cereal instead of spitting it back at him. He was much more patient and indulgent with his new daughter than he'd been with Lily when she was little, and I hoped Lil was oblivious to that fact, that it didn't cut into her the way it did me. I had insisted that Greg include her in the new family portrait he had taken with Heidi and baby Caroline, though it selfishly pained me to think of Lily in some other family without me.

"Mom? Dad wants to talk to you for a sec."

"I love you, sweetie," I said, but she had already handed the phone to Greg.

"Hey, Sadie. I hope you mailed that check for your part of Lily's school trip. The deposit's due Monday."

He might have developed a more easygoing attitude with his second family, but it didn't extend to me. I had sent the check on time—I always did, not that it would cause Greg any hardship if it came late. He had made partner at his firm and lived in a McMansion in a neighborhood of blandly reimagined French châteaus and marble fountains. We had planned to go through law school together but couldn't swing it without one of us working, so I'd supported him with the understanding that I would start when he finished. Everything changed when I unexpectedly got pregnant with Lily. Greg had assumed that I'd want to stay home with our baby, and I didn't know why he would assume that. It wasn't something I'd mentioned or even considered, but he insisted it would be impossible to care for an infant with him working and me in school, that I was being selfish. We'd moved to Shade Tree as a concession, so I could be close to my family.

Greg met his new wife, Heidi, at work—she was a lawyer who taught yoga on the side—and I wondered if he would pressure her to stay home when her leave was up, or if he'd softened his attitude on that, too, and would simply hire a nanny. Heidi wasn't the type to let Greg push her into anything, or make decisions for her, as I'd so often let him do for me.

I was grateful now for the time I'd had with Lily, regardless of how everything else had turned out. Greg had wanted to have more children right away and I'd wanted to wait, and as time went by, our marriage became as frustrating as the baby sweater I'd tried to knit for

Lil—a few dropped stitches, a pulled thread, and it was suddenly completely unrecognizable from the pattern I'd attempted to follow.

Becca had Gravy ready to go when I stopped to pick him up.

"I'm worried about him," she said. "He barely ate anything, but he threw up twice. I don't think that special senior food you got agrees with him. I gave him some of the Gravy Train we got from Shane's."

"Okay. Sorry he was sick."

"I almost called you earlier," she said. "It was awful—I thought he was dead. I dropped a biscuit pan on the floor right next to his head, and he didn't even flinch. And he's been peeing in his sleep, too," Becca murmured. "On the carpet or wherever he is. He peed on the new couch."

Gravy looked like an awkward cross between a Saint Bernard and a dachshund. He had shaggy brown and white fur, a flat snout, and drooping jowls. His legs were maybe four inches long and he could barely manage to balance his fat-laden body on top of them at times, yet he could somehow leap up onto the one piece of furniture Becca cared about. It seemed downright miraculous, and possibly spiteful.

"His vet appointment's next week," I said. "Maybe he's supposed to be on some kind of medication and Crystle didn't bother to tell us."

Becca was silent for a moment, picking hairs off Gravy's leash. I chewed on a hangnail, wishing the conversation wouldn't go where it was about to go.

"What did Kendrick say? Anything we didn't already know?"

"Yeah, actually. She said the coroner assumed it was a heart attack based on some prescriptions they found."

"So . . . is that our answer, then? But he never said he was having trouble. Why didn't he tell us? How long had he been having problems?"

"I don't know," I said. "We'd have to get Crystle's permission to see his records. Maybe he didn't say anything because he didn't want us to worry. Because of Dad." Our father had suffered a fatal heart attack at the grain elevator, time card in hand to clock out, still several years from retirement. It was fitting that he'd put in a full day's work before collapsing, and his death wasn't much of a shock given his refusal to quit smoking after bypass surgery. In many ways it was a relief. We no longer had to worry about Mom, the sole target of his volatile temper after Shane and Becca and I had graduated and moved out. Even after he was gone, a pit of dread would sometimes open up inside me when I entered my parents' house, and I'd have to remind myself that there was nothing to be afraid of.

The volume on the kitchen TV spiked abruptly and Jerry hollered from somewhere in the house for the boys to turn it down. Becca lowered her voice, even though no one could hear us. "Did you talk to her about Crystle?"

"Not really," I said. "She shut that down pretty well last time, on the phone."

I'd told Kendrick about Crystle's behavior at the funeral, about her not calling us when Shane died—how she'd accidentally dialed Becca hours later, a clamor of voices in the background, his body already gone. She'd dismissed my concerns with annoyance. *Fake tears aren't a crime*, Kendrick had said. *Not everybody cries. People grieve differently. Real life isn't like cop shows on TV.*

I'd left the furnace on all day to keep the pipes from freezing, but once I got home I turned it back down and made a fire. We'd never used the woodstove when Greg was here, but after he left, I figured it would help save on heating bills. I remembered the unpleasant childhood tasks of hauling wood and dumping ash, my clothes smelling like smoke after hanging laundry by the stove to dry, but I'd forgotten the good parts, the pleasure of basking in the intense wall of heat, of listening to the fire.

I got Gravy settled on Lily's old sleeping bag in the living room and moved an assortment of potted plants from the coffee table so I could eat a Lean Cuisine in front of the TV. The plants had come from Shane's funeral, two glossy peace lilies and one shriveled African violet. They were supposed to go to Mom, but she couldn't stand to look at them because they reminded her that Shane was gone. I'd saved the cards so we could write thank-you notes, which I still hadn't gotten around to doing.

The larger lily was from the power plant in Kansas City where Shane had worked for the past ten years as a welder. The other one was from Dave and Carla Gorecki. Dave had been one of his coworkers, the only one I'd met at the funeral. The lone violet, in a small woven basket, was from a Leola Burdett. The name was familiar, though I couldn't quite place it.

The smell of my dinner roused Gravy and he wriggled to his feet, sniffing my tray and then lumbering over to the door.

"You want to go out?" I asked. I clipped on his leash and opened the door, but he backed up and wouldn't budge. He stared out into the darkness, the chill wind lifting his ears, nose twitching.

I looked toward the woods but couldn't make out anything beyond the reach of the porch light. There was a far-off screech of a ghost-faced barn owl swooping through the trees, the hushed scurrying of unseen things, the plaintive howl of a dog or coyote. When I was little, Dad had convinced me that a coyote he shot dead in the field was actually a young wolf making its way toward the house. He claimed that wolves in the woods could tear a little girl like me limb from limb. Shane had stood behind him, shaking his head. *It's a lie,* he'd whispered later, squeezing my hand in the darkness when I couldn't sleep. *He's just trying to scare you. Wolves only eat bad people.*

I thought of the skull, of whomever it belonged to lying alone in the woods night after night as the moon came and went, scavengers going about their solemn work, and hoped that Hannah Calhoun would never have to think of Macey in the past tense the way I still had trouble doing with Shane.

CHAPTER 2

HENLEY

JULY

FOUR MONTHS EARLIER

M ost people in Cutler County could recount the highlights of
the Sullivan family's tragic history off the top of their heads.
They knew that Harlan Sullivan had stabbed his ten-year-old daughter, Emily, to death with a pitchfork, accidentally, when she hid in the
haymow to surprise him. They knew that Harlan's son, Earl, had given
up college to help run the family business when Harlan fell ill, and
that Earl's wife, Daphne, had died of cancer when their son, Jason, was
six years old. And whether or not people knew Jason personally, they
knew he was arrogant and spoiled, a gifted but lazy athlete, and a disappointment to his father.

Folks in Blackwater had grown up under the gaze of Emily Sullivan's statue in Sullivan Park and made their living working at Sullivan Grain or in its shadow. They relied on Earl Sullivan to sponsor the local Little League and to bid ridiculous amounts for homemade pies at the annual Fourth of July auction that paid for the fireworks display. Every spring, Earl sponsored the Emily Sullivan Memorial Essay Contest at Blackwater Elementary, inspired by the virtues his older sister had modeled in her short life. She had been a champion barrel racer in her age division, the only girl, and had survived a brutal fall, returning to competition as soon as the doctor would allow. After hearing a sermon about helping the less fortunate, she had boxed up all but a few of her dresses and shoes and hauled them to church in her wagon—a distance of several miles—to donate to orphans.

When Henley was younger, she had been fascinated by Emily's legend. She'd stood in the park face-to-face with Emily's statue and imagined what it would be like to have this fierce girl as her friend. When the river swelled and spilled over the floodplain, she thought of Emily in the park, alone and unafraid, water creeping over her bare feet, up to her knees, covering her dress and her resolute lips, unwavering as she kept watch over the town. And then Henley grew older and thought how unfair it was that Emily, who was dust in the grave, who had never been to Sullivan Park, which hadn't existed when she was alive, had her likeness rooted in one spot for eternity, to be defiled by birds and humped by drunk high school boys and drowned at the whim of the river. The poor girl hadn't lived long enough to disappoint anyone, and that had sealed her fate. Decades later, townspeople were still leaving flowers at her feet on Memorial Day, writing essays about her in school, and, in the case of Hannah Calhoun, standing before her statue on the news as she pleaded for her husband to return their nine-year-old daughter—tearfully invoking Emily, as if she were the patron saint of Amber Alerts.

In fifth grade, Henley had won the essay contest, imagining that Emily, had she lived, would have grown up to be mayor. She'd found the idea boldly optimistic at the time and now sadly pathetic—because she hadn't given Emily higher aspirations, and because, still, no woman in Blackwater had ever run for mayor. The essay prize was a hundred-dollar savings bond and a trip to the state capitol, which she had missed because her mother, Missy, had gotten the days mixed up.

Missy had a connection to the Sullivan family, like everyone else, though hers was more personal. She'd started keeping house for Earl as a teen after working in a summer jobs program he'd sponsored and had kept it up ever since, Earl generously welcoming her back every time she relapsed, disappeared, and then got clean again. Harlan had built the stately red-brick Colonial before he'd fallen ill, though he insisted on keeping the original Sullivan homestead—a shack, more or less—on the property as a reminder of their humble beginnings. Earl had had the big house completely renovated when he got married, rather late in life by Blackwater standards, after years of tomcatting around. That was in the eighties, and it was still a shrine to the style of that era, like the set of a John Hughes movie, a monument to his wife, Daphne, a one-time runner-up for Miss Kansas who had come to town to teach preschool and captured his wayward heart. Henley had grown up hearing stories about Jason, who was four years older than she was, from her mother. Missy viewed him by turns with exasperation, pity, and affection, likening him to a feral kitten that would spit and scratch, scared to let you see that it wanted to get close to you.

Henley's family, the Pettits, were well known in Blackwater, too, though for different reasons. Henley's grandpa was a drinker and ended up losing most of the family farm. His three sons, Henley's uncles, were delinquents from the start, graduating from schoolyard fights to petty theft to shady business ventures, or at least accusations of such, and his three daughters didn't fare much better, the two oldest girls marrying farmhands and birthing an ever-expanding crop of mischievous boys. His youngest, Missy—who'd surprised them by showing up when the other kids were nearly grown—had gotten pregnant with Henley at seventeen, father unknown. Each year on the first day of school, Henley's teachers had groaned when they called roll and saw her last name. Everyone in Blackwater knew a Pettit when they saw one, the honey-blond hair and wide hazel eyes, the freckles and sturdy frames, their genes refusing to be watered down over generations.

Earl Sullivan was no doubt seen as saintly for employing Missy. She owned her reputation by then, wearing rumors like illicit Girl Scout badges, and was glad for the opportunity he gave her, not just to earn a living, but to spend her days surrounded by fancy things— monogrammed silverware made of actual silver, an espresso machine that steamed your milk, central air conditioning—that she herself would never have.

Recently, Missy had hit a milestone, a two-year stretch of sobriety, which she and Henley had celebrated with cream horns from Why Not Donuts. Missy had started attending the Free Will Church again and mused optimistically about becoming a massage therapist or en- rolling in a vocational program to get certified in medical billing. Earl had offered to help her if she wanted to go back to school. Certain that better things were right around the corner, she decided to train Henley to take over the housekeeping for the Sullivans. Henley, who had just finished high school, had other plans, but they required money, which she didn't have, so she humored Missy and tagged along.

Her first day on the job was memorable, if nothing else. She was mortified when she pushed the vacuum into Jason Sullivan's bedroom, thinking the house was empty, and saw Jason stretched across the bed on his stomach, fast asleep, his lanky body bare as the day God made him. Her startled squeak woke him and he rolled onto his side, rub- bing sleep from his eyes as she tried to fumble backward with the vac- uum.

"What the hell?" he said, blinking at her.

"Sorry-sorry-sorry," she chanted, trying not to look at him, running the vacuum over her toe as she yanked it into the hall and wrenched the door shut. She heard him laughing.

"Well, good morning to you, too!" he called out. She flipped him off from behind the door.

It was hard to believe that had only been a week ago, one day before Missy relapsed, snorting crushed oxy off the coffee table and lighting out before dawn—or maybe Missy had been on the way down well before that, and Henley hadn't been paying close enough attention. They'd grown complacent in the airy farmhouse with the porch swing at the edge of what used to be Pawpaw's cornfield. The farm hadn't belonged to the Pettits in years, and the three boys had long since taken up residence near the salvage yard, but the small notch of land with the house, not worth much on its own, still belonged to the family, and Henley and her mother lived there for free—sometimes without electricity and running water if Missy forgot to pay—because Missy was the baby of the family, sweet and helpless as a knob-kneed foal, never quite strong enough to stand on her own.

Henley didn't know where Missy was now. When her mother was gone, the farmhouse was quiet, no Fleetwood Mac blaring in the kitchen while Missy burned popcorn on the stove and sang along in her clear, haunting voice, belting out the refrain like she was Stevie Nicks.

Henley opened the wide windows and listened as the corn whispered all around. She felt safe here, surrounded by the fields, the vast expanse of shuffling leaves the closest thing she'd seen to an ocean. The house still had some of Memaw's old furniture—the pieces Missy hadn't sold off—and her dainty crocheted doilies, yellowed with age, were still draped on the backs of the armchairs. The bathroom upstairs, with the baby blue toilet and tub, still held the lingering scent of Brylcreem and powder, though Memaw and Pawpaw had been gone for years, moving first to a state-run nursing home and then to the Blackwater cemetery.

Henley picked Pawpaw's old road atlas up off the floor and arranged herself in the love seat by the window, her bare feet resting on the sill, with a view of what used to be the Pettits' barn. She would miss the farmhouse and her family and the fields, but none of it was anything she couldn't live without. Charlie had already left town to attend welding school two hours away, rendering her lonely and bored and slightly hurt that her best friend had gotten out of Blackwater before she had, that she was the one left behind.

Their parting had been uncharacteristically awkward. There'd been an undeniable undercurrent of something more than friendship for a while now, and at times they'd crossed the line without admitting that it meant anything. Or rather, she hadn't admitted that it meant anything to her. Charlie had let her know how he felt, but he didn't press her for any sort of declaration or commitment. He had kissed her when he said goodbye, a real kiss, and she hadn't quite kissed him back, though as soon as he left, she wished that she had. She didn't know why she'd held back, except that it scared her a little to have something that might tether her close to home. They didn't talk about it in their late-night phone conversations, which weren't as frequent now that he was busy with school. Lately they had mostly been talking about Charlie's classes, and Missy, and she'd told him about her job at the Sullivans', about walking in on Jason. Charlie had called him a tool and changed the subject.

Charlie was supposed to call her tonight, but he hadn't yet. She flipped through the atlas to Colorado, tracing the ridges where the mountains were, gauging the elevation. She knew the air got cooler and thinner the higher you went, and that sounded good to her—breath that wasn't weighted with humidity and heat and the ever-present stink of fertilizer. All her life she had favored the cold, craving a true winter with lingering snow, not the schizophrenic Midwestern version interspersed with seventy-degree days that awakened mosquitoes in December and tricked plants into budding too soon, only to kill them with the next hard freeze. Missy hated cold weather, wishing she could wear sundresses and flip-flops year-round, and she'd once offhandedly remarked that Henley must have gotten her cold-bloodedness from her father, a statement Henley had dissected a dozen different ways in her diary, not sure if Missy was being literal or figurative (her mother had rolled her eyes when she asked).

She had wanted to leave for some time now, to take in the world beyond this stifling, landlocked place known for grain and Jesus and tornadoes, where everyone knew she was a Pettit and what that was supposed to mean. There was no chance that she would end up like Emily Sullivan, unwilling angel, forever trapped in Blackwater; she would rather leave everything behind and be forgotten.

CHAPTER 3

SADIE

NOVEMBER

I hated to miss any of my time with Lily, but I could tell how excited she was to be invited to a birthday sleepover with friends from her new school. They'd be going into Kansas City on Saturday, visiting the Nelson-Atkins museum, staying at a fancy hotel on the Plaza. A world away from the sort of sleepovers she'd had in Shade Tree, but a thousand times better than dragging her along with me, Mom, and Becca to help clear out Shane's house.

I'd been dreading this day, hoping it wouldn't be as bad as the first time we'd gone up there, to collect Gravy, days after Shane died. Crystle was in a rush to unload the poor dog, who flinched when she tried to pat him on the head. She'd told us on the phone that she simply wasn't able to care for him on her own. When she saw Becca's tears, though, the neediness in our mother's eyes, she had waffled. *I don't know if I can let him go. He's all I have left of my husband.*

She told us that when Shane's body was lying on the floor, Gravy had climbed into her lap to comfort her, something I didn't believe because the dog shrank away every time she got near him. That was one of the few details she shared about the night he died, claiming it was too difficult to talk about. We left empty-handed, but she ended up calling us back before we got a mile down the road. She acted as though it was the most charitable thing she had done in her life, giving us an incontinent dog that didn't seem to like her. When we asked if he had any food to take along, she stared at us blankly. She didn't know, she said, where Shane kept it, leaving us to wonder if Gravy had eaten in the past two days, though Becca easily located the bag of Gravy Train in the garage on our way out.

Today, Crystle had told us to arrive no earlier than ten, though there were already a slew of cars parked in the grass as Becca turned the van into the driveway at a quarter till. We passed through a stand of post oaks and the house came into view. It was clad in dark wood and resembled a rustic hunting lodge, perfect for Shane. He'd liked how it was set back among the trees, hidden from the road.

As we approached the house, I was surprised to see strangers crisscrossing the yard like industrious insects, carrying boxes to their cars, staring at us like we were trespassing. I assumed they were friends and relatives of Crystle's but wasn't sure why they were hauling things out of Shane's house, or why Crystle was letting them. In the driveway, a teenage boy with a mask of freckles and acne, dressed head to toe in camouflage, dug through my brother's toolbox with the fervor of a kid tearing into a Christmas stocking. A bearded man in coveralls hustled past us, toting a hydraulic jack and loading it into a hatchback car that was already stuffed with hunting gear and fishing tackle.

Crystle lumbered out of the garage in an off-the-shoulder top and jeans so tight she must have rolled them on like a condom. Shane had always been drawn to tough, sturdy girls, those with the stomach to field dress a deer and the strength to drag the carcass through the woods, and Crystle was the rare example who did those things in full makeup, her long hair aggressively streaked with Clairol highlights and styled to beauty-queen perfection with an arsenal of straightening and curling irons. Practicality prevailed, though, when it came to her nails. She kept them short, telling me once that acrylics got in the way, that fake nails were for prissy bitches who were afraid to get their hands dirty. It wasn't hard to understand what Shane had seen in her, the grit and the curves and the attitude, though I wished we'd had a chance to get to know her beyond the barbed surface. Becca and I had been ex-cited at the prospect of a sister-in-law, certain we'd like anyone who loved our brother, but Shane had come around less and less often after he started seeing Crystle and hadn't introduced her to us until they were engaged.

"God, I'm backed up," Crystle said, by way of greeting. She pressed a palm to her belly. "Everything's been thrown off, you know? Anyway. There's some stuff in the back bedroom you might want, stuff I don't care about. Here." She thrust a jar of Miracle Whip toward my mom. "You want it? Shane bought it right before he died. I can't stand this crap."

Mom, whose face had rarely registered anything other than slack grief since Shane's death, stared at her, uncomprehending. "It's not expired or nothing," Crystle grunted indignantly, and finally Mom's hand fluttered open to receive the jar. A scrawny, meth-eaten woman with ruined teeth and blood-red hair came up to whisper in Crystle's ear and they both turned around and went back inside.

"Oh, my word," Becca murmured, nudging me. Off in the side yard, a bonfire burned, a wide circle of embers pulsing around it. The air shimmered with its heat. A jumble of boxes, maybe empty, maybe not, waited their turn to be tossed into the flames. They had been at it for a while, the crowd of bustling strangers dismantling Shane's life. I hated to think how much of him had already been reduced to ash.

The front door was propped open, and we stepped inside to find an elderly man in a Kansas City Chiefs cap balanced on a ladder, taking things down off the wall. I had no idea who he was and he didn't offer any introduction. Three of Shane's framed drawings hung above the doorway, and my mom stared at them balefully. While Shane had been a below-average student in nearly every subject thanks to a maddening disregard for schoolwork, art class had revealed a natural talent.

"We want those," I said to the man, pointing. He eyed the nearest sketch, an assignment outside of Shane's standard repertoire of muscle cars and machinery: a cluster of bearded irises from Mom's front garden. I remembered the day Shane brought it home from school, all of us shocked, Mom flushing with quiet pride. The note on the back from the art teacher, next to the only A I could remember my brother receiving: *You are full of surprises.*

"You sure?" the geezer on the ladder snarked. His canine teeth were missing, giving him a rabbitlike appearance when he spoke. "It ain't no Picasso." He pronounced "Picasso" so it rhymed with "lasso." I wanted to shove the ladder, watch him fall.

"Yes," I said. "All of them."

While Mom and Becca put the drawings in the van, I wandered into the house and down the hallway to Shane's bedroom, passing several of the Pettit clan gathered in the kitchen. The meth-mouthed woman who had whispered to Crystle was in my brother's closet, rummaging through his clothes, so comfortable doing so that it made me feel as though I was the one who didn't belong here.

"Who are you?" she said, peeling scabs off her knuckles. Her face was pale, the skin around her nose and mouth flaky and inflamed.

"I'm Shane's sister."

"Oh. I never seen you before."

I didn't know what to say to that. I'd never seen her before, either, had never expected to find a stranger sorting through my brother's underwear.

"Them are Levi's," she said, pointing at a pile of jeans. "Name-brand. Get maybe five bucks each for 'em."

The woman burrowed farther into the closet, and Becca appeared, hissing in my ear. "They're selling his old clothes?"

"Makes you wonder what they're burning."

While Meth Mouth was occupied, I surveyed the bathroom. Crystle had used the bigger bath in the hall, leaving this one to Shane, and it was exactly what you'd expect from a bathroom no woman ever set foot in. The pattern on the Formica counter was worn away in places, grime caked around the faucets and drain, a cracked bar of Irish Spring resting in a basin sprinkled with whiskers and toothpaste spatter.

On the floor next to the shower lay a pair of jeans and a blue thermal shirt, crumpled like Shane had just stepped out of them. Were these the clothes he had worn that day? Had he taken them off when he got home from work to take a shower, just before he died? There were no towels in the room, clean or dirty, and the trash can was empty. It felt like anything might be a clue that we were missing, a puzzle piece that would click into place and explain how he'd died so suddenly.

Back in the bedroom, Becca clutched a picture of Shane and Gravy that she'd found on his nightstand. It was an old photo, Shane's dark hair still thick and combed to the side. Gravy wasn't nearly as portly in the photo as he was now. He'd shown up at the door one day as though invited, Shane surely not guessing that the stray dog would remain by his side for the rest of his life—that Gravy would outlive him.

Becca and I hauled out a couple of boxes of pictures and other personal items that weren't of any value to Crystle and went to locate Mom, who had gotten held up in the kitchen. She was trapped against the counter, stiffly holding a glass of murky tea or flat soda, listening to

Crystle go on about how she made Shane put the antique pie safe in an unused bedroom because it was so horribly ugly. The cabinet, its double doors ventilated with elaborate panels of punched tin, had belonged to Mom's mother.

Crystle got distracted by someone else, and as soon as she stepped away, I swooped in to grab Mom's glass, which was slipping from her fingers, and dump it in the sink. When I turned around, Becca was watching Mom carefully. She leaned in and murmured in my ear. "This isn't good for her. Maybe we shouldn't have let her come."

Our mother looked dazed, her eyes clouded, hand extended like she was still holding the glass. She was in her seventies, but until recently had never looked her age, one small thing she allowed herself to be prideful of. She bristled when Becca tried to coddle her, something my sister had been doing more and more since Dad died — wanting to put a rubber mat in the tub so Mom wouldn't slip, offering to get her one of those emergency necklaces like you see on commercials, with an oversized button to call for help. I'd found Becca's concern premature and almost laughable. Compared to the clients I worked with, I wasn't worried about Mom at all. She was one of the most capable people I knew — she could rewire a lamp, swing an axe, sew her own clothes, kill a spider barehanded. It was disconcerting to see the toll Shane's death had taken, to watch her shrink inward, her strength visibly waning.

"It's crowded in here," Mom said, the first words she'd uttered since we arrived. Becca and I led her down to Shane's basement workshop to get away from everyone for a minute. The welding tools and supplies had been cleared out, but the two gun safes were still there, each large as a refrigerator. Shane loved his firearms, though he wasn't the type to keep a pistol on the nightstand; all his weapons were meticulously cleaned and stored when he wasn't using them. Becca's husband had ribbed him about it, asking what he'd do if someone broke in and he didn't have time to run downstairs and open the safe. Shane had laughed, flexing his sizable biceps and asking Jerry if he'd like a demonstration.

A beefy guy with a buzz cut and goatee paced back and forth in the corner, tapping on his phone. His cowboy boots were ostrich skin, the bumpy flesh resembling an eruption of boils, and his belt buckle was large enough that I could read the word RODEO from across the room. One of Crystle's brothers. He stopped pacing and stared at us unabashedly. Mom picked up a notepad from the workbench and let out a small moan. Shane had doodled in the corners and begun a sketch of Gravy in the center, though it was only half finished and would stay that way. Mom tore the page from the notepad and folded it carefully into her purse.

"Hey, where's Grandpa's rifle?" Becca said. The rack where Shane had displayed it was empty.

Crystle's brother stuffed his phone in his pocket. "All the guns got loaded up this morning," he said. "Headed to the pawn shop."

"But that one's not worth anything to anybody but us," I said. "You can't even fire it."

He shrugged. "So go buy it back."

"Come on," I said. "Maybe they haven't left yet."

The three of us made our way back upstairs and out to the yard. Crystle had obviously told us to come late so she could haul things away before we arrived. We couldn't find anyone who knew anything about the guns—or anyone willing to tell us—and Mom excused herself to go wait in the van, saying that she felt a migraine coming on. Becca and I walked up to the garage, where a cluster of Crystle's cousins were admiring Shane's '78 Firebird Trans Am. I recognized them from the funeral.

"Took him years to restore it," I said.

"That right?" The tallest guy in the group stepped forward. I didn't know his name, but I'd heard one of the others call him Big Boy. His belly protruded like a massive tumor, and he wore suspenders to hold up his pants. "She's a looker. Should fetch a fair price."

"We're not selling it," I said.

He snorted. "Well, Crystle is. She done sold the truck and put the car on Craigslist."

"But it's not hers to sell." Becca moved closer to me, so we were standing shoulder to shoulder.

Big Boy fingered his suspenders, his jowls twitching. "Darlin', everything's Crystle's now. That's how it works." He spoke slowly, as though explaining to children. The rest of the cousins stood behind him, smirking.

"Where's the title?" Becca asked. Big Boy shrugged.

I opened the passenger door and ducked inside to dig through the glove box. "Here," I said, holding up the slip of paper for him. "It's got a Transfer on Death to our mother."

"Transfer on Death?"

"It means she gets it when he dies."

He scanned the form and then flicked it back at me. "It's stayin' put for now, anyhow. Ain't got the key to get it started."

I didn't know if that was true, but it didn't matter. "That's no problem," I said, pulling out my phone. "I'll call AAA and have it towed."

"I don't want it," Mom whispered when Becca and I climbed into the van to tell her.

"We'll figure something out," I said. "We can't leave it here." The Firebird had been Shane's most prized possession. He'd loved that car far longer than he'd loved Crystle, and I wouldn't let her sell it.

Mom's eyes darted to various points in space, not wanting to look at us directly. She curled up in the seat with her head cradled in her hands, and Becca and I left her alone, heading back out into the cold to wait for the tow truck. The bonfire was still blazing unattended, and we wandered over to peek into the boxes that hadn't yet been burned.

"They're all full of papers," Becca said. "I can't tell if it's trash."

"It's Shane's," I said. "Let's take whatever we can carry."

"Vultures," Becca muttered, eyeing the assorted relatives and strangers milling around the house. The wind kicked up, clacking a bare tree branch against the roof and swirling the smoke from the fire. Ash flitted through the air like a flurry of moths. "Does it not seem wrong that Crystle's selling or burning or giving away every trace of her husband less than a month after she put him in the ground?"

"*Everybody grieves differently*," I said, mocking Kendrick. I knew it was true that some embraced death more easily than others or found unusual ways to heal, but I hated to watch Crystle disassemble her life with Shane and move on before it had fully sunk in for us that he was gone.

I thought of our mother, when Becca and I came to tell her that Shane had died, how she had struggled to accept it. How grief came in slow tides of shock and disbelief and then wave upon wave of sorrow, interspersed, at first, with brief lulls where you could almost forget that it was real. She'd been robbed of the one thing she felt she was owed after so many years of nursing and bathing, cooking and sewing and cleaning, doling out discipline and love in careful measures. Dying before your children, she had said, was supposed to be a mother's greatest blessing.

Becca and I had promised to help Mom go through the boxes we'd brought back from Shane's. After Dad died, she'd given up partway through sorting his belongings, filling the basement with musty cartons of unknown contents, waiting for a heavy rain to seep through the floor and destroy it all so she wouldn't have to make decisions about what to toss and what to keep.

Mom still lived in the battered three-bedroom house where we'd grown up, paint peeling off the old aluminum awnings, asbestos-shingle siding peppered with mildew. The yard was shaggy. Weeds had kept growing until the recent cold snap, and Shane was the one who usually mowed it. A neighbor came by with his brush hog the day after Shane died, but he'd mowed right over the dogwood sapling Mom had won in a drawing at the bank, and she told him not to come back. She'd been saying since Dad died—it had been a dozen years now—that she should sell the house and move into an apartment over in Blackwater (a regular apartment, not one specifically for old people, God forbid) but then she'd be out planting tomatoes and pruning the pussy willows and sticking new weather stripping around the drafty front door, and it seemed fairly obvious that she would never leave. Not because she loved the house—she was forever grousing about the lack of a decent porch—but because it was familiar.

After so many years, she no longer saw the outdated linoleum in the kitchen, the hideous mirrored tiles glued to the dining room wall, the pea-green sink in the bathroom. A dog named Brownie (all of our pets had been unimaginatively named after their most obvious characteristic: Spot, Fluffy, Shorty) had ripped up the carpet in the living room, and she had smoothed it down with packing tape so that no one would trip on it, saying she wanted to wait and replace it right before she moved. She would stay, unless something happened to upheave her life in such a way that she couldn't go on there. If Dad's death hadn't done it—or Shane's—nothing would.

She'd settled into a simple routine after Dad died. I'd thought at first that she was depressed, because she stopped cooking and sewing, two things I'd always thought she enjoyed. When I asked her about it, she'd been indignant. Decades of necessary seamstress duties—stitching everything from Halloween costumes to prom dresses, constantly altering our clothes to make them last a little longer—had eroded any joy she got from her sewing machine. Same with cooking. She now relished making dinner for one, a Banquet potpie in a foil pan that could go right in the trash, no dishwashing required, nobody bothering her while she ate. The house was quiet and empty, devoid of people and pets after a lifetime of crowding, and she didn't seem to mind.

Becca and I carried in the crates of old yearbooks and cassette tapes and photo albums—all sentimental things Crystle didn't want—and the boxes of papers that we'd saved from the fire. Becca said she'd let me have the antique pie safe because she knew I wanted it, even though she was technically next in line. Mom sank into her recliner, staring out the window at the silver Firebird in her driveway, and then closed her eyes so she wouldn't have to see it. She either fell asleep or pretended to, leaving Becca and me alone at the kitchen table to sift through what Shane had left behind.

We quickly realized that the papers, which we'd thought might be trash, were actually organized by year, and it looked as though Shane had saved every vaguely important document or piece of mail he'd ever received—an inefficient system, maybe, but I was impressed that he had a system at all. I kept my mail in a pile on the counter, cleaning around it and watching it grow until the inevitable avalanche forced me to do the necessary culling and filing.

"Do you remember a girlfriend named DeAnne?" Becca asked, picking through a stack of greeting cards.

"Nope."

"How about Lindsey? Or Tara?"

"Never heard of them," I said. "Are they from his Alabama days?" Shane had wanted to get as far away from home as possible after graduation, and he'd found his escape through a trade school in Birmingham. He earned his welding certification and didn't move back until after Dad had died.

"Yeah. Looks like he was keeping Hallmark in business." She held up a Valentine card covered in lacy hearts. "I wonder if any of them know. That he's gone. Or any of his old buddies, the ones he hasn't seen in a while. There are letters from some of them."

"Probably not," I said. "Maybe it's better that way." Shane wasn't into social media, so we didn't have an easy way to track down his old friends. I envied them, that they could continue to think of him from time to time, imagining that he was out there somewhere if they wanted to get in touch. I still caught myself picking up the phone to text him, not wanting to remove his name from my contacts because that felt too final, too real. As though erasing him from my phone was somehow worse than burying him.

"That's weird." Becca frowned.

"What?"

"His mortgage. It was going down with every statement, like you'd expect. Then here it jumped up, higher than where it started."

"What year was that?"

Becca handed me the paper. "Two years ago. Around the time he and Crystle got engaged."

"He must have pulled out his equity and refinanced."

"Yeah, but what do you think he needed all that cash for?"

"My guess would be Crystle." He'd bought her a modest engagement ring at first, but she'd talked him into exchanging it for something flashier, the new diamond larger and surrounded by a halo of smaller gems. Right after their engagement, her car had broken down and he'd replaced it with a new Jeep. Shane was frugal in many ways, packing bologna sandwiches for lunch every day and putting a box fan in the window rather than running the air conditioner, but when it came to women and cars, he was easily convinced to open his wallet.

"Look at this," Becca said. "About a year ago, he took out a personal loan."

"I bet that was when he helped Crystle go into business selling those leggings. That didn't last long."

"Just long enough for her to quit her job," Becca grumbled. She'd bought several pairs of Crystle's leggings to be nice but never wore them after the first pair she tried on split a seam along the crotch.

Crystle had switched from leggings to selling essential oils, then diet supplements, not sticking with anything long enough to come out ahead.

"Hey, are there credit card statements in there?" I asked.

"Everything's in here," she said. We dug through the most recent boxes and compared. His credit card, bank, and mortgage statements all tracked a steady decline in his finances from the time he and Crystle had gotten together.

"He worked so hard," Becca said, getting up to stretch and rub her eyes. "And then he was just moving backward." She opened Mom's nearly empty fridge and scooted aside a few cans of store-brand soda to get out the iced tea. "Don't you think it's strange, too, that Crystle's name's not on any of this? The house? The checking account?"

"I don't know. I mean, plenty of people keep their finances separate when they get married."

"I guess," Becca said, pouring two glasses of tea. "You want something to eat?"

"Nah, I'm okay." It was getting dark, nearly dinnertime, but our late lunch of gas station hotdogs was still churning in my stomach.

"Good," Becca said, carefully opening and closing cabinet doors so as not to wake Mom. "Because there's nothing to eat here but saltine crackers and bouillon cubes. Maybe we should run and get her some groceries."

"I can do it when you head home," I said. "The boys'll want you there to tuck them in." I missed putting Lily to bed on the nights she wasn't with me. She still liked for me to read to her, sometimes library books that seemed too mature for her but weren't, other times she'd surprise me and choose an old favorite, a picture book like *Scrambled Eggs Super!* by Dr. Seuss, something she'd probably be embarrassed to admit to anyone. I knew she was safe at Greg's, but that wasn't the same as being able to see her foot poking out of the covers, hearing her sigh in her sleep when I peered in to check on her.

Becca handed me a glass of tea and sat back down. "Yeah, Jerry has a hard time wrangling them into bed. And he's probably sneezing like crazy from having Gravy there all day." She started stuffing papers back into the appropriate boxes.

"Maybe he just hadn't gotten around to putting Crystle's name on everything yet," Becca continued. "I'm sure he wasn't thinking he'd die anytime soon."

"It's possible," I said. "Or maybe things weren't going well between them. Maybe he wasn't sure the marriage would last."

"Wouldn't he have said something to us, though?" Becca asked. "Wouldn't he have told us if they were having problems?"

"I don't know," I said. "Did he ever say anything to you about their relationship?"

She shook her head. Shane had always kept his personal life private, even from us. I'd never thought of it as intentional, just a guy thing, not wanting to tell his sisters about his girlfriends. When we were all together, we played cards, horsed around with the kids, watched Royals games. We texted stupid memes back and forth, things to make one another laugh. He didn't talk about his job or his friends or what he did when we weren't around. He'd barely mentioned Crystle before they got engaged—he only said something when Mom wondered aloud why he hadn't been coming around as often. If there had been some sliver of uncertainty between Shane and his wife, something that kept them from going all in as most newlyweds do, I didn't know anything about it.

"One more box," I said, "and I think we're done for the night." I opened a storage tub that Shane had helpfully labeled JUNK. At the top were old *Field & Stream* and *Hot Rod* magazines, and beneath those, a mishmash of mementos and trinkets: loose coins, Matchbox cars, Mardi Gras beads, warped cardboard coasters from various dive bars, some with phone numbers scrawled on the margins. Buried in the jumble was a kid's craft project made of paper plates and yarn and

Popsicle sticks, like something Lily would have brought home from preschool. A heart with the words JESUS LOVES ME was pasted unevenly on the front, and a child's name was inscribed in crayon on the back, the letters long and gangly like they had kept growing after they were drawn. CHARLE. Charlie or Charles, I assumed, didn't know how to spell his own name.

"Who's Charles?" I asked, holding up the craft to show Becca. She looked at it with wide eyes and shrugged.

I wondered what else Shane had kept from us, what more we might discover. His art teacher's words floated in my head, the note he'd left on Shane's unexpected rendering of flowers. *You are full of surprises.*

CHAPTER 4

HENLEY
JULY

The next week, Henley went to clean the Sullivan house alone. Missy hadn't come home, and Henley suspected that her mother had hooked up with her old friend Ellie Embry again. Ellie, who hadn't changed since junior high, when she and Missy had cemented their friendship by getting caught drunk-driving a tractor, still had a year-round suntan, a complete lack of interest in getting sober, and the ability to make terrible ideas sound enticing. Henley hadn't mentioned Missy's absence to her uncles, wanting to give her mother a chance to come back on her own. Plenty of times over the years, Raymond and Junior had hunted down their baby sister and extracted her from whatever dark den she'd holed up in, and they would surely do it again if it came to that.

The Sullivan house felt empty, though it had felt that way the last time, too, and she wondered if it was partly because of Daphne's loom-ing absence—if a house without women, without a mother, had an inherently different feel. Henley considered skipping Jason's bedroom altogether, but she hadn't washed his sheets the week before, for obvi-ous reasons, and she didn't want to give Earl anything to grouse about. She had no interest in a career as the Sullivans' housekeeper, but Earl paid better than any job she could find in town, and she needed to stay in his good graces for a while, at least.

Jason's door gaped open several inches. She hammered her knuck-les on the thick wooden slab and called hello, and when she heard nothing but the whoosh of the air conditioner laboring to keep the big house cool, she let herself in, parking the vacuum on the plush carpet. The bed was empty, the covers twisted up like a pack of wild dogs had been burrowing in them.

She hadn't gotten a good look around before, when Jason had rolled over and startled her, but the room was the same as the rest of the house, opulent and outdated, with a preppy argyle wallpaper border and shiny brass sconces and a matching suite of heavy oak furniture. Thick brocade drapes blocked the sun, and an enormous flat-screen television hung on the wall, video games strewn on the floor below. A Kansas City Royals pennant was tacked above the bed. On a shelf weighted down with baseball trophies and track medals was a framed photo of Jason at maybe two years old, wearing a tiny seersucker suit and sitting on his mother's lap. As she maneuvered around the balled-up socks and empty energy drink cans on the floor and began to strip the bed, Henley noted the same feral scent that all boys' rooms seemed to have, a musk of sweat and pheromones and wet dreams. She wasn't sure why she'd thought the rich's dirty laundry would smell any differ-ent, any better.

She wondered how long Jason would be sticking around. Most peo-ple assumed he was home from college for the summer, working for his dad before going back for a fifth year, but Missy had told her he'd all but flunked out and was nowhere near a degree, that Earl was fed up with his partying and laziness and complete lack of gratitude for all he'd been given and was determined to reform him into a responsible adult who could run the company one day. According to Missy, Earl had taken control of nearly every aspect of Jason's life—setting his work schedule, managing his finances, testing him for drugs. She imagined Jason was taking that as well as a cat takes a bath.

In search of a laundry basket for the sheets, Henley opened the closet door and the light flicked on automatically. It was a sizable walk-in, the floor covered in mounds of discarded clothing. The few things still hanging were encased in plastic dry-cleaning bags like cocoons waiting to hatch. She backed up and bumped into something that hadn't been there before, and when she whirled around, Jason stood in front of her, warm and damp from a shower, a towel low on his waist.

She instinctively tried to move away from him but there was nowhere to go. Blood rushed to burn her cheeks.

"Had to come back for another look?" he said, a cocky grin spreading across his face. He still had a taut, muscular athlete's body, though she knew that life would start to catch up with him before long, that he'd begin to look like all the other former high school stars—bald and flabby, strutting around like they'd just stepped off a ball field rather than a cornfield. The illusion held within the confines of Blackwater—schoolyard kings were forever royalty in this little town.

"You should try getting dressed before noon," Henley said. She took a step forward until they were almost touching, and he gave in and stepped aside, allowing her to move past him.

"I see you're working hard," he said, jutting his chin toward the silent vacuum.

She rolled her eyes. "Hard to vacuum in here with your shit all over the floor."

The words came out without any thought and she didn't regret them. She was starting to get the feeling that if Jason tattled to Earl, Earl might take her side.

"Huh." He looked amused, like he was enjoying the pushback. "Missy says the same thing." He plucked a T-shirt off the back of a chair and pulled it over his head, taking his time rolling it down over his chest. "She here today?"

"No. She wasn't feeling well," Henley said, looking away.

"You wanna go for a swim?" He grabbed a pair of trunks off the floor. "It's my day off and I'm bored as hell out here."

"I've got work to do," she said.

Jason smiled, a dimple appearing. He pulled the shorts up and dropped the towel in one swift motion as Henley pretended not to notice. "You could take a break. Missy does."

"My mom does not go swimming with you."

He winked. "She would if I asked her."

Henley knew Missy had a soft spot for Jason, feeling bad that he'd had to grow up without his mother, and the way she talked about him sometimes made it seem like he was still a little boy, not a man in his twenties. Maybe he was right and Missy would entertain his every whim, but unlike her mother, Henley felt no obligation to placate him. She scooped up the dirty sheets. "Thanks anyway."

Later, as she wiped down the kitchen counters, she watched him lying on the diving board, the sun glinting on his wet skin, the Sullivans' fields stretching out beyond the crisp aqua rectangle of the pool all the way to the hazy horizon. She'd never given it any thought before, that despite her mother's close relationship with Jason, Henley didn't know him at all. Jason sat up, cupping a hand over his eyes, looking toward the house. He probably couldn't see her watching him through the window, but she ducked down anyway.

She didn't feel like going home and seeing that Missy still wasn't there, so she headed over to her uncles' place in the '77 Buick Skylark they'd restored for her sixteenth birthday. It was one of the last model years, Raymond insisted, before Skylarks started to look like something your grandma would drive. Junior, Raymond, and Denny had started Pettit Brothers Auto Body & Salvage together with proceeds from selling their last remaining acres of the farm, and Raymond and Junior, only ten months apart, lived on the property. Denny was currently serving a stretch in Leavenworth for assault with a tire iron, his double-wide empty since his third wife had gotten fed up and his youngest daughter, Crystle, had gotten married and moved out.

The garage was set back from the gravel road, a chain-link and scrap-metal fence blocking off the entrance to the salvage yard. There were no customers around and the side door was propped open with a cinder block. Raymond's legs stuck out from under his truck, where he was changing the oil. She knelt down to say hello and then headed to the old soda machine that Raymond stocked just for her, so no matter which button you pushed, whatever flavor you chose, a Dr Pepper dropped down the chute. Raymond was the only one who didn't have kids of his own, and he'd taken it upon himself to step in and do things for Henley that a father might have done.

An oversized map of the United States hung on the wall next to the soda machine, red pushpins stuck in all the places she dreamed of visiting. Grand Teton, the Continental Divide, Denali, Glacier National Park, the Sawtooth Range.

Henley had talked about wanting a map, and this one had appeared in the shop around the same time that an identical one was stolen from the social studies room at her school, the top edge jagged where it had been torn from the wall-mounted roller. Raymond hadn't said a word, he'd just winked and handed her a box of pins.

Henley perched on the old wooden stool in the shop, the seat worn smooth as glass, and Junior came out of his office to join her.

"You doin' good?"

She nodded carefully. She didn't want to see the disappointment on his face, the lack of surprise, if she said anything about Missy, though he'd surely find out before long.

Junior popped his knuckles, working from left to right and back again, the joints making a sound like billiard balls smacking together. Black lines rimmed his nails and etched the cracked skin of his fingers. They were the hands of someone who worked hard, if not always aboveboard, and no amount of Lava soap could clean them.

"When you plannin' to head out on your trip?"

"End of summer," she said. "I'm saving up a bit. Helping out at the Sullivans'."

His eyebrow went up and he stroked his graying beard but said nothing.

Shane walked in then, his work boots clomping on the concrete, the sound echoing through the open space. He was built like a lumberjack, bulked with muscle through the chest and shoulders, his T-shirt tight in the sleeves. His dark hair had thinned to the point that he'd recently given up and started shaving his head, though his ruddy cheeks and easy grin gave his face a still-boyish appearance. She'd seen an old picture of him in his high school football uniform, his jaw sharp, blue eyes focused intently on the camera, doing his best not to smile.

He'd first come out to the salvage yard years before, looking for parts for an old Trans Am he was restoring, and had struck up a friendship with Raymond and Junior over their mutual love of muscle cars, his teasing nature keeping things light when her uncles got worked up over something, which they were prone to do when whiskey was involved. Shane was respectful, always asking Henley about school and looking her in the eye, never trailing his gaze down to check out her boobs like some of the men who hung around the garage drinking and talking shit with her uncles.

He was older and bordering on dull by Crystle's standards, but he'd fallen for her coarse mouth and Amazonian beauty—those lush Pettit hips that Henley had initially thought a curse—and patiently courted her for a good long while before she decided to marry him. Crystle's previous beaus had mostly been freewheeling rodeo boys high on Adderall, and Henley had to wonder what Shane had done to wear her down—if Crystle had fallen in love over time or simply made a calculated decision, weighing her prospects as she neared thirty and betting on the long-term value of a loyal man with a steady job.

Shane nodded hello, but there was something off about him. He was always telling her corny riddles, the kind you'd read on a Popsicle stick, the stupider the better. *Hey, Henley, what has thirteen hearts but has never been in love? Hey, Henley, what has a thousand ears but can't hear?* He'd pause dramatically before revealing the punch line (*A deck of cards! A cornfield!*), and then he'd make the goofiest expression, trying to get her to laugh or roll her eyes and groan. He had no jokes for her today. Instead, he mumbled something vague about the heat, his smile uneasy, and when Junior returned with two beers and gave her a look, Henley slid down from the stool and said her goodbyes without glancing back. She'd learned a lot about business from her uncles. Mind your own. Stay out of others'. Don't ask questions you don't want answers to.

Still, she couldn't help wondering what was going on with Shane. She moved slowly, hoping she might overhear something, but the men were silent as they waited for her to walk out the door, the harsh sunlight momentarily blinding her, the crunch of gravel beneath her feet obliterating any words that might have followed her out of the darkness.

CHAPTER 5

SADIE

NOVEMBER

On Monday morning, I called Lily before she left for school, to see how her sleepover party had gone. "It was so embarrassing," Lily whispered, and I wondered where she was in the house, maybe hiding so her stepmother wouldn't hear. "I'm the *only* one who doesn't wear a real bra. I've got these stupid sports bras from Justice and that baby nightgown and *nobody* shops at Justice here, they all have bras and pajamas from Pink."

Did eleven-year-olds really shop at Pink? I had no idea. It wasn't long ago that Lil had begged me to buy the "baby" nightgown, which featured a smiling cartoon sloth and cost more than a child's pajamas should—more than anything I wore to bed. Of course no one saw what I wore, so it didn't really matter. When I was Lily's age, I slept in one of Becca's old stretched-out T-shirts.

Lily had never been one of those kids who were in a hurry to grow up. She'd shown no interest in makeup and still slept with her stuffed animals. Only last year, I'd given her a stack of books on puberty with titles like *Is This Normal?* and *What's Happening to My Body?* and she'd been horrified that these things would one day happen to her. Now she seemed upset that they hadn't yet.

"I'm sorry, honey," I said. "I know what it's like, wanting to wear the same things as the other girls—"

"And there's nothing to eat here, Mom," she interrupted. She'd only recently switched from Mommy to Mom, and it was still jarring at times. "I wanted cereal and there wasn't any milk but the weird kind Heidi likes, and I used the last of that, and then Dad was mad."

"What? I'm sure if they're out of something, they'll go to the store soon."

"No, they're doing this diet where they only eat, like, olives and pine needles for thirty days, and it's making them all crabby, and Heidi won't buy anything that has . . . I don't know, sugar? Starch? Flavor? It'll be too much of a *temptation.*"

"Hm. You can get school lunch today, right? I'll talk to Dad."

"Thanks, Mom! Love you. Gotta go. Wait! Tell him to get Pop-Tarts. Bye."

Lily was still adjusting to her new environment, preferring to use me as a go-between rather than broaching issues directly with her dad and Heidi. It couldn't be going too badly, though, as she hadn't yet said anything about wanting to come home, something I secretly longed for.

I dialed Greg's cell on my way to work. I could tell from the background noise that he was at the gym. He liked to ride the stationary bike while watching the morning news. "Hey," I said. "Just making sure you got the check for Lily?"

"Yeah," he said. "Thanks."

"So, she called this morning saying something about food . . . a diet?"

Greg groaned. "Yeah. I know, I shouldn't have snapped at her. Things were hectic, and I was running late. And it's not a *diet*, it's a complete reset of your eating habits, and you might want to think about trying it yourself."

"She was worried there wouldn't be anything for her to eat for the next thirty days. She asked for Pop-Tarts."

"Don't worry," he said. "I promise we're not going to starve her. I'll take her to the store tonight; she can pick out whatever she wants."

"Great, thanks. I know you wouldn't let her go hungry. Listen, can I talk to you a minute about some legal stuff?"

"Regarding?"

"Shane."

"Oh. Sure, if it's quick."

"How hard would it be for us to go around Shane's wife to get his medical records?"

"Why? What's going on?"

"There's too much to get into over the phone. Just generally, is it even possible?"

"Well, that depends. Is there some pertinent reason to get your hands on that information? Are you worried about hereditary conditions that could affect you or Lily?"

"We just want to know the cause of death. It was ruled natural, but that was a guess. No autopsy was performed."

Greg was silent for a moment, and I could hear his bike churning. He was ten pounds lighter now than when we were married. He'd been sedentary throughout law school, always studying, and then working long hours when he'd started his job at the firm, too busy to go to the park with Lily and me. He and Heidi liked to go for runs together in their neighborhood, the baby strapped into a sleek jogging stroller.

"You think his death wasn't natural?"

"I don't know that it wasn't—it's just that we don't have the whole

story, and his wife won't tell us anything. She's acting strange for someone whose husband just died."

"Okay. Look, it's not like that kind of thing never happens, but why
kill someone when you could just get a divorce? There weren't any
kids involved, so she wouldn't have been worried about custody, and if
he was supporting her, she almost certainly would have gotten some
maintenance payments."

You know how ugly divorce can be. I didn't say it out loud, but he
probably knew I was thinking it. Divorcing a lawyer was not something
I'd recommend to anyone.

"Listen, Sadie, I know you wouldn't pursue this if you didn't think
there was something to it, but it doesn't sound like you have a lot to go
on here. The spouse is all-powerful, unless you have some compelling
evidence to get around that. If you're wanting to hire someone, it could
get expensive, and no matter what you do, nothing will bring him
back. Will it be worthwhile if nothing's likely to change?"

Greg had managed to reduce the situation to a balance sheet,
weighing decisions in dollar signs. I supposed that was why he was so
good at his job.

"We're talking about my brother, Greg. We can't just forget about
it. We want to know what happened."

"I get it," he said. "Nobody likes uncertainties. I hope you get everything straightened out."

I knew he was right, that suspicion wasn't much good without evidence to back it up, and our only evidence was open to interpretation:
Crystle wasn't mourning properly; she'd driven our brother into debt;
she wouldn't tell us anything. Detective Kendrick had insisted that we
were lucky—however Shane had died, his body was intact, and we'd
been able to bury him, to see him one last time. Whatever my family
was going through, Hannah Calhoun had it so much worse. I wondered if there had been any progress in identifying the child's skull.

Though I wasn't sure she'd even want my sympathy—she might

view me as an intruder, an unwelcome witness to her grief—I had a sudden urge to reach out to Hannah. I typed up a brief message as soon as I got to work, using the last email address I had for her and hoping it was still valid. I told her I was here for her, that if she needed anything, I'd show up in a heartbeat. I signed it "Love, Sadie" and clicked Send before I could change my mind.

Gravy lay on his side like a bloated corpse, not even looking in my direction. I jiggled the leash. "Come on, time to go to the vet. We'll get you all fixed up." I tried to sound enthusiastic, but he continued to ignore me. He probably knew that I was lying, that there was only so much fixing up that could be done at his age.

I wedged my hands underneath him to pry him off the frozen grass, and he flipped over and growled, agitated. Luckily, I was prepared. I took the cold remains of a Jimmy Dean sausage biscuit from my coat pocket, unwrapped it, and held it in front of his nose. He wasn't impressed.

"Seriously, we're gonna be late." I'd left work early to make his appointment on time, but I'd gotten stuck behind an enormous tractor on the way home from Blackwater and wouldn't be terribly surprised if I got stuck behind another one on the way back. I pulled gently on the leash until he skittered to his feet and began to slide, unwillingly, across the yard. I opened the car door and he promptly flopped onto his belly.

"That's it," I said, tossing the biscuit onto the seat and hoisting Gravy's wriggling body in after it. He flung his head from side to side, his teeth clacking, unable to gain purchase on my coat sleeves. I slammed the door before he could slide back out. When I got in my seat, he was morosely eating the biscuit wrapper, leaving the sausage to grease up the upholstery.

"Did you bring the urine sample?" the receptionist asked when we arrived, already five minutes late. She could tell by my face that I hadn't, sighed, and handed me an empty Cool Whip container, directing me out to the side yard.

The potty area was heaven for Gravy, who roused at the scent of piss from a hundred different dogs. He snuffled at the grass, changing direction every two seconds. It was unbelievably difficult to collect urine from a dog whose belly was about two inches off the ground. To make it more challenging, Gravy was sprinkling a few drops here, a few there, taking forever to produce a decent sample. I started to call Becca to complain but hung up. She had texted earlier to tell me both boys were sick with a stomach bug, and I didn't want to bother her when she was dealing with that.

"I'm sorry," I told the vet minutes later, wiping my hands on my jeans. "I hope there's enough to test. I've never done this before, Doctor . . . ?" I glanced at his name tag. Theodore Hayward, DVM. The name conjured an elderly man wearing an ascot, perhaps leaning on one of those canes with a fancy gold handle. In reality, Dr. Hayward didn't appear to be much older than me, early forties at most. He had sympathetic brown eyes and dark hair that was beginning to gray at the temples. There were dirty paw prints on the sleeves of his lab coat.

"I'm Theo," he said, smiling gently. There was something calming about him, and even Gravy stopped sniffing and fidgeting and sat down, his ample rear planted squarely on my feet. Dr. Hayward set his clipboard on the counter and clasped his large hands together. They looked strong and capable, like they'd have no trouble pulling a stuck calf or hoisting an irritable overweight dog onto the exam table. "I saw the note on your file," he said. "And I'm so sorry for your loss. I'm not actually Gravy's vet—the doctor he used to see retired last year, and it looks like Gravy's overdue for vaccinations, so we'll get that taken care of today. And he's having some trouble with incontinence?"

"Yes."

He bent down to stroke Gravy's back and carefully probe his under-belly. "We'll rule out an infection before trying incontinence meds. Are there other concerns?"

"Yes. Yeah. I'm worried he might be depressed, if that's possible."

"It is," he said. "It's hard for pets to lose someone, just like it is for people. Has his behavior changed in some way?"

"I don't know. I mean, he doesn't seem like himself, but he's getting older, so maybe that's all it is. Maybe it's nothing."

Guilt swelled inside my rib cage and filled my throat. I hadn't seen Shane or Gravy much in the months before he died, and I couldn't remember the last time I'd asked him how Gravy was doing. Or the last time I'd asked Shane how *he* was doing. I should have done a better job, been a better sister. We'd been so close when we were growing up, he and Becca and I. We always knew when he was in trouble back then—and he was, much of the time—because we were a team. We helped one another. If something was wrong, I should have known. Tears stung and fell, and I tried to stop them but couldn't.

Dr. Hayward murmured sympathies and let me cry, his expression patient and understanding, even as I blubbered like he was a therapist, telling him how much Shane had loved his dog, and that having him with us was like holding on to a piece of our brother.

He handed me a box of tissues. "Take care of him, and love him, and enjoy the time you have. We'll do what we can to make sure he's as healthy and comfortable as possible."

By the time the doctor was finished, Gravy had been diagnosed with an allergy-induced skin condition, a urinary tract infection, and kidney failure. The words "kidney failure" had me near tears again, but he assured me that it was still manageable; he might live another year, maybe more. He would need to eat a low-protein, low-fat diet, which ruled out his beloved Gravy Train. Dr. Hayward suggested boiling chicken in water and pouring the liquid over cooked rice. He told me to keep him posted and offered Gravy a diet dog treat, the poor dog wriggling away from it as though it were a hot coal. I told myself I would do anything to help Gravy, even if it meant putting more effort into cooking for him than I did for myself, though part of me wondered if it was worth it. Even if we were able to prolong his life, Gravy didn't seem to be enjoying it much without Shane.

I tossed the assorted pill bottles and prescription shampoo into the backseat and deposited Gravy in the front with the now familiar routine of him snapping at me ineffectively, like a hobbled gator. He was even more grouchy than usual after a round of shots and a blood draw that had required Dr. Hayward to try three different legs before finding a good vein. I rolled down his window and let the frigid air rush in. As we neared the turnoff to Shane's house, Gravy began to perk up. His ears lifted and his tail began to swish back and forth. He thought he was going home.

"Sorry, boy," I told him. "We can't."

His stamped his front feet, a high-pitched keening building in his throat. I hadn't seen Gravy so excited since he'd come to live with me. I still had a key to Shane's house—we'd exchanged spares when he first moved in. And the house was likely empty after the weekend's purge, making its way through probate so Crystle could sell it. She'd moved her things out immediately after his death, claiming she couldn't sleep in a place where she'd found a dead body.

I crunched onto the gravel road, passing Pettit Brothers Auto Body & Salvage and continuing deeper into the woods, the landscape a muted palette of winter browns and grays but for the sumac tangled in the ditch, blood-red berries clustered on dead branches. There were no cars in sight as I pulled into the long drive, Gravy clawing frantically at the armrest, wanting out. I made the mistake of opening the door before clipping on his leash, and he flopped out onto the ground, taking off for the house before I could wrangle him. I hadn't realized he could still move that fast.

The property had the hollow, uneasy feeling of abandonment. The post oaks loomed over the front yard, their leathery brown leaves, shaped like ghosts with outstretched arms, blowing into drifts on the ground. Crystle hadn't liked living this far from the paved road, too far out for city sewer or trash service or snowplows, but Shane had loved it and Gravy had too. He sniffed his way along a worn deer path and veered toward the front door, his miniature legs moving double time. He scratched at the doorframe, which was marked with deep grooves from years of demanding to be let in.

"Don't you want to run around?" I asked him. "Mark your territory?" He whined, focused on the door. "He's not in there," I said, wondering if Gravy could tell that Shane was gone, or if he sensed some version of my brother's presence that I couldn't, something more than a lingering scent.

I dug the keychain out of my pocket and unlocked the door. Gravy trotted inside and disappeared down the hallway. It was dark in the living room, all the curtains drawn, and it took my eyes a moment to adjust as I stepped inside. The space was empty except for Shane's recliner, which sat in the middle of the room where it always had, surrounded by indents in the carpet where the rest of the furniture had been. Gravy hadn't bothered with the chair, or the spot where Shane had taken his last breath, and I didn't pause there, either.

I moved down the hallway to the kitchen. I didn't see Gravy anywhere, but the pantry door was ajar. I pushed it open farther and stepped into the narrow space, a tiny window letting in light. I hadn't thought to check the pantry when we'd come for Shane's things, but like the rest of the house, it had been cleared out, straight into trash bags, most likely, if there was nothing worth selling. A low growl came from behind me and I wheeled around.

"Jesus," Crystle said, towering over me in the doorway. She wore a thin, glittery sweater that showed a black bra underneath, and spike-heeled boots with impossibly narrow pointed toes. Gravy kept his distance, growling from the hall.

"You're lucky I didn't shoot you," she said. "Want to tell me what you're doing in my pantry? You need to borrow a cup of sugar?"

"I thought Shane might have had some of our grandma's dishes," I lied. "I didn't find them in the boxes we took home."

Crystle glanced at the shelves and then stared pointedly at me. No dishes of any kind, nothing but a box of cornmeal and an ancient deep fryer grimed with grease and dog hair.

"Got some dishes over here," Crystle said, swiveling to the cabinet near the sink and pulling out a stack of plain white plates, part of a set I'd given to Shane as a housewarming gift. "Go ahead and take 'em."

"Crystle . . ." I eased out of the pantry. "Since you're here. There's something I wanted to ask you."

Her eyebrows lifted, the tails penciled into sharp points. Gravy whined.

"Could you sign a release so we can access Shane's medical records?"

"What for?"

"Detective Kendrick said we'd need your permission."

"Why's she talking to you?"

"Had he been sick?" I asked.

She snorted. "Allergies, but that was his own fault, because he kept the damn windows open all the time. I was taking care of him. What, you want to blame me for not knowing his heart was gonna give out?"

"We just want to know how he died. Don't you?"

She slapped the plates down on the counter so hard I thought they would break. "I know how he died," she said. "Alone, on the floor, his eyes wide open. You ever see something like that? You ever walk in the front door and find your whole world gone to shit?"

Gravy had stopped whining at us and now faced the dark hallway, muttering, his tail low. A puddle of urine darkened the carpet at his feet. He let out a small bark, his hackles rising.

"You think we didn't love him, too?" I said. "We lost him, same as you."

Crystle got in my face, blocking my view, looking me dead-on. Up close, her irises were a stunning hazel, green fractured with gold, her breath laced with stale smoke. "Get out of my fucking house," she hissed. Gravy yipped, and Crystle turned around. Her brother, the one we'd seen in the basement over the weekend, appeared in the doorway, pushing up his sleeves. Gravy was barking furiously, backing up into the kitchen, and I squeezed past Crystle to get to him.

"Stay the hell away from me," she said, shoving my shoulder with the heel of her hand before I moved out of reach. I fought the urge to turn around and shove her back, instead grabbing Gravy's collar and dragging him out of the house, his teeth snapping at me the whole way, my heart ricocheting in my chest.

I called Becca from the car to tell her about my run-in with Crystle—that she'd responded about as well as expected when I asked for Shane's records—and she said Gravy and I should come by. It took her a minute to answer the door when we got to her house. She'd decorated the front porch for Thanksgiving, turning pumpkins into turkeys with a kit from the craft store. The orange birds had fat dangly wattles, googly eyes, and feather fans. An extension ladder leaned against the gutter, probably as far as Jerry had gotten in stringing the Christmas lights like she'd asked him to.

"I think the boys are finally done puking," Becca said when she let us in. "They're passed out on a shower curtain in the bedroom watching *PAW Patrol*—I couldn't get the sheets and blankets washed quick enough to keep up with them."

"Poor things," I said. "And poor you."

Becca shrugged, heading for the kitchen and opening the fridge. "It's fine," she said. "I'm sorry you had to deal with Crystle. That sounds way worse. You want something to eat?"

"Don't fix anything on my account," I said. "I know you had a long day."

"No trouble at all," she said, pulling out a stack of Lunchables. "Jerry's bowling tonight, so I don't have to cook, but I need a little something in my stomach. Soak up the liquor." She snorted.

"Are you *drunk*?" I asked. Becca had never been much of a drinker. She'd been known to get light-headed after a single wine cooler.

"Maybe a little." She handed me a foil pouch that looked a lot like the Capri Suns I used to pack in Lily's lunch. "It's a margarita," she said. "Jerry got them at Walmart and I thought I'd try one. They're better than you'd think."

We sat on the living room floor and Becca opened the Lunchables on the coffee table, crackers and bright orange cheese and little circles of pink glistening meat, all nestled in plastic trays.

"Is that ham or turkey?" I asked.

"Doesn't matter," she said, stuffing cheese in her mouth. "They all taste the same. How'd it go at the vet?"

"Okay," I said. "Got some pills to fix what's fixable. I ugly-cried in front of the doctor for a good five minutes, which was embarrassing, but he was nice about it."

"But Gravy's okay?" He had flopped on the rug, his legs splayed out to the side, and was already snoring.

"He's got some problems, but he's as good as expected for a fifteen-year-old dog." Becca looked relieved, and I decided to save his full diagnosis for another time.

"And the vet was nice?"

"Yeah. He was great. Wouldn't mind having him for my doctor. He's a better listener."

Becca smiled coyly. "Any chance he's single?"

"Wow, you know, somehow that never came up in our conversation about incontinence and depression."

Becca sighed. She had recently decided that it was time for me to date again and had already tricked me into an uncomfortable double date with her and Jerry and one of Jerry's work friends. The guy had spent the whole night texting his ex-girlfriend. Becca thought she was being helpful. I wasn't opposed to meeting someone, but blind dates and websites felt artificial and awkward, and living in a small town limited my options. I was aware that I hadn't done the best job of picking a partner the first time around, and I didn't want to repeat my mistakes. Being single was preferable to being stuck in a bad relationship. I'd married Greg in part because he was nothing like my father, which, as it turned out, wasn't enough to ensure a happy marriage.

We ate in silence for a minute, *Wheel of Fortune* playing on the muted TV.

"Oh, my gosh," Becca said, grabbing my arm. "I have to tell you what happened to me the other day."

Her cheeks were bright pink, and I was starting to wonder how many margarita pouches she'd had before I showed up.

"I was in the shower," she said, "and I looked down, and there was a gray hair. *There.* Did you even know that went gray? I mean, I guess it makes sense, but I never thought about it. Jerry just said the other day that he hopes I never wear granny panties—and now I *literally* look like a granny!"

That was about the last thing I'd expected Becca to say, and laughter took hold in my gut, shaking me until it rattled up my throat and out. It was hilarious, the thought of Becca as an old lady. She was only five years older than me. In my head, Becca and Shane and I were still kids, wearing one another's hand-me-downs, our dark hair styled in identical shaggy bowl cuts with Mom's kitchen shears.

"Hey, remember that time we got a bag of secondhand underwear from church? Those big old briefs?"

Becca shrieked. "Oh, my god! Were we really so poor we couldn't buy underwear?"

"We must've been," I said. "Didn't Mom make you some pants out of a pair of Dad's old work pants?"

"Yes! I hated those stupid things! I couldn't wait to grow out of them."

"They were so ugly! What ever happened to them?" I asked. "All your stuff got passed down to me, but I don't remember wearing them."

Becca laughed so hard she went mute. She slapped the floor, doubled over. "I burned them," she wheezed.

"You what?" I was laughing again because she was laughing. I tried to imagine Becca, the most prudent and well behaved of the three of us, setting her pants on fire.

"I put them in Mom's rag bin. They were *done*. And she took them out and stuck them in your dresser drawer and I just couldn't stand the thought of you having to wear them." Becca's eyes gleamed, her face rosy from laughing, though she wasn't laughing now. "I stuffed them in the trash and took it out to burn. And when it all burned down I picked through the ashes and took the snap and the little metal teeth from the zipper and I buried them so nobody would ever find out."

Becca had always tried to keep us out of trouble, concealing the evidence of our minor indiscretions as best she could. After she repaired the angel figurine that Shane and I had broken, she'd put the superglue back exactly where she had found it and rolled masking tape over the carpet to collect any tiny ceramic shards where the wing had hit the floor and broken off. Our father was quick to raise his hand when his temper flared, firmly believing that he could whip the wickedness out of us, so it was in our best interest to behave, but Becca had been the only one of us with the forethought and restraint to consider repercussions before she acted.

One summer our garden produced an ungodly surplus of green beans, so many that Mom ran out of canning jars, and we were all sick of eating them for every meal, the pods so tough and hairy that the only way to make them edible was to boil them until they fell apart and all the flavor leached out. The three of us were grumbling as we picked our way through the rows, Becca and I dreaming up ways to end the scourge—salting the earth, praying for aphids, dousing the plants with weed killer—when Shane said he had a better idea, grabbed the bucketful we'd just picked, and spun in a circle, flinging the beans out into the field. Then he reached down and yanked one of the plants up by the roots, swung it above his head like a lasso, dirt pelting down on us, and let it fly. We'd whooped and hollered, enjoying a gleeful moment of rebellion, though Becca ended up convincing us to pick all the beans back up before Dad found out and salvage the plant the best we could. I understood now. We didn't have much. Letting something go to waste was a sin. The pants that had already been cut down could have been further winnowed for their useful parts—the snap, the zipper, the fabric. Becca knew that and burned them anyway, for me.

"It sucked," she said. "Being thirteen years old, wearing hand-me-down undies and old workpants. I wanted a pair of Guess jeans *so bad*. I thought when I was a grown-up, everything would be different. I could buy cool clothes, go out whenever I wanted. And look at me now!" She wiggled her fingers through the holes in her baggy John Deere T-shirt, raised her leg to show off the bleach stain trailing down her yoga pants. "On the floor eating Lunchables, dressed like a bag lady. Thirteen-year-old me would be *pissed*."

"Being a grown-up is a huge disappointment," I said.

"Nobody told me about gray pubes!" Becca bellowed, forgetting to keep her voice down for the boys.

We were laughing again, sobbing. "This is it, Becca," I choked, bits of cracker spraying out of my mouth. "This is as good as it gets. We're living the dream."

"You want another margarita?" Becca asked, getting to her feet. "'Cause I sure do."

"Absolutely."

"Be right back," she said. "I'm gonna check on the boys while I'm at it."

I sucked my drink pouch dry and grabbed the remote. *Wheel of Fortune* was over and the news had come on. There was a shot of winter woods, yellow crime tape strung between tree trunks, writhing in the wind. Then live feed of a reporter on the scene, her pale face and red jacket brilliantly lit against the darkness behind her. Her mouth moved silently, the captions on the screen spelling out the discovery of more bones in the woods where the skull had been found. I turned the sound back on in time to hear the word "homicide."

A photo of Macey Calhoun appeared on the screen, the same shy smile I remembered, her gaze seemingly focused on the photographer rather than the camera, a bright green bow in her reddish hair. She had been positively identified.

"Oh, no," Becca said, returning with our drinks. She knelt down next to me and grabbed my hand. "No, no, no."

I squeezed Becca's hand so hard I couldn't feel my fingers. I imagined a solemn procession as Macey's bones were ferried to the morgue, no lights, no sirens. How it must have been when Shane was taken away. Everyone moving slowly, methodically, no sense of urgency for the dead. I couldn't claim to know what Hannah was going through, how it felt to lose a child, though I could imagine the rough outlines of her pain. The way grief opened up inside you like a crypt, a dark pit with room for one, the torment of questions that might never be answered, secrets the dead alone could know.

CHAPTER 6

HENLEY
AUGUST

Henley rocked on the porch swing, sweating, the night air draped over her skin, thick and prickly as one of Memaw's afghans. A russet moon rose up from the corn, and she wondered where Missy was, if she was still with Ellie Embry, partying in some filthy trailer out in the sticks, wearing borrowed clothes, her phone lost in a stranger's field, sold for quick cash, or maybe buzzing in her pocket, Henley's face flashing on the screen and then going dark when Missy didn't answer.

Missy had known Ellie forever. She'd once gotten out her old yearbooks when Ellie came over, flipping to all the pictures of the two of them together: in matching overalls for Twin Day; secretary and treasurer of Future Farmers of America; driving a tractor in the homecoming parade. They were pretty and flirtatious, qualities that allowed them more popularity than they might have had otherwise, their families not being well-to-do or particularly respected in town. In the pictures, Ellie was willowy with flaxen hair, Missy flaunting her burgeoning hips and sly smile. They smoked cigarettes in the school parking lot at lunch and rode around in Ellie's pickup on the weekends, putting a hundred miles on the odometer every Saturday night, cruising the loop between Casey's and the car wash.

That was before Missy got pregnant and Ellie got into meth. The Ellie that Henley knew was unrecognizable from the yearbook photos, her yellow hair now lank and brittle, hollows in her cheeks where they sucked in around missing molars. She had a tanning bed in the living room of her trailer, and it reminded Henley of a casket. Ellie would emerge from it bleary-eyed, like a vampire arising for the night, her skin the color of cured ham. She always told Henley that a tan took off ten pounds, though Ellie was already unpleasantly thin. She'd moved on from meth to oxy like most everyone else, though she didn't discriminate, according to Missy, against Vicodin, fentanyl, or heroin. Henley hadn't seen Ellie in a while, since Missy had started taking her sobriety seriously, or pretending to.

Junior would go out searching for her mother if she asked him, finding no irony or guilt in the part he played in his baby sister's plight. *We're just middlemen*, he'd explained to her matter-of-factly when she was old enough to realize that Pettit Brothers did more than fix fenders and salvage cars. He had no trouble squaring his part in the drug trade, where doctors sold prescriptions, pills were dispensed, cash collected. It was a business, one side of it blandly sterile—white-coated MDs writing scrips with scrubbed hands, pharmacists filling bottles. Her family was on the dirty side, where things got personal and decidedly more risky—face-to-face negotiations, wads of crumpled bills changing hands, the administration of punishment for unpaid debts and other infractions.

Junior had never hooked Missy up and had scared most everyone else out of dealing to her, too (Denny had slipped one time and paid with a fractured jaw), but he reckoned that junkies, his sister included, would find a way to get what they wanted. It was something in your wiring, and while you might attempt to trip the circuit or ground the current, what you couldn't do was rip it all out and start fresh like you'd do if you renovated a house. No matter what you tried, the old connections would still be there, waiting to spark, start a fire, burn you out. It was hard to find a family in town who hadn't been touched by the scourge in some way. It had become an inescapable part of the landscape, and if there was no reconciling it, Junior figured, you might as well squeeze out a profit.

Henley's phone pinged, but it wasn't her mother.

What r u wearing?

She didn't recognize the number. Her muscles tensed, her eyes instinctively scanning the edge of the field. *Who is this?* she typed.

Jason.

Why are you texting me?

Just wanted to give u a head's up so u r dressed when I stop by. Unlike when u show up at my place with no warning. :)

You're coming by? A flutter of nerves was tamped down by irritation. So presumptuous. She hadn't given him any encouragement the other day at the house, and while she'd mentally revisited the image of him sprawled in bed naked a few times and detailed it in her diary, he had no way of knowing that. He probably assumed every woman he met wanted to screw him.

U ask a lot of questions. :) OK with me coming over? Just to say hi. If not I'll keep driving.

Fine. Come by. She figured it might be entertaining. A story to tell Charlie later.

Headlights lit the corn moments later as Jason's Ford pulled into the drive. He parked and walked up to the house, taking the three porch steps in one stride. "Howdy," he said, the swing creaking when he lowered himself down next to her. "What are you up to tonight?"

"You're looking at it," she said, tucking her feet up beneath her. He smiled at her and she cocked her head to the side. "Why are you here?"

He stretched his arm out across the back of the swing, not touching her, not quite. "I was thinking about you. Have been since I opened my eyes and saw you in my room."

She'd been expecting him to make a joke, but he looked serious. She wasn't sure how to feel about it. There was no doubt she found him attractive, but she still thought of him as the spoiled, ill-behaved brat Missy doted on at work, someone who seemed hell-bent on wasting all the opportunities he'd been given.

"Don't you have . . . friends to hang out with?" she asked.

"Yeah. Don't you?"

She rolled her eyes. Her friends had scattered after graduation, getting married, starting jobs, moving to the city. Charlie had promised to come back for a visit as soon as he could, but he'd been too busy and didn't have a car at school. She was bored. And so was Jason. He'd told her as much the other day when he invited her to swim.

He gestured at the house. "Is Missy around?"

She shook her head.

"Want to go for a drive?"

As much as she tried, she couldn't think of a reason not to.

They navigated a labyrinth of back roads, kicking up plumes of gravel dust, fireflies swirling in their wake, winding up at Lonesome Hill, an old cemetery out in the country where kids came to drink and play truth or dare and scare themselves with Ouija boards.

Jason lowered the tailgate and they sat together, waving away mosquitoes. "You ever come out here?" he asked. "With all those friends of yours?"

"Yeah," she said, leaning back on her hands. "What else are you gonna do when you finally get to drive and realize there's nowhere to go?"

They gazed out over the lichen-covered headstones, sweeps of loosestrife growing wild in between.

"You asked if I have friends to hang out with," he said. "And I don't really, not like I used to. I mean, I know people. But the guys who stuck around here are all farming, starting families. I don't hang out with anybody from the grain elevator after work. Nothing in common, really. I'm just kind of on my own right now, you know?"

"Yeah." She'd felt it, too, since school got out, the vacuum that threatened to swallow anyone who didn't leave right away. She was mired in small-town purgatory, a lonesome in-between that drove people to have babies or pop pills or take a job shoveling grain, anything for the sensation of moving forward in a place you couldn't escape.

"What about you?" he asked. "You have any big plans, now that you're done with school? Missy was always talking about you wanting to get out of Blackwater. Kinda figured you'd be gone by now."

She shrugged. "I'm saving up."

"Okay. Let's say you had a free ticket. If you could pick any place, where would you go?"

"I don't know."

"Sure you do."

She carved her thumbnail into a bug bite on her thigh, pressing an X into her skin. *Make a cross on it,* Memaw used to say. *Jesus'll take out the itch.*

"By this winter," she said, "I want to be out in Colorado, working in a resort town, learning how to ski. Figure I can get a job bussing tables or cleaning hotel rooms and take it from there." She hadn't told anyone that she'd decided on Colorado years ago when Ellie Embry, high on paint thinner, whispered in her ear that Henley's daddy lived there. Whenever she asked Missy about her dad, her mother claimed not to know or care, but Ellie had always hinted otherwise. Henley loved the cold, and all it took was four rolling syllables, *Col-o-ra-do*, to set her fixation on the mountains. She imagined her father as a ski instructor for no particular reason—perhaps he'd moved there to train for the Olympics?—only realizing years later that Ellie had probably said it as a joke, to get her to shut up and stop asking.

"That's your big dream—to go somewhere else and clean up after people like you're doing here?"

She scowled at him. "You wouldn't know, but most people have to start at the bottom. I'll do whatever I have to do to get out of here."

"Relax, I'm just messing with you," he said. "I think it's cool. I wish I had some kind of plan."

"I don't get it. Can't you do whatever you want? I mean, if money's no object?"

"It's not that simple," he said, tapping his fingers on the tailgate. "My dad's got me locked down these days. Trying to straighten me out, I guess. I don't have access to anything but my paycheck, and he makes me put part of that in a savings account I can't touch. He keeps threatening to revoke my trust if I don't do what he wants, and basically what he wants is to turn me into him, you know? My only hope's that he'll keel over before he cuts me out of the will." He smirked. "I used to wish sometimes that Missy was my mom. She was always so laid-back about everything."

"Yeah. Well. She's got issues of her own."

He rearranged himself, folding up his long legs and turning so he could sit facing her. "She using again?"

She flinched as though he'd probed a bruise. Jason had grown up with Missy, knew her nearly as well as she did. There was no point in lying. "I guess," she said. "I don't know. I haven't seen her. I've been texting her but haven't heard back."

"That must be hard," he said. "I figured maybe she was done for good this time."

"Yeah, me, too," Henley said. "Wishful thinking." She'd been telling herself Missy would come back any day, that she'd find her mother on the couch, blasting her favorite Fleetwood Mac album, flipping through an old issue of *People* magazine, painting her nails with glitter polish. And if she didn't come back, it wouldn't matter, because Henley would be gone soon anyway. But Henley was still here, and Missy wasn't, and that hummed in the background like the ever-present drone of combines at harvest time.

"I don't remember my mom much," Jason said. "I feel bad about it. Like, I *should* remember. There are pictures of her all over the house, you know? But I barely remember what it was like, having her around. One time, I was crossing the quad up at school, and I thought I *smelled* her. Sounds stupid, right? She'd been gone for like twelve years. But this lady walked by, and something clicked in my brain, and everything came flooding back. She smelled exactly like my mom, this random combination of who knows what—hair spray, dryer sheets, some kind of lotion she used to wear, I don't even know what it was called. And I *followed* this lady, not even thinking about it. Followed her all the way to her car, freaked her out. I don't know what I thought I'd do when I caught up to her. Give her a hug?" He smiled half-heartedly. "Crazy, right?"

"No," she said. "I think of my pawpaw when I smell Brylcreem. If I close my eyes, it's like he's there."

He brushed a moth from her hair, and it left dust on his fingers. "Missy might not be here now," he said, "but she's still out there. That's something."

They talked until she began to drowse, her head nodding, and she would have stretched out in the truck bed, luxuriating in the cool pre-dawn breeze that swayed the loosestrife, and slept, but Jason murmured that he had to get back. They drove along the empty country roads, the sun firing up the eastern fields by the time they parked at the farm-house.

"I'd like to see you again," he said.

"Yeah."

He threaded his fingers through her and traced his thumb across her palm. "'Yeah'? Such enthusiasm."

She had imagined once or twice what it might be like to kiss him — a harmless mental exercise that she'd indulged in, understandably, after seeing him sprawled naked in his bed — but she hadn't anticipated the rush it would bring, the sense of disorientation after he pulled away, as though the world had tilted and clicked back into place at a slightly different angle. Jason leaned across her to open her door and she slid out of the truck, her legs wobbly as she climbed the porch steps and watched him drive away. She went upstairs without peeking into Missy's room to see if she'd returned and fell into sleep without thinking of her.

CHAPTER 7

SADIE

NOVEMBER

I was surprised to see a message from Hannah in my inbox three days after I'd written to her: *There is something you can do for me. I need cigarettes. I'm staying out at the farm and I can't hardly leave the house.*

I wrote back to let her know I'd come by right after work, and to ask if I could bring dinner, groceries, or anything else, but she didn't respond.

I left work slightly early in an attempt to beat the evening crowd at Walmart, but the dark parking lot was already congested by the time I got there. Judy, the elderly greeter who always seemed to be working no matter what time or day I came in, nodded from her scooter as I walked inside. She looked a hundred years old, her back painfully humped, thin peach-colored fuzz on her shiny scalp, garish splotches of blush smeared on her sunken cheeks. I smiled and asked how she was doing, but she didn't respond. She never did. I wondered if she worked because she liked being around people or because she couldn't afford not to.

I grabbed a few things I needed for the office and then took a detour across the store to pick up some of the margarita pouches like the ones I'd had at Becca's. On the way to the register to get Hannah's cigarettes, I passed the lingerie department, such as it was. I chose a tiny training bra for Lily, hoping it would suffice even though it wasn't from Pink and regretting it when the cashier accidentally rang it up with the work supplies and had to call someone to split out the transactions. While we waited for the manager to arrive, the lane light flashing, the cashier stared at my assortment of purchases, as though trying to figure out how the cigarettes, liquor, tiny bra, zip ties, and industrial stapler fit together.

Hannah's family farm was on the north side of Shade Tree. Her grandparents had still lived there the last time I'd visited, when we took Macey and Lily to see a litter of newborn kittens in the barn a lifetime ago. The grandparents had both passed away in the intervening years, and I didn't know who lived there now.

The yard was still decorated for Halloween. There was a giant inflatable spider staked by the driveway, half deflated. Cheesecloth ghosts dangled from the trees, and a jack-o'-lantern had rotted into mush near the porch. Broken remnants of gingerbread trim hung from the eaves of the old farmhouse like loose teeth, and a plastic tarp had been draped over the steep front gable to keep the roof from leaking.

A woman I recognized as one of Hannah's aunts cracked the door a few inches, a squirming, half-naked toddler in her arms.

"Hi," I said, awkwardly waving the carton of cigarettes. "I'm Sadie. Hannah's expecting me." She didn't make eye contact, though she moved aside so I could squeeze into the dusky foyer, the child shrieking. A narrow staircase and narrower hall split the space.

Once the door was shut, she took the cigarettes from me and jerked her chin toward the back of the house. "Go on and sit. I'll see if she's up to it."

The dark hall led to a living room. A SpongeBob cartoon played on a bulky console TV in the corner, the sound turned low, and a man looked up from the tattered velvet sofa, his feet propped on a coffee table, e-cigarette in his mouth. Even in the dim light, his hair and beard were a vibrant red. The room held a faint stench of decay, like the inside of my car when Lily had left a half-eaten yogurt under the seat.

"Oh, hey," he said, blowing out a cloud of candy-scented vapor.

A little girl dressed in footie pajamas and a tutu burst into the room, hollering. "Hi! Hi! Look at this. Look what my doll can do!" I smiled at her as she held on to the headless doll's arms and flipped its body around like it was doing gymnastics. As I glanced around the room, I noticed more dolls. Doll *parts* would be more accurate. Doll heads with spiky cactuses poking out of the top; a string of pink plastic torsos hanging in the window; disembodied arms and legs glued together to form a picture frame.

The guy noticed me staring. "My girlfriend sells those on Etsy," he said, pulling out his wallet to offer a business card. "I'm Chad, by the way. Hannah's cousin."

I perched at the opposite end of the couch, on the verge of introducing myself, when the little boy Hannah's aunt had been holding earlier barreled into the room and knocked his sister down. They both started wailing. Chad didn't attempt to intervene, though from their reddish hair, I guessed the kids belonged to him.

"You're Sadie, right?" he said. "Shane Keller's sister?"

The kids stopped crying as quickly as they'd started and began working together to pull ancient volumes of the *World Book Encyclopedia* off a tall, flimsy bookshelf that I hoped was not about to fall over and crush them.

"Yeah," I said. "Did you know Shane?"

"I did, I did. Hey, I was sorry to hear about what happened." Chad sucked on his e-cig and blew fog up toward the ceiling. "It's a shame."

The girl scooted up onto the couch next to me and bounced her doll in my lap.

"I like your dolly," I said. "What's her name?" The girl dug down between the couch cushions and collected a handful of grit, cat hair, and what looked like Lucky Charms cereal and stood up to sprinkle it over Chad's head with a gleeful squeal. I covered my mouth, trying not to laugh, and she beamed proudly at me.

"Molly. The grown-ups are talking. Go play with Granny." Chad clenched his e-cig between his teeth and eased the girl off the couch. He brushed crumbs off his face. "Kids, you know?"

Molly clutched her doll to her chest, spinning in circles. She reminded me of Lily at that age, when she would drive me crazy talking nonstop all day long, constantly imploring me, *Look, Mommy. Watch me.* The thing she had wanted most in the world was my attention. I wondered if it made things harder for Hannah, having a little girl here.

"I'm so sorry about Macey," I said.

Chad's expression darkened, and he shook his head. "Roger always was a waste of flesh."

Hannah's aunt hollered down the hall: "Go on up." I guessed she was talking to me, so I said goodbye to Chad. His daughter followed me to the foot of the stairs and wrapped her arms around the newel post, watching wide-eyed as I headed up the steps.

Hannah was waiting in a doorway and closed the door behind me as I came in. Her eyes were rubbed raw, her light strawberry hair matted like she hadn't brushed it in days. She wore pajama pants and a ratty cardigan that she wrapped and rewrapped around her narrow rib cage, pulling it close to her neck as though she couldn't get warm enough.

"I'm so sorry, Hannah."

"Thanks," she said mechanically, tearing open a package of Marlboros.

"I hope those are okay," I said. "I didn't know what kind."

"It's fine," she said. "You want one?"

"No. Thank you."

She lit her cigarette and took a deep drag. "All they got around here is those freaking fake things, tastes like cotton candy. Makes me nauseous. You mind cracking the window?"

"Sure." I crossed the room to pry open the stubborn sash, and cold air eased in. Hannah sat cross-legged on the twin bed and I sat at the edge. The simple block quilt on the bed was hand-tied with pink yarn, the flowered fabrics faded and beginning to fray at the seams. A sewing table was wedged in where a nightstand might go, and much of the floor space in the cramped room was taken up with storage bins and fabric remnants. A hastily prepared guest room.

"I wish I had something stronger right now," Hannah said, ashing into an almost-empty Gatorade bottle. "I keep telling myself Macey wouldn't want that. That was the whole reason Roger said I was an unfit mother. He didn't believe I'd stay clean. But I did. I didn't give in all this time I've been waiting for her to come home. But I don't know now. It'd be so much easier if I couldn't feel this," she said. "If I could just be numb."

"Is there something else I can get you?" I almost mentioned the margaritas I had in the car before realizing how stupid that would sound, offering alcohol to someone in recovery. I had no idea whether Hannah still drank. She had invited me out for drinks at the Barred Owl once, years ago, but I hadn't gone.

She shook her head, not looking at me. She was quiet for a few minutes, nursing her cigarette down to the filter. I didn't know what to do or say, whether she wanted me to stay or go.

"I had to leave my place," she said. "News crews showed up to get

shots of it. *Here's the shitty trailer where that poor little girl used to live.*"
She finished the cigarette and dropped the butt down into the bottle,
swirling it around in the purple liquid at the bottom.

"I knew it was a possibility," she continued. "I've known it since the
beginning, since I hadn't heard from her. She had my phone number
memorized, her grandparents', too. I was sure she'd call me if she
could, find a way to get back to me. You'd think that'd make it easier
when the news comes, right?" Her voice faded to a gravelly whisper.
"But it doesn't. Not one bit. I kept imagining her coming home. All
the things we'd do. She wanted to get her ears pierced." Hannah looked
up at me. "Remember when we took the girls to Walmart that time,
and I wanted so bad to pierce her ears, and the lady whipped out that
big-ass stapler thing and Macey started screaming?"

"Yeah," I said. "I remember." Lily had started bawling, too, even
though I'd had no intention of piercing her ears, and we had to hustle
them over to the frozen foods aisle and rip open a box of Popsicles to
calm them down. *Well,* Hannah had said, once the girls' sobs had
stopped drawing stares, *that didn't go quite like I pictured it.* We had
burst out laughing.

Our friendship had revolved around our children, though I'd probably enjoyed our playdates as much as Lily and Macey had. At the
time, I was eager for any excuse to get out of the house and talk to another woman. Hannah and I were opposites in some respects—
motherhood had exacerbated my tendency toward caution and worry,
while she remained free-spirited and impulsive—but the two of us had
clicked in a way that neither of us had with the other stay-at-home
moms. It had felt like we were on the verge of crossing the invisible
threshold from a superficial friendship to a real one, though we never
got the chance. On the way home from the Barred Owl, Hannah's car
had been T-boned on the highway, and everything had changed after
that.

"Well, she told me she was finally ready. She had the studs picked out and everything. Little gold hearts. We were gonna go on her birthday." She rubbed her eyes with the hem of her cardigan, her shoulders sagging. "I feel like it's my fault. . . . I shouldn't have let him take her that weekend. Sometimes she wouldn't want to go, and he blamed me for that, but he hadn't been around, hadn't made the effort to be part of her life when I was in rehab. I didn't want to piss off the judge, make things worse than they already were. I had to let her go with him. Things got so nasty between Roger and me, with the divorce. But I didn't think he'd do this."

"It's not your fault, Hannah. You couldn't have known." The temperature had dropped, the cold air still spilling in through the open window.

Hannah glanced sharply at me. "What about you? You knew him nearly as well as I did, back in school. Did you think back then—did you *ever* think—that Roger would do something like this? Did you see something I missed?"

I wondered if that was the main reason, aside from the cigarettes, that she'd asked me to come. Roger and I had ridden the bus together since kindergarten, and he and Shane had been close friends for years. Every day of high school, Roger wore Wranglers with a Skoal-can impression in the back pocket and his Future Farmers of America jacket, navy blue with bright yellow embroidery. I remembered him explaining to me, with great seriousness, that the FFA emblem was not a gold medallion, as it might appear, but the cross section of an ear of corn. He'd been part of homecoming court senior year with a group of guys who wore cowboy hats and boots with their tuxes. His crowd had keg parties in an abandoned barn and tucked lumps of spearmint chewing tobacco in their lower lips, spitting the juice into Pepsi bottles. He'd seemed like a decent guy, hardworking, genuine. Had plans to take over the family farm, but his parents had sold the land. He'd been bitter about that, which was understandable. Hannah had alluded to his prickly temper early in their marriage, though I'd never seen it for myself.

"No," I said. "Nothing. I don't think anybody could have predicted this. Are they . . . are they sure it was him?"

Hannah pushed her hair back from her face. There was red polish on her painfully short nails, most of it scraped off. "I don't know, but that's what everybody's thinking. They're looking for him. Alive or dead. Detective said people . . . when they do this, they might kill themselves after."

She lit another cigarette. "I know I was a shitty person when I was high," she said. "I wasn't me for a while. But I really could have used a friend after rehab. Everybody who was still alive scattered like roaches in daylight."

I'd long felt guilt for abandoning her, though the dissolution of our friendship had been a gradual progression, much like her addiction. She hadn't woken up one day and started shooting heroin in the alley behind the Conoco. She'd gotten hooked on oxy like plenty of other people, after her car accident left her with lingering pain and a generous doctor kept refilling her prescription with an increasing number of pills. Macey was in kindergarten at the time, and I helped Hannah out, giving Macey rides home from school some days, or taking her and Lily back to our house to play. One afternoon when I tried to drop Macey off, Hannah wasn't home. I couldn't reach her by phone for hours, and Roger was at work, so we ended up keeping Macey overnight. Greg had wanted to report Hannah to the Department of Family Services.

I hadn't realized until that day how serious it was, and things got worse from there. She became increasingly unreliable, and Macey went to stay with her grandparents. Without our kids' playdates to tether us, I rarely saw Hannah, and it wasn't until a string of overdoses from fentanyl-laced heroin killed several people across the county—

including two women Hannah had been hanging around with—that she finally got help. She messaged me once after finishing rehab, but Greg hadn't wanted me or Lily anywhere near her. I didn't argue, though I couldn't help wondering what might have happened if I'd accepted Hannah's invitation to go to the bar the night of the accident, if I might have ended up in her position just as easily.

"I wish things would have gone differently," I said.

"I was glad," Hannah said. "When you got divorced. Thought it brought you back down to my level. Stupid, right? Like any of that matters now."

"No. I get it." I'd been embarrassed, to some extent, about coming back to Shade Tree without accomplishing the things I'd set out to do. I'd spent my teen years loudly declaring my desire to leave and never return. My two best friends were single and childless, attending grad school on opposite coasts, and I was suddenly a small-town stay-at-home mom. I was lonely, and being with Hannah was easy. She didn't care what degrees I had or didn't have. She'd spent her senior year of high school planning her wedding and picking out baby names. She never judged me for caving in to Greg's demands, giving up my career to raise Lily; she didn't consider it a failure to move back home and start a family. Then her own family had fallen apart, and maybe she'd felt like she was the failure, that I somehow thought I was better than her. And maybe I had thought that, in a way, in certain uncharitable moments.

"She was shot," Hannah blurted. "They didn't say that on the news, but they told me. My baby was shot." Hannah was crying. "It would have been quick, they said. No suffering." She pressed her sweater to her face, muffling her words. "How am I supposed to believe that, that she didn't suffer?"

I moved closer and wrapped my arms around her, feeling her bones shudder beneath a thin veneer of flesh. I held her and rocked her until she stopped shaking.

"I'm sorry I haven't been around," I said. "But I'm here now. If you need a break—if you need to get out of here—you're welcome at my house anytime."

She nodded, snuffling. "I'm sorry about Shane. I should have said something back when it happened."

"It's okay. You had enough to worry about." I looked around, found a crumpled tissue on the floor, and handed it to her. After a while, she got up to shut the window and stood there, staring out.

"Did Roger hate me that much?" she asked. "Did he hate me so much he killed her and left her there to punish me?"

I didn't have an answer.

I half expected Chad's little girl to still be waiting at the bottom of the stairs when I left, but she and her brother must have been put to bed. A single bulb burned in the entry, the rest of the first floor dark and hushed except for the unmistakable voices of a *South Park* rerun drifting from the living room as I let myself out the front door.

I sped home along the winding blacktop, the dead fields stretching out on all sides, switching the radio back and forth between static, sermons, conservative talk shows, and country music, in search of distraction, the Kansas City stations just far enough away to fade in and out like fickle ghosts.

Hannah's words echoed in my head, along with the image they conjured: Macey lying alone in the woods as the seasons passed, spring to summer to fall, her small body dwindling down to bone. I couldn't help thinking of Shane, on the floor in his living room. How long had his body lain there, cooling? How long before Crystle had come home and called the ambulance? And how long after that before she had accidentally dialed Becca? *I didn't mean to call you*, she'd said. Becca had heard people in the house. A crowd, like Crystle was having a party. *He was cold*, Crystle said finally. *He was already cold when I found him.*

CHAPTER 8

HENLEY
AUGUST

The sun glanced down through the cottonwoods at the edge of the river, dappling Jason's tanned skin, still wet from their swim. He held one hand behind his back. "Close your eyes," he said.

"Why?" She'd been spending so much time with him that the days had begun to warp, and she alternately felt like she'd known him forever or that he was a stranger who evoked a dizzying case of déjà vu.

"I got you something. This is our anniversary, you know."

"Anniversary of what?"

"Our first kiss. It was two weeks ago."

"Guess I forgot," she said. "I didn't get you anything. Because two week anniversaries are not a thing."

"I forgive you." He smirked, taking her hand. "Now close your eyes."

She could tell when it touched her skin that it was some sort of jewelry. Her eyes opened to a delicate gold chain spiraled in her palm, a fat diamond at the center.

"It was my mother's," he said.

"No," she blurted. Two weeks together did not warrant a diamond — certainly not his dead mother's — and it made her uneasy that he thought it did.

"Really, it's no big deal. My dad keeps her jewelry in a box in his closet. He can't stand to look at it, but he won't get rid of it, so it's just gonna sit there until he dies." He drew her hair away from the back of her neck and fastened the necklace, the stone nested in the hollow of her throat. "It'd be a waste, don't you think, to keep it hidden away, when it looks so beautiful on you?"

She shook her head, unconvinced, though her fingers snuck up to touch it. "I can't keep it."

"Think it over," he said.

They lay down on their damp towels, looking out across the water. A knotted rope hung down from a nearby tree, and it made Henley think of Charlie. When they were twelve years old, they'd gone fishing out near her uncles' camper and heard screaming and splashing down-river. They crept around a bend to see a group of older kids taking turns swinging out over the river on a rope. They were about to turn around and go back when one of the girls stepped out of the water and they saw that she was topless. It was Henley's cousin Crystle. Henley and Charlie had hidden in the weeds and watched, mesmerized, as Crystle's friends stripped down, laughing and shrieking, flinging their suits onto the shore. Later, when the big kids had gone home, Henley had asked Charlie if he wanted to try skinny-dipping. They agreed to jump in with their clothes on and then take them off underwater. After splashing around shyly for a few minutes, careful to keep their bodies concealed beneath the surface, Henley's dress got caught in the current and Charlie swam to retrieve it. Their fingers had touched when he gave it back to her, and his face had pinked up.

"What are you thinking about?" Jason asked.

"Nothing," she said. He moved closer and began to massage her shoulders, his strong fingers expertly working the tension out of her muscles. She'd been surprised by how attentive he was, how thoughtful. He would show up at her door with a Dr Pepper from Casey's and a bouquet of black-eyed Susans and Queen Anne's lace picked from the ditch. They went on long drives through the country and played cards at the kitchen table with the windows thrown wide, listening to the insects and night birds singing. He wanted to stay with her in the empty farmhouse, but Earl had pitched a fit that first night when Jason had taken her to Lonesome Hill and hadn't come home until dawn. They hadn't gone anyplace where people might see them together, and she preferred it that way, so they didn't have to deal with the looks they might get or have to explain themselves to anyone. That's why they'd come to the old Gunderson farmstead to swim. The property was in foreclosure, so no one was around, though kids sometimes snuck out there to drink at night, the river access hidden away, the channel wide and deep.

"Tell me something you've never told anyone," he said, bending to kiss her neck. He was always saying things like that. *Tell me your favorite memory. Your worst fear. Your deepest regret.* Like he wanted to know all there was to know about her. She'd never been with someone who didn't already know her, who hadn't known her for her entire life. The novelty was strangely exhilarating.

"You go first."

He stretched out behind her and pulled her against his chest, so they were both facing the water.

"Did you know," he said, "that when I was in junior high, I got sent away to a school for troubled kids?"

"No. Why? What did you do?"

"I hit my dad with a baseball bat. Fractured his hand."

"No you didn't."

She felt him nod, the stubble on his jaw brushing her ear. "I got mad. He wasn't going to let me play ball because I wasn't keeping my grades up. I didn't really think, I just swung."

"That's crazy. How long were you there?"

"I straightened up pretty quick," he said. "They called it a 'therapeutic' school, but it was like a prison. Everything was a privilege that had to be earned with good behavior—hot water, blankets, salt. Had plenty of time to think things over. I apologized as soon as they let me call him, but he made me stay the whole semester. He told everybody I was at a fancy boarding school, and then he told them I came back because I got homesick."

"And you never told anybody the truth?"

"No."

The sun angled lower, blazing over their tangled legs.

"Your turn," he said.

She had plenty of family secrets that weren't hers to tell, and few of her own that she wanted to share with anyone. Secrets were secret for a reason. He'd revealed something deeply personal, though, and she wanted to be fair. "You know my friend Charlie?" she said.

"I've heard you mention him. He moved away, right?"

"Yeah. Anyway. He was my first. And I was his. We never told anybody. We were always just friends, and then one night it was different."

"When was that?"

"When we were sixteen."

"Where?"

"Where? Why does that matter?"

"You've got to tell the whole secret."

"Fine. My uncles' camper, on the river."

"Where on the river?"

"The very end of Hatchery Road, if you really need to know."

"Just once?" he said. "You never thought about doing it again?"

"No," she said. "I told you, it's not like that between us."

"I bet *he* thought about it."

"Jealous?" she asked teasingly. She couldn't see his face, figured he was only joking.

"I'm hot," he said, pushing himself up and offering his hand. He grabbed the knotted rope hanging down from the tree and passed it to her. "Ladies first."

Henley swung out over the green water, closing her eyes as she fell. Jason dove in after her. "Let's try something," he said as they bobbed on the surface. She raised her eyebrow suggestively, wondering what he might have in mind.

"Not that." A slow grin spread across his face. "Come on. Trust me." They climbed up the bank, dripping, and made their way back to the rope. "Let me take you down to the bottom."

"What do you mean?"

"I'll hold on to you and you hold still. Don't try to swim. Don't fight it. Just let me take you down and back up."

"Why?"

"To show how much you trust me," he said. "You do, right?"

It wasn't something she had thought about. She liked the way he looked at her, the heat that spread through her body when he touched her, the way he had opened up to her and gotten her to open up to him. When they were together, it didn't matter that she was a Pettit and he was a Sullivan, that her mother was an addict, that everyone in town thought he was an arrogant ass. She liked him, but she wasn't sure she trusted anyone enough to drag her to the bottom of the river.

He took the rope in one hand and extended the other toward her. "Please?"

She hesitated. "Are you being serious?"

"I want to show you," he said. "You can trust me like you've never trusted anyone."

She wasn't scared, exactly, despite the sense of unease prickling up her spine—she didn't think for a second that he would do anything to hurt her—but she couldn't quite grasp why he was pushing her to do this. She looked into his eyes, an intensity focused solely on her, and shrugged. "Fine," she said. "Let's do it."

He lifted her up, careful not to let go of the rope, and she wrapped her legs around his waist. He embraced her, pinning her arms to her sides. It was still a new feeling, his body pressed against hers, and she felt herself flushing. "Don't fight it. I'll keep you safe," he whispered in her ear, and then they were flying out over the river. Her stomach dropped when he released the rope, and panic overtook her as they fell. Their bodies pierced the bright surface, rocketing down toward the chilly depths.

They hovered near the bottom, her eyes pinched shut, toes kicking mud, and he gripped her tightly as she instinctively squirmed. For a sickening moment, she wondered if she'd misread everything, if he might be as reckless as people said, if he would, for some unknown reason, hold her under until they both drowned. In her heart, she didn't believe it. She forced herself to relax and hold still, to show that she trusted him, and as soon as she did, he launched them upward with powerful kicks, surfacing and gulping air, and then his mouth was on hers, kissing her, Jason doing all the work to keep them afloat. It went against every instinct not to swim for herself, but once she broke through the dark curtain of fear and doubt, it was intoxicating— surrendering control, allowing herself to trust him with her life.

His lips moved along her neck, igniting her skin, and she wanted him so urgently that she was on the cusp before they fell onto the sedge grass, his body stretched over hers, his muscles taut and trembling.

"I've got you," he whispered, burying his face against her throat, his breath hot in her ear as his fingers traced her jawbone, her clavicle, looped into the necklace and tugged just enough that the chain nipped her flesh. "And I'll never let go."

CHAPTER 9

SADIE
NOVEMBER

G ravy had shown his displeasure at my coming home late from Hannah's by knocking the African violet off the coffee table and chewing the basket into sharp little bits of confetti. It reminded me that I still needed to thank the people who had sent flowers to the funeral, so on my morning break at work the next day, I googled addresses for Dave Gorecki and Leola Burdett.

Once I found Leola, I remembered why her name had sounded familiar. She lived way out on what old-timers called Wildwood Lane, though it had been thirty years since all the county roads had been rechristened with numbers. I'd accompanied another social worker on a home visit to the Burdetts' when I was new to the job and Leola was needing assistance following hip replacement surgery; she'd been embarrassed about asking for outside help. I had no idea how she knew Shane. Her number was listed, and I decided to call her.

She answered right away, and as soon as I explained who I was and thanked her for the plant, she told me she was glad that I'd called.

"I have something for you," she said, her voice wavering. "Something of your brother's. I don't get to town much, but you're welcome to drop by anytime."

"I could come today, on my lunch break."

She seemed a bit startled that I'd taken her up on her offer so quickly but said that would be all right.

Wildwood Lane turned from asphalt to gravel to dirt, meandering between fallow fields and overgrown tracts of invasive honeysuckle as it angled north and east of town. The unmarked cutoff to Raccoon Ridge Conservation Area, where the skull had been found, was blocked with an orange-and-white-striped barricade.

When I reached Leola's, the midday light filtered through a gauze of dull clouds, washing the property in the faded tones of an old sepia photograph. The weathered farmhouse had a tin roof and a small porch, firewood stacked waist-high between the posts. A chipped cast-iron tub sat upended and half buried in the front yard, providing a shrine for a Virgin Mary figure in flowing robes, and the flowerbeds around the house's foundation were crowded with spinning whirligigs, gazing globes, and an assortment of stone angels.

I knocked on the storm door, which rattled in its frame and set a chorus of dogs to yipping inside the house. The inner door opened and a frail woman with a long white braid appeared, three tiny dogs bouncing up and down at her feet.

"Hello, Mrs. Burdett? I'm Sadie." The wind picked up behind me, cutting through my jacket and setting all the whirligigs in the yard to squawking.

"Leola," she said. Her voice warbled like a bird's, a soft drape of flesh beneath her chin quivering as she spoke. "You can come on in."

She pushed open the storm door with a creak, and the little dogs sprang toward me, scraping at my boots with tiny claws. They were some sort of cartoonish Chihuahua mix, with bug eyes and long hair. I stepped inside, doing my best not to trip on them. The front room of the farmhouse had faded yellow-and-green floral wallpaper and carpet that had been worn down to the backing in a path from the door to the hall. A potbelly stove sat on a brick platform in one corner, an overflowing ash bucket next to it, waiting to be dumped. Leola was bundled in a thick shawl, an ankle-length housecoat with a lace collar, and a pair of men's loafers, and while I'd thought at first that the cold air had blown in with me, it quickly became apparent that there was no heat coming off the stove. I pulled my hands up into the sleeves of my coat to keep them warm.

Leola sat down and the dogs bounced up onto the sagging couch and huddled at her side, growling at me with sidelong glances as I took a seat in a recliner with dishtowels draped over the armrests.

"I am so sorry about your brother," she said. "He was a fine young man."

"Thank you," I said. "And thank you again for sending the violet. It was so thoughtful." I left out the part about Gravy destroying it.

"It was a small thing, after everything he'd done for us. I wanted to come to the visitation," she said, "but I'm afraid I don't get out much anymore." One of the dogs turned circles beside her on the couch, making a little nest in the shawl.

I didn't want to have to ask, but it seemed like she wasn't going to say it without prompting. "I was wondering, Leola . . . if you could tell me a little bit about how you knew Shane? I feel like I should know, but . . ."

"Oh," she said, fiddling with the collar of her housecoat. "I shouldn't have expected you'd know me by name. I'm Charlie's granny. I half-way raised him."

Charlie. I remembered the child's craft I had found in Shane's things, the misspelled name written in crayon that wasn't quite Charlie or Charles. A tingling sensation spread from my chest out to my fingertips.

"I'm sorry," I said. "I don't know Charlie either."

Leola eyed me carefully, studying my face as though questioning the clear family resemblance. Same blue eyes, same ruddy cheeks, hair so dark it almost looked black. "Were you and your brother not close?"

I'd thought we were. We saw Shane at Mom's house for every holiday and nearly every other weekend before he started dating Crystle. I'd always felt close to my brother, but maybe the tight bond we'd shared as kids had loosened so gradually that I'd failed to notice. Dad's belt, in a way, had bound us together, united against a common threat. Once we'd escaped the pressure cooker of our childhood home, there had been no need to cling so tightly to one another.

"He didn't talk a lot about himself," I said. "I don't know why. I wish he had. Or that I'd asked the right questions."

"Well," Leola said. "He didn't run his mouth like so many fools you see now. One of the things I liked about him."

"So how did he get to know you and your grandson?"

Leola patted one of the dogs with an unsteady hand, a wadded tissue cupped in her palm. "Charlie used to live out by your brother, back when his mom still had custody, and he really took to Shane. Stuck to him like a bur, and I was glad for it. My daughter-in-law couldn't handle him on her own—she never was much for mothering. Shane was a good influence on him. He'd spend hours tinkering with that old car, teaching Charlie how to fix things. Really turned him around, got him on a good path. I didn't hear the story till years later,"

Leola said, "but the first time they laid eyes on each other, Charlie was in Shane's driveway smashing his taillights with a tire iron. He was only about seven or eight years old." She shook her head, a faint smile on her lips. "Shane told him he'd have to help fix it, and he'd show him how. I think your brother saw a bit of himself in Charlie. Wanted to help. And look at him now—off at the technical college. That's Shane's doing."

One of the light bulbs in the overhead fixture flickered and buzzed, and Leola leaned forward to spread her liver-spotted hands over the photo album that lay open on the coffee table. She turned the pages carefully, running her knobby fingers over each picture until she came to one of Shane.

I couldn't tell exactly how old the picture was, but he still had most of his hair. He grinned proudly, crouching next to a little blond boy, his hand on the boy's shoulder. On the ground in front of them was a Pinewood Derby car.

"That's Charlie," Leola said. He had a wide gap between his front teeth and an unruly cowlick at his crown, like he'd forgotten to brush his hair. "It was doubly hard on him, I think, losing Shane after he'd already lost his daddy."

"Your son?"

Her jaw worked back and forth. "Yes. Years back, accident at Sullivan." She flipped through the album to the last picture before the pages went blank, a more recent shot of Charlie leaning against a dilapidated pickup, his hair in his eyes, limbs long and gangly.

"That's Charlie now?" I asked.

Leola nodded. "Tall as all get-out."

"I don't remember seeing him at the funeral."

She looked down at the dogs. They appeared to be sleeping. "He couldn't stand to go," she said. "He didn't quite get along with Crystle."

"Oh," I said. "Did something happen? Or . . . ?"

Leola hesitated, weighing her words, as though deciding how candid to be. "He didn't like the way Crystle treated Shane, and Crystle didn't like him saying so. He figured she'd be peacocking around the funeral, making it all about herself."

"Do you think he'd be willing to talk to me?" I said. "I understand if he wouldn't want to, but if he and Shane were close . . . there are some things I'd like to ask him."

"I'm sure that'd be fine," she said. "He'll be back to visit soon. I'll let you know. Pardon me a minute." She attempted to get up from the couch without disturbing the dogs, but they hopped down and trailed her out of the room. She returned with a battery-powered lantern and handed it to me.

"Shane's. Been meaning to give it back to him and hadn't got around to it. Power went out in a windstorm back in the spring, and he didn't want me using the old kerosene lamp. Thought I'd trip over a dog and set the house afire." A sad smile deepened the grooves around her mouth. "He made a joke of it, of course, like he wasn't serious— didn't want me to feel as old and useless as I really am—but he worried about us. Looked after us. That's the kind of man he was."

"Why don't you keep it," I said, giving the lantern back to her. I dug in my bag for a business card. "My cell number's on here, and the office number, too. Call me if there's ever anything you need help with." She tucked the card into the pocket of her housecoat without glancing at it. "Can I stoke the fire for you before I go?" I asked. "Or bring in more firewood? It's getting colder out there."

Her thin lips pressed together and she shook her head. "Thank you all the same."

I'd offended her, possibly, with my offer. Social workers weren't always welcome. It wasn't uncommon, people too proud to accept help from anyone other than family. It showed how much she'd thought of Shane.

————

I'd planned to go straight home after work, but Becca was in Blackwater, having dropped the boys off at her in-laws' for an overnight visit, and she wanted to meet up for dinner and hear more about Charlie and Leola than I'd been able to tell her on the phone.

Two police SUVs drove past me on the way to the Blackwater Diner, the kind with the low-profile light bars on top that make it easier to sneak up on you. Main Street was nearly deserted, and the SUVs rolled through the intersections without coming to a complete stop. Becca was waiting for me when I arrived. The diner had a comforting retro feel, with red vinyl seats and Formica tabletops and slabs of cream pie in a glass-front cooler at the counter. It was Lily's favorite place to eat, and it felt strange going there without her. Aside from Becca and me, the early dinner crowd included a few overall-clad farmers and a cluster of gray-haired women wearing turtlenecks and Christmas sweaters. Johnny Cash played low over the speakers, fry grease crackling in the back.

Becca ordered the special, a breaded pork tenderloin sandwich the size of a catcher's mitt, served with onion rings and coleslaw. I ordered two slices of pie, chocolate cream and buttermilk chess, and when our food arrived, we divided it all in half to share.

"You look nice," I said. Becca had mascara on, a blouse she'd clearly ironed, shoes with a slight heel. She had curled her hair and might have even spritzed it with hair spray.

"Thanks," she said, smacking her palm on the ketchup bottle to get it going. "It's the first time I've left the house in days and I wanted to feel human. You go too long without wearing shoes and a bra, it's hard to go back."

"That sounds like a proverb," I said.

"Well. You start to get philosophical after watching five episodes of *PAW Patrol* back-to-back."

"Hey, you're lucky," I said. "Remember when Lily was that age? How much she loved Barney? Greg's mom got her that horrid *Barney's*

Best Manners DVD and she watched it on repeat. I was ready for a lobotomy."

"It's weird," Becca said, using a knife to cut up a monstrous onion ring. "Today I was wondering how long I should wait before going back to work—you know, whether we should keep trying for a third or start looking into preschool for the boys so I can work part-time. And for the first time, I didn't get teary-eyed thinking about not being home with them every day."

Becca had always wanted enough kids to fill a minivan, though she'd had trouble conceiving the boys and had been worried that she was getting too old, that she was running out of time.

"I think kids are wired to drive you just crazy enough that you'll be willing to let them go to kindergarten."

"Makes sense," Becca said, taking the bun off her half of the sandwich to rearrange the lettuce and remove the anemic slice of tomato. "Do you think if Shane hadn't . . . do you think he and Crystle would have had kids?"

"I don't know. She's not exactly maternal. I don't remember Shane ever talking about it."

"I don't either," Becca said. "He would have been a great dad."

"He was always so good with Lily and the boys."

Becca nodded, sniffing. "I wish they were older. You know? So they'd remember."

"Yeah."

"Did you talk to Mom about Charlie yet? I think it'll make her happy."

"Happy might be a stretch."

"You know what I mean, Sadie. It's a nice surprise. I like knowing Shane had that in his life, since he never got to have kids of his own."

"But why didn't he ever mention him? If this kid was so important to him, why didn't he share that with us?"

Becca scrubbed grease from her fingers with a napkin. "I don't know."

"It's not the same," I said, "but it makes me think of stories you read in the news, where some guy has two different families who don't know about each other, and you wonder how they could possibly not know."

"Maybe it's not as big of a deal as we're making it out to be," Becca said. "He might not have thought it was worth telling us that he was helping out a neighbor. It's just something you do, no need to brag about it."

I knew it wasn't realistic to expect him to tell us everything. Becca and I talked about plenty of things without including him, and we all kept pieces of ourselves secret from one another, intentionally or not. Still, there was a slight pinch of hurt or betrayal that, for whatever reason, he'd kept the two parts of his life separate. His old family and his new one. The one he was born into and the one he chose.

People filtered into the diner, filling up a few of the booths. I recognized Brody Flynn, who worked dispatch at the police department, talking animatedly to the waitress as she made her way to our table. She paused to listen to him, clamping our check between her teeth as she pulled her ponytail tighter and adjusted her scrunchie. She sighed wearily as she approached our table and tucked the bill under the ketchup bottle.

"You hear the latest?"

"No." Becca's forehead furrowed in anticipation of bad news. We didn't have to ask *About what?*

"Brody said they found Roger Calhoun. What was left of him. 'Skeletal remains,' he said."

"Where'd they find him?"

"Out in the woods, not too far from where they found Macey."

Acid burned my throat, the lingering sweetness of chocolate pie turning bitter as I thought of Hannah. She must know—surely they'd told her before they let the news get out. I wondered if this was the answer she would have chosen from the dwindling list of possibilities, each one wretched and heartbreaking—if it was better for Roger to be dead than alive.

"Murder-suicide," the waitress said. "Isn't that what you call it? Can you imagine? Why couldn't he have just shot himself, spared the little girl?"

"Pure spite," one of the Christmas-sweater ladies behind us piped. "Wanted to punish the mother—take her baby, leave her alive. Worse than killing her. She probably wishes she was dead."

"Or, maybe she did it." The voice was soft and musical, belonging to a bird-boned woman in a sequined sweatshirt that read JESUS IS THE REASON FOR THE SEASON. "Hannah. Killed 'em both and made it look like the husband. Probably wanted to get 'em out of her hair so she could go back to partying."

"What?" Becca looked horrified.

"She's a junkie," the woman said. "Left her daughter with the grandparents while she was out doing drugs. Bill and Martha go to my church, poor souls. They're sorry they ever let Macey go back to her mother. Don't trust her one bit. Won't let her in their house."

"Huh." The waitress tilted her head, considering. "I did hear she was out at the Barred Owl riding the mechanical bull a while back, like nothing was wrong. While Macey was missing."

"It's not right," the woman said. "She didn't deserve to be a mother."

"You don't know anything about it," I snapped. The sweater ladies swiveled toward us and gawked. "About her. You don't even know what happened."

"And you do?" the woman in the Jesus shirt asked, her eyes magnified behind bifocals.

Becca touched my arm, and I didn't say anything. Everyone was quiet for a moment, and then the waitress sauntered back toward the counter. The sweater ladies turned around and resumed chattering among themselves. It wasn't lost on me that Hannah was being judged the same as I'd judged Crystle. The proper way for a wife or mother to grieve. The correct behavior to exhibit when someone you love is gone and you have to keep on living. How should the guilty behave, and the innocent, so you could tell them apart? What about the rest of us, those grieving outside the spotlight?

I took out my phone and texted Hannah. *I'm so sorry.* Three little dots popped up in the bubble, as though she was writing back. They hovered there, disappearing and reappearing, once, twice, three times, and then they were gone.

HENLEY
SEPTEMBER

Labor Day weekend was always spent on the water. Her uncles had kept an old camper at their spot down by the river for as long as Henley could remember, and it had survived floods, rodent infestations, and the general abuse of scores of Pettit cousins. The long strip of pebbled shoreline was reshaped each season by crests and currents, the water cool and golden green in the meandering shallows. A circle of driftwood logs and folding chairs was arranged around a blackened firepit, and a clothesline hung between two trees, sagging beneath the weight of drying towels. A long-gone girlfriend of presently incarcerated Uncle Denny had strung a dream catcher on a cottonwood branch, and it dangled there still, its unraveling web clogged with high-water debris. Junior and Raymond had found the girlfriend to be too much of a hippie, and the woman had gone packing after Crystle had elbowed her in the gut in a fight over cigarettes, Denny siding with his daughter.

Raymond had Bud Light in the Styrofoam cooler and a six-pack of Dr Pepper for Henley, though she knew he'd let her have a beer if she wanted one. She lounged on the shore in an inner tube, her feet in the languid current and her hair looped in a knot to keep it off of her neck. She was thinking of Charlie, who was supposed to be there with her. He had made plans to come home for the holiday weekend, but at the last minute his ride had canceled. Or at least that's what he'd said. She had pretended not to be disappointed when he told her, part of her wondering if he had simply decided not to come — if he'd been distant recently because he was busy with school, like he'd claimed, or because he'd grown tired of waiting for her to decide how she felt about him. She'd looked forward to spending time together on the water, where they had made so many memories. They'd shared their first kiss on this very shore, the fire drying their damp swimsuits, woodsmoke scenting the night air.

Crystle and Shane and the other cousins began to arrive as Junior was starting up the fire. Crystle wore a Chiefs cap and mirrored aviators that masked her mood. Her hair hung down in two thick braids that framed the cleavage ballooning out of her camouflage bikini. She had brought a bowl of Suddenly Salad and a thermos full of marshmallow vodka. She cracked open one of the Dr Peppers and dribbled some into the thermos, swirling it around and taking a long slug.

Henley was never sure if she preferred Crystle drunk or sober. While prone to moodiness either way, the drunk version was both more fun and more volatile. Crystle dragged a tube into the shallows and flopped down on it, grinding the butt of her thermos into the pebbles so it wouldn't tip over. She made an irritable groaning sound and hollered at Shane to fetch her tanning oil out of the Jeep. He shook his head and did as he was told. His wife's moods and demands had little effect on him, and Henley wondered if Crystle did things to make up for it in private—if she had been serious when she told Henley that certain bedroom acts could make a man overlook all manner of flaws and sins. Henley doubted all men were that simple, but she couldn't think of a better explanation for why Shane put up with Crystle.

As Raymond and Junior set to work getting hotdogs ready to roast, no one mentioned Missy's absence. She wasn't the only one missing, of course. Denny was in jail, and the two older aunts, plagued with health problems from arthritis to diabetes, weren't much for the river these days. The littlest cousins—Junior's and Denny's grandkids—ran free, oblivious to their elders. They had formed their own tribe, playing chicken in the current, throwing rocks at turtles sunning on a deadfall, sneaking the Hershey bars meant for s'mores and eating them all before dinner, their chocolate-smeared faces lacking remorse. The next generation of Pettits, well on the way to earning their reputations.

It was near dark when Charlie showed up, everyone gone except for Shane and Crystle and the uncles and Crystle's brother Dex, who always wore a rodeo buckle and bragged about his roping prowess but hadn't competed in years. Henley hopped up to burrow into Charlie's chest and then pummel him.

"You said you weren't coming!"

"Shane found me a ride into town," he said.

"Get that schoolboy a beer!" Shane hooted, stoking the bonfire. "Damn proud of you, kid."

Charlie cracked a wide grin, and even in the fading light, Henley sensed he was blushing. Shane had helped him get into the program, and she knew his pride meant more to Charlie than anyone else's, including hers.

"You hungry?" Henley asked, dragging him to the camper. "We can see what's left."

They sat together in the tiny dinette, Henley switching on the lantern and ripping open a bag of Cheetos. She remembered that she was wearing the necklace Jason had given her, and her hand flew up to cover the stone. Jewelry wasn't something Charlie was likely to notice, but if he did, she'd tell him it was fake.

"How's it going?" he asked, planting his elbows on the table.

"Fine. Boring. What've you been up to? I haven't seen you in forever." Their legs brushed together under the table, neither of them pulling away. He looked different somehow, older, if that was possible, his hair shorter than he usually wore it and carefully combed.

"Just busy with school," he said. "Fall semester started." Mosquitoes drifted in through the open door and swirled around the lamp.

"You like it? Is it everything you thought it would be?"

"Yeah," he said. "I mean, it's better than regular school. We still have tests and homework, though, and you know I'm not too good at that stuff."

"Program's not that long, right? You can make it."

He shrugged and nodded, crunching a mouthful of Cheetos.

"How long are you in town for?" she asked.

"Not long—I go back tomorrow night. I wanted to come, though. To check on Granny. And see you." His hand lay inches from hers on the tabletop, his fingers lightly tapping. She detected something in his shadowed face, a seriousness in his voice.

"So you missed me?" she teased.

"Yeah," he said. "It gets a little lonely, being someplace you don't know anybody."

"There any girls at tech school?" she asked.

"Girls? Yeah," he said, laughing. "Lots. Not in welding, though. Maybe one or two. Why? You thinking about coming down to join me?"

She'd never considered it seriously, though Shane had made the same pitch to her that he'd made to Charlie. The technical programs were shorter and cheaper than regular college and almost guaranteed to land you a job. Shane had given her a brochure, creased down the middle from being folded in his pocket. She wondered where he'd gotten it, how long he'd carried it around, waiting to give it to her. She'd thanked him and thrown it away without ever opening it.

"You could, you know," Charlie said. "I know it's not as far away as you were wanting to go, but at least you could get out of here."

Henley's phone buzzed and she felt herself tense involuntarily, like she was bracing for something. Jason, wanting to meet up.

Can't tonight, she texted. *At the river with my family.* He'd been texting her constantly lately, anytime he wasn't at work and they weren't together, and it was starting to wear on her.

"You want a drink?" Charlie asked, getting up.

"Sure. Thanks." Her phone buzzed again. *Can I come?* She didn't answer. Charlie returned with two Buds and opened one for her. They clinked their cans together.

Another text. *Pretty please?* Followed by puppy dog faces. Then another. *I really want to see you.*

Maybe later, she texted back.

I'm already out that way, he texted. *I'll swing by and say hi. Promise I won't stay long. See u in a minute.*

She was confused for a moment, not sure how he knew exactly where she was, and then she remembered all the questions he'd asked about her uncles' place, after she told him what she'd done in the camper with Charlie.

"What's up?" Charlie asked. "You're scrunching up your face something awful."

She hadn't realized. "Nothing," she said, forcing a smile. "Just—a friend coming over."

"Anybody I know?"

She sipped her beer, avoiding his gaze. "You know Jason Sullivan?"

Charlie squinted, reaching out to smash a mosquito on his beer can. "Who doesn't." There was no judgment in his voice, nor any teasing. He didn't even sound surprised, as though it had somehow been inevitable that Jason would find his way to her eventually. He kept his expression neutral, though disappointment showed in his eyes.

"It's nothing," she said. "Just having some fun."

"All right," he said, the corner of his mouth turning up in a half smile. He rose to his feet and brushed Cheeto dust off his jeans. "I'll leave you to it."

"No, stay. Finish your beer." Even to her own ears it didn't sound sincere. As much as she wanted to spend time with Charlie, she didn't know what would happen if Jason showed up and saw them there together.

"Nah," he said, bending to hug her goodbye. "I'll catch up with you later." She squeezed him extra hard before letting go, pressing a kiss to his cheek. He stopped to clap Shane on the back on his way out, and Henley could hear the muffler rattling even after the truck had disappeared into the dark.

She joined the others around the fire, where Crystle was laughing loud enough to scare fish out of the river. She'd finished her vodka and switched to beer, and Junior had gotten out the pipe.

"Henny Penny!" Crystle howled, her eyes watering. "Sit your sweet ass down. We were just talking about Dalmire." Crystle snorted and near choked and started giggling again. Junior kicked in, too, his laugh dry and wheezy like an asthmatic having an attack.

Henley knew the story well, though she'd never found it that funny. Dalmire had once been a friend and customer of the Pettits. During the brief time that Dalmire had been saved by Jesus Christ, he had gotten up on a moral high horse, by Junior's reckoning. Shortly thereafter, Dalmire had gone back to buying drugs from them, because he liked his oxy and his fentanyl, and he had subsequently disappeared. Something unpleasant had happened to Dalmire. Supposedly he had jumped out of a moving car to escape some men he owed money to, cracked his skull on the way out, and ended up in a hog trough. Junior and Raymond were coy about whether the men in question were, in fact, themselves. There was a long bone—which Henley suspected came from a cow or deer—that was always lying around the shop, being put to various uses, and the uncles joked that it was all that was left of Dalmire. For a long spell, it was used to hold the door of the chicken pen closed while the latch was broken. When the bone slipped down and the chickens got out, they would blame their former friend. *Goddammit, Dalmire falling down on the job again.* And they would laugh so hard Junior'd about piss himself. *Half worthless, always was, no different now.*

"Jason Sullivan's coming over," Henley said, cutting through the laughter. "If you can't say anything nice, don't say anything at all."

"What?" Crystle said. "That Sullivan boy? Oh, I'll be nice to him." She giggled and flicked her tongue through her teeth. "I'll be real nice."

Dex chuckled and Shane shook his head, scraping the bowl of the pipe with his fingernail.

Junior thumbed the wheel of his lighter. "Hey, come on now, when are we ever not nice?" Even Shane busted out laughing. Junior steered the conversation to the time Pawpaw tried to make moonshine, and Raymond beckoned Henley away from the fire.

"Listen, you're gonna do what you're gonna do. But I hope you know a Sullivan man'll never make an honest woman of a Pettit."

Henley smirked. "I don't need a man to make me anything."

Her uncle shook his head, grinning, his silver tooth showing. "That's my girl. Got a sass mouth like your mama." He paused, stroking his beard, the smile fading. "Take it she ain't back yet?"

"No."

"I'll be making a visit up to Ellie's place shortly. She'll be all right."

"Raymond?"

"Yeah?"

"When I leave . . . when I'm gone. You'd come find me and bring me home if I ever got in too much trouble, wouldn't you?"

"You know it, darlin'." He squeezed her arm and kissed her forehead and let her go.

Her uncles worried, especially Raymond, but they knew, too, that she was stronger than Missy. That she could hold her own.

Jason came into the firelight bearing gifts. A case of Boulevard beer, which he handed off to an unimpressed Junior, and a king-size bag of Skittles, which were Henley's favorite. After introductions were made, Jason and Henley retreated to the river's edge and spread out a quilt. He pulled her down onto his lap, lacing his fingers through hers and pressing his lips to her wrist.

The air was still dense with the heat of the day, though Henley knew that soon enough the first cool night would come, and even though the days might be sweltering well into October, summer would be over.

"You still thinking about leaving?" Jason murmured, opening the Skittles for them to share. "You haven't mentioned it lately."

Henley nodded, unwinding her hair, shaking it out over her shoulders.

"I'll come with you."

She smiled gently. "That's sweet."

"No. I mean it. I was thinking, I've got some things I could pawn. Get us a little startup cash to get going."

She eyed him dubiously, scratching at a rash of chigger bites on her ankle. "What about your dad?"

"I don't want to spend the rest of my life shoveling grain. He can't keep me here forever."

She didn't know what to say. She hadn't really thought about what it would be like to have him go with her. She chewed her lip.

"Don't you want me to?" He played with her hair, gathering it loosely into his fist and then letting it fan down.

"I don't know . . . I just always thought it was something I'd do on my own."

"But now you don't have to."

She opened her mouth to reply, but he didn't give her a chance. He kissed her, his mouth sweet from the candy, his hand sliding down her rib cage to the small of her back and drawing her closer. She felt the stirring that his touch always elicited, a desire that blinded her to anything but what she wanted in the present moment, and that was him.

He pulled her up and whispered into the cup of her ear: "Come on." The others were still gathered around the fire, getting worked up over cars or baseball or whatever pointless thing they were talking about, paying no attention. Jason led her to the camper, easing the door closed behind them. It was sweltering inside with the breeze cut off, sweat instantly slicking her body. He pushed her back against the door and lifted her up, her legs around his waist. A thought flickered in her head, that he wanted to do this because this was where she had been with Charlie—not just once, as she had told him, but a few times more—and he wanted to reclaim it for himself, like a dog marking his territory. Still, her body lit up and she let it.

When it was over, and she was leaning against the door catching her breath, she noticed that the conversation outside had grown heated. Jason lay on the floor, his eyes closed. She pulled on her shorts and cracked the door.

Shane was hollering like she'd never heard him, jabbing his finger in the air and slurring his words, and Crystle whacked him across the chest, her rings glinting in the firelight. "Calm down!" she roared. "Chill the fuck out!"

Junior grumbled something inaudible to Dex that seemed to rile him. Dex and Crystle were the only kids from Denny's second wife, and they always stuck up for each other. Dex's hair was a little darker, eyes more brown than green, and Junior often expressed doubt that Denny was his father, that he was a Pettit at all, something that pissed Dex off to no end. He leapt out of his chair and he and Junior went chest to chest. Raymond switched on the boom box, drowning everything out, an old cassette of some big-haired metal band, Ratt or Twisted Sister or Quiet Riot, they all sounded alike to Henley. The music screeched in her ears, and she watched Junior's mouth move, his palm smoothing his beard. Her muscles tensed across her shoulders and down her spine, waiting for something, though she didn't know what. Shane and Crystle moved toward the river, and she could tell they were still fighting, glowing cigarette tips swirling through the darkness beyond the fire. It reminded Henley of the Fourth of July, when she would write her name across the night sky with sparklers, her hand working in furious swoops to get the last letter out before the first one disappeared, the smoking remains of her name still burning bright when she closed her eyes.

Fingers curled around her ankle and she yelped. Jason's hands, their unbearable heat moving up her thigh. She shook him off. "Get up. It's time to go."

CHAPTER 11

SADIE

NOVEMBER

I tried to reach Hannah after hearing the news that Roger's remains had been found, but she didn't respond to any of my messages. I was worried about her and hoped that she wasn't alone, that she had someone to talk to, even if she didn't want to talk to me. I regretted buying her an entire carton of cigarettes, if running out was the only thing that would get her to call.

All week I looked forward to Lily coming home for the weekend. I bought three different flavors of Pop-Tarts, put clean sheets on her bed, gathered ingredients to make her favorite pie—lemon cream—and queued up Netflix movies for us to watch. I spiffed up Gravy for her arrival, too, or tried, anyway—I stuck him in the bath and inadvertently spilled most of his medicated shampoo when he knocked the open bottle off the edge of the tub. I called in a refill to the vet's office on Thursday and was surprised when Dr. Hayward rang me back that evening after I got home from work.

"Hey, did you run out already? Just wanted to make sure you're only using it twice a week."

"Oh, yeah—I spilled it."

"Ah," he said. "It happens. So . . . how's Gravy doing? Notice any changes, good or bad?"

"Not really, not yet. He hates the rice, though. Even with the chicken water on it." I didn't mind boiling chicken for the dog every day, but it didn't seem to be doing any good.

"It might take him a little time to get used to it. I've got samples of some different kinds of prescription food for him to try, if you'd like. You could get them from me when you pick up his shampoo tomorrow."

"That'd be great. But it probably won't be until next week—my daughter's coming for the weekend, and I won't have time after work."

"Sure." He almost sounded disappointed. "Hey, if it'd help, I can drop everything off on my way home tonight. I'm heading out now, and I live right outside Shade Tree."

"No, you don't have to do that."

"It's not a problem. Save you a trip."

I hesitated, wondering if it was common for him to make deliveries and whether it was a good idea—no matter how nice he seemed—to tell him where I lived. Of course, he would already have my address on file. That must have been how he knew I lived in Shade Tree.

"We could meet on the square," I said. "So you don't have to go too far out of your way."

I'd already put on the flannel pajama pants and ratty college sweatshirt that I wore when I was in for the night, and it seemed silly to change for Dr. Hayward, so I zipped up my coat and coaxed Gravy out for a potty break before I left.

While Shade Tree's town square was no longer the commercial hub it had once been, the park and pavilion at its center were still the heart of the community, where all important events were held: the annual Easter egg hunt, the photographing of high schoolers dressed up for prom, the farmers' market on Saturday mornings in the summer. In recent years, the oak trees in the park had become diseased and started to rot, and the city was struggling to raise enough money to cut them down and plant new ones. A string of vacant storefronts surrounded the square, old two-story buildings with high ceilings covered in decorative pressed tin. The upper-level apartments, once coveted for their tall windows overlooking the park, were all empty save for the birds that came and went through the broken glass. The mayor's grandson had died of an overdose in one of those abandoned rooms and wasn't found until a foul puddle had leaked down to the floor below.

On a typical day, there was little evidence of life. The barber pole outside Corner Cuts was still lit up on Tuesdays and Thursdays, old-timers gathering there for barely needed trims and an opportunity to gab about crops and weather. The VFW hall held the occasional bingo and beer night, and the community center, in what had long ago been a grocery, hosted wedding receptions and dwindling class reunions. On a weeknight, the streets were deserted, the only light coming from the lone streetlamp near the park pavilion.

A Lincoln SUV gleamed beneath the streetlamp, and Dr. Hayward waved as I pulled up and parked. There was a moment of disconnect seeing him outside his office, wearing jeans and a leather jacket instead of a lab coat, like when you're a kid and see your teacher at the grocery store for the first time. He came around to my window and I rolled it down.

"Thanks," I said, taking the bag of Gravy's supplies from him.

"No problem," he said, his hand on the door, his face inches away, his eyes peering into mine. "Like I said, it's on my way." Something shifted in my chest, the moment feeling strangely intimate, and I dropped my gaze. His jacket had a rich luster under the streetlight, and I had the urge to reach out and stroke the leather, to see if it was as soft as it looked. He was watching me expectantly, and my face warmed, though he couldn't have possibly guessed what I was thinking.

"Oh." It occurred to me what he was waiting for. "I need to pay you. I wasn't even thinking when I left the house. I'm not sure I have any cash on me."

"No, it's fine, I just put it on your account."

"Okay. I appreciate it." I was about to roll up the window, but he was still standing there with his hand in the way, like he wanted to say something. The cold bled into the car and I clicked the heat up higher.

"Was there . . . something else?"

He cleared his throat, his expression uncomfortably pinched. "You don't remember me at all, do you?"

"What do you mean? Should I?"

"I wanted to say something the other day, but it didn't seem like the right time to bring it up. Shane and I—we were friends, back in school. Before I moved away?" He watched my eyes for any sign of recognition. "Remember that typing class prank?"

"Who could forget that?" Dad had lost it, tearing into Shane, and Mom had tried to get between her son and the belt, receiving a stinging welt that cut across her face. Theo shoved his hands into his pockets, and I realized he must be freezing. "Do you want to . . . it's cold." I gestured to the passenger seat. "If you want to talk a minute."

"Sure."

The car rocked slightly when he climbed inside, his ears and nose pink from the wind, the scent of snow clinging to him. It was rare to have someone in the front seat with me—Lily still preferred the back—

and the sudden proximity to Theo somehow felt awkward now that I knew who he was. A few dry snowflakes floated down outside, dusting the windshield.

"We landed in detention together quite a few times," he said. "Talking in class. Too many tardies. A few fights. There was this guy we didn't like. Real jerk. He'd grabbed my backpack and stuffed it in a urinal. I had some fireworks at home, and Shane got the idea to scare the crap out of him. We sat behind him in typing, and the next day when the teacher said go and everybody started their speed test, Shane set the firecrackers off right under the guy's chair, and everybody hit the floor."

I hadn't heard the reasoning behind it. I only remembered Shane pacing by the front window, the dread in his eyes as he waited for Dad to come home, the sound of the belt whistling through the air before it struck him.

"Shane confessed right away, but when I saw how upset the teacher was, I got scared and denied I had anything to do with it." Theo squinted, looking both ashamed and apologetic. "I imagine if it was anywhere else but Shade Tree, your brother probably would have been expelled, but he only got suspended for a few days. And he had to come in on a weekend and repaint the stripes in the parking lot. Do you remember that?"

I shook my head. It was a minor punishment, I imagined, in comparison to the whipping.

"I still feel bad about putting it all on him. I wish I'd apologized when I had the chance."

"I'm sure he didn't hold it against you," I said. "He got into plenty of trouble on his own."

"Well, I was like that, too, but not so much after that. I guess it scared me straight." He smiled wryly.

"At least something good came out of it," I said.

"Yeah. It's too bad we didn't cross paths at the clinic," he said. "I moved back about a year ago. I figured I'd run into him sometime, we'd grab a beer, catch up. How was he doing, before?"

"He had a job that he liked. Got married last year. No kids."

"Your family still around? I remember your sister."

"Yeah. Mom's still in the old house. Becca's nearby. We're all still here," I said. It was getting stuffy in the car with my coat on and the heat blasting, the windshield beginning to fog.

"And what about you?"

I shrugged. "Nothing too interesting. I'm in social work. I have a daughter. That's about it."

He looked out the window, at the snow drifting down.

"I remember one time I was out at your place, shooting cans with Shane. We were blasting heavy metal, mouthing off. You told us to quiet down, you were trying to study. Waved this big Latin book in my face. You were maybe in eighth grade. Shane said you were the smartest one in the family. That you'd be the first to go to college. He was proud of you."

The memory materialized when he described it, hazy, nothing I'd thought of in years. I'd gotten the dog-eared book at a library sale after one of my teachers mentioned Latin would be useful to anyone wanting to pursue a career in medicine or law. All I knew about careers at the time, aside from farming, came from television. The lawyers on *Law & Order* were smart and serious and made enough money to afford nice suits, and that was the shallow origin of my lofty goals. I was tired of being poor.

"You weren't a bad shot," I said. "I remember."

"Shane was better," he said. "Cans'd jump right off the rail, every one hit dead center."

He swung the door open, white clumps pelting his jacket and blowing in to melt on the dash. His smile was kind and sincere, the dome light reflected in his eyes. "Well, thanks for listening to my belated confession," he said. "I hope Gravy likes the food." Then he was gone, the door slamming shut, the car dark and smelling faintly of warm leather and fresh snow.

An unfamiliar car blocked my driveway when I got home, and I flicked on my brights, approaching cautiously, one hand on my phone. A Hyundai hatchback with a tiny donut spare on the left rear instead of a regular tire. I cut around it, driving through the grass, and as I got closer, the headlights illuminated a small figure huddled on the porch. Hannah, knees pulled up to her chest, hair tossed by the wind, a cigarette burning between her fingers. I parked and got out.

"You said come by anytime," she said, her lips chapped and bloodless.

"I meant it," I said, helping her up. She dropped her cigarette, ground it out with her heel, and followed me inside.

"I need something. A drink. My aunt doesn't keep anything in the house. I can't go into town."

"Are you sure you want to do that? Can you . . . ?"

"I can handle a drink, do you have something or not?"

"Yeah. Yes."

Hannah trailed me to the kitchen and leaned against the doorframe, pressing her palms to her temples like she was trying to crush her own skull. Gravy, lying on his side under the kitchen table, opened one myopic eye and watched her without getting up. I handed Hannah a margarita pouch and she stabbed the straw in without question and drained it flat.

"They're done, finally," she said. "Took longer than they thought, but they're done collecting their evidence. Looking for clues. They didn't want me out there, before, but I want to go now, to the woods. Where they found them."

"Hannah . . . why don't we sit down for a minute? It's dark. It's starting to snow. You just had a drink."

She didn't move. Her wool coat gaped open, a flimsy summer

blouse underneath, her clavicle exposed. She was too thin. "You can drive," she said. "If it makes you feel better."

"I'll take you in the morning."

"You said you were here for me." Blue veins showed beneath her ashen skin, her features sharp and delicate, like Macey's. Desperation lit her eyes. "You said anything I needed. I need to go see where they found my baby. And I can't go alone. I need you to come with me."

The snow was too dry to stick to the road. It swirled and flew sideways and collected in the leaf-clogged ditch but left a clear path for us. We started down Wildwood Lane, branching off well before Leola's house onto an overgrown path mostly used by hunters this time of year, to access conservation land. We parked in the rutted lot and Hannah led the way into the woods, sticker bushes tugging at our pant legs, depositing tiny burs that would have to be picked off later, one by one. We followed a sloping glade until it ended abruptly in an outcropping of stone. Below, in a narrow gully, was the cedar thicket where the woman had found Macey's skull.

The spot couldn't have been more than a quarter mile from the road, the thicket inaccessible enough to keep anyone from wandering by and discovering the bones until the hunter sought a private place to relieve herself. Hannah stopped just short of the drop-off, snow dusting her shoulders and catching in her hair. Yellow tape still flapped from a tree trunk, though in the darkness there was little evidence of the investigation, nothing to indicate that a crime had taken place.

I pulled my hood up to cover my ears and wedged my hands deep into my pockets.

"Gunshots," Hannah whispered. "Both of them. I thought he killed her. That's what I thought, maybe, before they found him. And after. That he killed her and then himself." She wiped her nose on her coat sleeve. "I'd been thinking about it for so long, imagining every different way it might have happened, like one of those choose-your-own-adventure books, but every choice leads to the same fucking end."

I touched her arm and she didn't pull away. The cedars shuddered as the wind swept through the gully.

"It wasn't Roger," she breathed. "They didn't find the gun."

"Oh, Hannah . . ."

"They were shot. Here. Or not, maybe. It's not so far, they said . . . that they couldn't have been carried. Killed somewhere else and dumped here. It'll be in the news, I guess, before long. They're not treating me like a suspect yet, but I'm sure it's coming."

I wanted to tell her she was wrong, that no one could possibly think she'd had anything to do with it, but I couldn't. I remembered the waitress at the diner, the elderly woman. How they'd so quickly blamed Hannah. Accused her of being a bad mother. People would talk. People who didn't know her, and people who did.

"I wished he was dead," she said. "During the divorce. I know I said it out loud, I don't know how many times, who heard me. Everything would be easier. When you've got a kid with somebody, that's for life, you can't escape. Feels like this weight crushing you and you can't breathe and you'd do almost anything to get out from under it. I said I wanted him dead, but I didn't really mean it. Chad offered to take him out for me, to shoot him through the balls, and we laughed about it."

Her arms hung loose at her sides, her coat flapping open. I wanted to button it up against the wind, like I might do for Lily, pull up the collar, insulate her from the cold.

"We brought Macey camping out here one time," Hannah said. "Before me and Roger split up. That little campground way over on the other side. She didn't like the woods at night. All the noises—owls, coyotes, things moving in the trees. I told her we could go home, but she didn't want her daddy to know she was scared. I had to sing her to sleep. Had her arms locked around my neck all night till I thought she'd choke me." Her words caught in her throat, and I could feel her shivering, tremors rocking her slight frame. "She was out here, without me. She would have been so scared. I wish I could have been with her, instead of Roger."

Her breath heaved in and out, a ragged rhythm. "I don't feel her here," she said, her face gray in the faint moonlight. I squeezed her shoulders, wishing there was more I could do. "I thought I might . . . that there might be something out here. A feeling. Like I might under-stand what happened. Like she could tell me somehow. But there's nothing. She's just gone."

CHAPTER 12

HENLEY

SEPTEMBER

Henley yawned as she dusted the picture frames in the hallway that led to the master bedroom. There were dozens of them, Daphne Sullivan looking out from each one, the camera seeming to focus on her regardless of who or what else was in the picture. Daphne had been especially photogenic, with her bouncy golden hair and expressive eyes and the smile of someone who had never met a stranger. There was an engagement photo with her left hand placed strategically on Earl's lapel to showcase the glittering princess-cut diamond on her ring finger. A snapshot of Daphne with glorious feathered 1980s hair, posing with her preschool students. A radiant pregnancy portrait, her belly firm as a melon beneath her gauzy white dress. There were no photos of her after she'd fallen ill, here or anywhere else in the house. Henley imagined that was Daphne's doing. She would have wanted Jason and Earl to remember her vibrant, glowing, alive.

Henley had gotten a late start, up half the night fretting over her own mother, who had managed to get into trouble before Raymond and Junior could track her down. Raymond came by to tell her, sparing no detail, knowing she'd hear about it anyhow as the story worked its way around town, embellished and exaggerated by each mouth that spat it out.

Missy had been involved in a failed robbery at the Casey's convenience store, though it seemed most likely that Ellie had attempted the crime alone after Missy chickened out or became incapacitated, overdosing on a mix of fentanyl and heroin in the ladies' restroom. Ellie, not even bothering to disguise herself, had approached the counter with a loaded Ruger hidden behind a bag of pork rinds. The Casey's clerk had struck her in the head with a stapler, knocking her flat and cracking her eye socket, and Missy had been revived with a dose of Narcan before both of them were taken to the hospital, Missy's hair clotted with vomit and Ellie's pink ruffled blouse stained with blood. Henley felt faint when Raymond told her Missy had nearly died.

Her mother had gotten into trouble before, but this had her shaken. It was unclear whether Missy would end up in rehab or jail, and Henley hoped for both. Wherever they put her, she'd be safer locked up, and Henley hoped she would stay there awhile.

Henley carried the cleaning caddy into the master bedroom, her shoes sinking into the mauve carpet that covered the entire suite, including the bathroom. She scrubbed water spots from the brass fixtures and shell-shaped sink, wiped toothpaste specks from the mirror, lifted the toilet lid, which had a furry mauve cover that had probably been there since before Daphne died. She knew she should probably take the cover off and wash it, but she didn't care. How had Missy been able to stand it, cleaning this house for so many years? Henley was more than ready to be done.

When she finished the bathroom, she paused at the double doors to the closet. She had never gone inside—Missy claimed she only vacuumed it once a month, and Henley doubted it was necessary as often as that—but she remembered what Jason had said, about Earl keeping a box of Daphne's jewelry stashed there. It wouldn't hurt to look. She poked around on the shelves until she found it, a large leather box, the drawers lined with velvet. There were glittering bracelets, ruby earrings, strands of milky pearls, thick chains of herringbone gold. In the ring compartment was the princess-cut solitaire Daphne had been wearing in the engagement photo and a wedding band crusted with diamonds.

It occurred to her for a fleeting moment that she could fill her pockets, pawn it all across state lines, and disappear into the mountains by sunrise. She thought of the modest heirlooms Memaw and Pawpaw had left behind: a silver-plated class ring; an engraved pocket watch with a chain. One look at those keepsakes could bring back memories of Memaw's floured hands kneading dough for yeast rolls, tractor rides on Pawpaw's lap, pressing her ear to the breast pocket of his overalls to hear the watch's steady tick next to his heart. Her fingers went to the stone around her neck, the one Jason had given her. She had forgotten to take the necklace off before coming to the house today, and standing in the closet Earl had shared with Daphne, sorting through the jewelry he kept in her memory, she knew she couldn't keep it. It meant something to Earl that it would never mean to her, and it hadn't been Jason's to give.

She reached up to unfasten the necklace and heard the click of a door closing. She froze, her stomach lurching, and had to remind herself that she'd done nothing wrong. Earl wasn't normally at home when she was there, but she'd gotten a late start, and there shouldn't be anything strange about her emerging from his closet. He had likely seen her car outside and knew she was there. Still, she didn't want to face him if she didn't have to. Despite Missy's insistence that Earl had a soft heart, Henley didn't know him well enough to feel comfortable around him and had always found him intimidating.

She waited, regulating her breath, her feet mired in the spongy carpet, until she heard a jangling smack from the direction of the bathroom. It sounded like a belt buckle being dropped on the counter, like Earl was getting undressed. She pushed the closet door open a crack and peered through. The bathroom door was slightly ajar, the light on inside, and Henley figured that if she was quick, she could sneak out without Earl seeing her. She shoved the cleaning caddy into the corner and darted out of the closet, her breath leaving her as Earl stepped out of the bathroom, dressed in his boxers and undershirt.

"Henley," he said, not appearing the least bit startled. "There you are."

She had rarely been so close to him. He was even taller than Jason, with the same sharp jaw and sinewy build, though he could easily pass for Jason's grandfather, his hair gleaming silver and his sun-worn face lined like a farmer's.

"Hi," she said, managing a small smile, because she wasn't sure what else to do or say. Earl was watching her with intense interest, his eyes bright as a bird's, and a spasm of panic clenched her chest as she became acutely aware that the diamond necklace was still clasped around her neck. His gaze traveled down and back up, his expression shifting slightly. Did he recognize it? He had to. And she had just emerged from the closet where he had kept it hidden. She could tell him that Jason had given her the necklace and hadn't told her it was Daphne's, but she'd be lying, and Jason would suffer the consequences. She could tell him the truth, that she'd meant to give it back, though he wasn't likely to believe her.

"Henley, Henley, Henley," he said, his words soft and unhurried.

"Why don't you sit down? We can talk." He stepped around her, his arm brushing hers. "I was about to pour myself a drink." He opened the antique wormwood cabinet next to the dresser, revealing a small bar. "Can I get you one as well?" He turned back toward her. "It's all whiskey, I'm afraid, but I've got quite a selection. I'm partial to the Macallan."

"No, thank you," she said, waiting awkwardly while he poured the liquor into a tumbler. He'd asked her to sit, but there was nowhere to sit aside from the huge canopy bed, and she felt more comfortable with her feet on the floor. She wished he would just get it over with — fire her, or ask her to apologize, or whatever he planned to do now that he thought she was a thief, if that's what this was all about.

Earl took a long swallow and sighed, crossing the room to set his drink on the nightstand. She noticed that his gait was slightly unsteady. He leaned against the bedpost and shook his head.

"It's been hard without Missy here," he said. "You don't realize how much you appreciate that womanly touch until you're living without it. But you're here, now."

The liquor smell on his breath was sharp and astringent, the whiskey obviously not his first pour. Missy had told her that he drank too much sometimes and got sloppy, usually if something was troubling him, or Daphne was on his mind, and she'd have to help him to bed. He was studying her face with a gentle smile, though his expression was distant, as if his focus lay elsewhere. Her panic eased. He was drunk. Maybe he hadn't noticed the necklace at all.

"She was ready to move on one way or another. It was her idea, mostly, you taking her place. I wasn't sure a young girl like you would be interested in taking care of an old man like me, but here you are. And I'm glad you're here."

"Yeah," she said, inching backward. "Thank you . . . for the job."

"Thank *you*," he said, taking her hand in his. There was a tenderness in his voice. "You don't know how much I needed this today."

She tugged her hand away, but before she could move beyond his reach, he fumbled toward her, pressing his mouth onto hers and losing his balance, his momentum knocking her backward onto the bed. As soon as she registered his weight on her body, she shoved back, wedging her arms between them and pushing him up off her chest. "What are you doing?" she hollered, wriggling free. Earl looked at her, confused, grabbing at her wrist as she got to her feet. Henley jerked out of his grasp, banging the side of her head on the bedpost, and a horrified expression manifested on Earl's face.

"Oh, god," he said. Henley backed toward the bedroom door, pressing her palm to her stinging ear. "Your mother," he slurred. "I thought—and you were here waiting—" She bolted and he came after her, his hand clawing out and falling short. "Henley!"

She ran down the hall, the carpet muffling her escape. "Wait!" Earl called after her as she fled down the staircase. She sprinted out to her car, her breath ragged in her throat, leaving the front door of the Sullivan house wide open. She burned down the blacktop, pushing the car to seventy-five, the wind tearing through the open windows, slowing before she hit gravel to check the rearview mirror with blurred eyes, but no one was chasing her.

CHAPTER 13

SADIE

NOVEMBER

Lily and I took Gravy out for a long walk on Saturday morning. It was freezing, but the sky was clear, the sunshine blindingly decadent after a string of dreary days. I had hugged Lily too many times when Greg had dropped her off the night before, and she had finally squirmed away, declaring that she was half starved and rooting through the cabinets for junk food. She ate two Pop-Tarts as an appetizer and half a frozen pizza for dinner, making me feel a pang of guilt when she complained about the healthy meals Heidi made, and then fell asleep on the couch before our movie finished. I had to wake her up to go to bed. It seemed like it wasn't so long ago that I could carry her up the stairs, but at some point, without me noticing, she had gotten too big for me to lift her. One of the many small milestones of motherhood, of our children outgrowing us. Now, as I watched Lily playing in the sun with Gravy, I wondered how many other little changes had slipped by me, unnoticed.

"Should we head back now?" Lily asked.

"Want to cut down to the creek? He's still going strong." Gravy seemed to tap into hidden energy reserves when Lil was around.

"Through the woods?" Lily paused to tug at her socks. They were so low they were getting swallowed up by her shoes, but she no longer liked the kind that covered her ankles.

"Yeah. I think he can handle it. Look at him." He was actually pulling on the leash. "Maybe the new food's starting to do him some good."

"Is it safe, though?" Her dark eyes were uncertain. She fidgeted with her bangs, which were smashed to her forehead beneath her stocking cap.

"Sure," I said. "Why wouldn't it be?" We had walked down to the creek all the time when she was little, sending leaf boats down the current and hunting tadpoles.

"Dad said Macey was found in the woods."

"Oh, sweetie." I reached out to squeeze her hand. "Yes, she was, but I don't think it had anything to do with the woods not being safe. We don't know exactly what happened. We're on our own property here." She stayed rooted in place, unconvinced. "We've got a guard dog."

She didn't smile. "Mom."

I tried to remember the last time she'd called me Mommy. I felt like I was already forgetting how it sounded. "We're safe here," I said.

"How do you know?"

I didn't know how to tell her that there are no guarantees, that mothers, despite their efforts and intentions, have no magical ability to protect their children, though she was already beginning to sense that on her own.

"Come on. Let's see if it's frozen."

Gravy led the way down the overgrown path, seeming to know where he was going despite never having gone this way before. I loved the fresh smell of the cedars, the way the trees closed in around us, encasing us in a hidden world, the delight in Lily's voice as she laughed at Gravy and told him, possibly for the first time ever, to slow down. The creek, when we reached it, was an unimpressive trickle, the edges clotted with ice, and Gravy trotted right into the frigid water and began to lap it up.

"Look, he loves it," I said. Lily followed him along the creek bed, careful to keep her tennis shoes out of the water.

"How's social studies?" I asked. "Did you get your project back yet?"

"Yeah," she said. "I got an A. Heidi helped me with it."

"That's great. So everything's going okay at Dad's?"

"Yeah," she said. "He works a lot, but Heidi makes him come home so we can eat dinner together. She's picky about things. Like food, obviously. And keeping my room clean." She rolled her eyes. "And she's super crabby if she misses her morning yoga. Did you know she can stand on her head? And she's trying to teach me to meditate. She says it's good for anxiety."

"Nice," I said.

"It's harder than you'd think," she said. "You have to sit still, and breathe, and if a thought comes into your head, you just let it go. She said it takes lots of practice."

"I'm sure it does."

The sun barely penetrated the wooded valley, the shadows deep on either side of the creek. You couldn't hear traffic from the far-off road, or the wind chimes clanging back at the house. There was only the breeze ghosting through the branches, and the screeching of jays, and the muted gurgle of the water. Lily stopped here and there to examine an interesting rock, to pull her socks back up again. She'd forgotten her earlier worries, no longer thinking about her safety. She was still a little girl in some ways, like Macey, not yet expected to always be on guard, not listening for footsteps, not looking over her shoulder like I was, as mothers were required to do.

Mom was asleep in her recliner when we arrived for lunch, a *Hoarders* marathon playing on the TV. She liked the show because it made her feel better about her own clutter. *A dead cat!* she'd say. *My knickknacks might be dusty, but I'd notice a dead cat behind the bookcase!* On the side table next to her chair, carefully distanced from a sweating can of diet soda, lay the sketch of Gravy she'd torn from Shane's notepad. The edges were curled like she'd been holding it in her palm.

"Grandma." Lily sat on the arm of the recliner and tugged her sleeve, and Mom startled awake with a gasp.

"Just resting my eyes," she said, squinting at us.

Lily hugged her. "Smells good in here."

"Well, since you were coming, I fixed something nice. Found a hambone in the deep freeze and cooked up a pot of bean soup."

I didn't want to know how old the hambone was. She used to make ham and beans all the time when Dad was still alive, ladling it over slices of white bread. None of us kids particularly liked it, but it was comfort food, bland and familiar.

"Is Becca on her way?" I asked.

"I reckon so," Mom said. "Lily, I need you to come in the kitchen and clear off the table for me before she gets here. She starts thinking I can't keep the place up on my own and she'll ruin lunch talking about nursing homes."

I stayed in the living room, digging into the cracks of the recliner to find the remote and switch off *Hoarders*. It was too depressing watching a frail elderly couple argue about how many storage bins of old magazines they could keep while a sewage leak rotted away the floorboards in the background.

I set the remote on the table and picked up Shane's drawing. It wasn't detailed like any of his finished work, just a pencil sketch, the sort of thing you might doodle absentmindedly while talking on the phone. It was smudged, and I imagined Mom tracing her fingers over the lines, knowing it was the last thing her son would ever draw. The lead had smeared into the indentations of whatever he'd written on the pages above, and I pressed the edges of the paper to flatten it. A few letters stood out, in block print rather than his usual sloppy cursive and drawn with a heavy, deliberate hand. I looked more closely, trying to make out words, tilting the paper to catch the light.

The front door cracked open and then slammed full force against the wall as Becca's boys, Colton and Logan, burst in and ran to find Lily and the dog, Becca hollering from the driveway for them to slow down. I set the paper down and went to see if Becca had anything she needed me to carry.

We all ate together at the kitchen table, then Becca and I waited until Mom retired to her recliner. Lily took the boys outside before we started on the dishes, the running water masking our voices so we could talk.

"Mom seems like she's doing okay today," Becca said. "I think it helps, having the kids around. She didn't mention Shane."

"They're definitely a good distraction," I said, though we both knew Mom's silence didn't mean Shane wasn't on her mind. His car still sat right outside the front window, where she could see it from her chair. She had covered it with an old canvas tarp.

"Leola said I can talk to Charlie when he's back in town," I said. "And I called Dave Gorecki, the guy we met at the funeral. I'm going to stop by and see him tomorrow when I take Lily back. He probably spent more time with Shane than anyone—five days a week for the last ten years. Maybe he can tell us something useful."

"But do you think we're making it worse for ourselves, and for Mom?" Becca said. "Digging into his private life? Is that what he would have wanted?"

"I don't know." I couldn't help thinking that if we found the right pieces, it would all fit together and make sense. I couldn't move on, not knowing.

I peeked in on Mom, who was snoring lightly in the recliner, *Hoarders* turned back on, the volume too loud. I moved closer, wanting to get another look at the piece of paper—to see if the letters were truly clear enough to read, or if my mind had just been putting shapes together and forming words that weren't there—but it lay clasped in her hands, her fingers curled protectively around the edges.

On the way back from dropping Lily off on Sunday (early, so she could go with Greg and Heidi to the *Nutcracker* matinee), I took the beltway to the south outer suburbs. After twisting through a labyrinth of subdivisions, I found the Goreckis' tidy split-level, one of two dozen nearly identical homes that had probably been surrounded by fields when they were built decades earlier, but were now crowded by a proliferation of chain stores selling mundane necessities—Batteries Plus Bulbs, Big O Tires, Mattress Firm—things everyone had to buy but didn't enjoy shopping for.

Four concrete stepping stones, each decorated with a child's name and handprint, sat among frozen mums in the flowerbed next to the tiny front porch. Gorecki answered the door dressed in church clothes. It looked like the same gray suit he'd worn to the funeral—noticeably tight, shoulders pinched, waistband cutting into his soft belly.

He nodded hello, his lips pursed, his bulbous forehead and small round eyes reminding me of a parakeet. He pushed the screen door open wide, ushering me in from the cold. Once inside, he didn't invite me up or down the split stairs, so we stood awkwardly in the cramped foyer. Four school-bus-shaped frames on the wall chronicled the Gorecki children's young lives, each window in each bus representing a new school year, new teeth, new haircuts, new blemishes. Two of the buses were nearly full. I admired the Goreckis' organization and follow-through. I'd had good intentions, evidenced by all the scrapbooks and picture frames I'd bought over the years and stashed in a closet, but I'd never even finished Lily's baby book.

"I've got to pick up my wife and kids about noon," he said. "When Sunday school's over." He held up the church bulletin clutched in his calloused hand.

"I won't take much of your time," I said. "I wanted to talk to you before, at the funeral, but I didn't get a chance. The whole day was a blur. I meant to thank you for coming. I know you probably had to take off work to be there."

"It was a lovely service," he said.

He was lying. Being kind. We had expected that Shane would be buried near family, but Crystle had chosen a cemetery in Kansas City. The service was quick and impersonal, the funeral director mistakenly calling Shane "Shannon" several times. As we sang "Amazing Grace," a deer had emerged mere feet from the tent and stepped unhurriedly across the lawn. The peaceful animal had appeared for a moment like a sign from Shane, ruined when the funeral director grumbled that the place was overrun with them, a nuisance they couldn't keep at bay.

We were rushed away from his casket with a warning that reminded me of the bartender's closing-time classic: "You don't have to go home, but you can't stay here." *Now please*, they'd said, *move your cars or they'll be towed.* They were on a strict schedule that didn't allow for tearful lingering.

The entire time, Crystle's family had crowded on one side of the tent while we were on the other, like at a wedding except in reverse, the couple arriving together and then separating, the words *till death do us part* ending not with a kiss but with one of them going into the ground.

"Since you would have been among the last people to see him, I wondered if you could tell me about that last day—what happened, anything he might have said, whatever you remember. Really, anything is helpful."

"Uh, sure," he said, brushing back his thin straw-colored hair with his palm. "It was a normal day. He clocked in on time—he always did. About an hour into the shift, he said he wasn't feeling too good, that he was going home. He looked a little sweaty, maybe, a little pale."

An orange cat appeared at the top of the stairs, a bell tinkling on its collar as it moved. Gorecki glanced up at it and flinched slightly when the cat hissed at him.

"Did Shane say anything specific about his symptoms?" I asked.

"Not that I recall. I figured he must be pretty miserable to leave work over it, though. He didn't like to use sick time unless it was absolutely necessary. Got perfect attendance the last couple years."

"Was that the first day you noticed him being sick?"

Gorecki squinted, tapping the church bulletin against his palm. "He wasn't a big complainer—not the type to make a fuss about feeling poorly. But he'd seemed a bit off for a while," he said. "Quieter than usual. I just assumed he was . . . you know. Going through a rough patch with Crystle again. He never liked to say too much about personal matters, but he'd tell me things now and then, when he thought I might have some insight. I've been married going on twenty years. I told him the first year's a big adjustment, that it takes some work, but it's worth it." His gaze flicked to the school bus frames on the wall, all those pictures of his children.

"Rough patch? What happened between him and Crystle?"

Gorecki's face pinked up a bit. "He didn't tell you?"

"What did he say?"

He hesitated, absently rolling the bulletin into a tight scroll with his stubby fingers.

"Please? I know he might have told you in confidence, but we're just trying to make sense of what happened. It's been really hard on our mom, not knowing."

He looked down at his shoes, worn-out oxfords, the leather deeply creased across the toes, yet freshly polished. "I guess it doesn't matter now. He'd thought she was messing around on him a while back. She denied it was what it looked like, blamed it on the guy. Said he was harassing her, wouldn't leave her alone. Shane was pretty upset over it, but I think they worked it out." Gorecki wiped his mouth with the back of his hand and swallowed hard. The orange cat zipped down the stairs and disappeared into the lower level, its bell jingling madly. "With the way he was acting, I thought that might've come back up again."

"Who was the guy? Did he say?"

"I don't recall. It's been a while." Gorecki looked me in the eye. "We didn't spend much time together outside of work—a beer now and again—but he was there every day, worked hard, always had a smile ready, or a joke, always listened when I talked about my kids, which I probably did too often. It's different without him there. I miss him. I'm really sorry."

"Thanks," I said. "I'm glad you were there for him, that he had someone to talk to." The wind shrieked outside, a bitter draft sheeting in under the front door. I tried to remember if Shane had ever mentioned Gorecki by name and couldn't. Another piece of his life that had been invisible to me.

Back in the car, I cranked up the heat and called Becca to give her the update, and we decided it wouldn't hurt to tell Kendrick, even if she wasn't likely to listen. I was grateful that the detective didn't answer, so I could lay out my concerns in a voicemail without her interrupting to tell me that I'd been watching too much TV. Crystle's lack of tears wasn't a crime, but combined with her infidelity and the financial concerns, it seemed like it might add up to something, or at least warrant a closer look at Shane's case.

CHAPTER 14

HENLEY
SEPTEMBER

There was a mark down the side of her face where she'd struck the bedpost; no longer red, as it had been the day before, but the blue hint of a bruise. The oval mirror above Henley's dresser was an antique that had belonged to Memaw. It was tarnished with black spots where moisture had damaged the silver backing, the edges covered with stickers Henley had affixed to the glass when she was younger. She studied her clouded reflection, wondering how she would look in ten years, twenty, fifty. If she'd still be seeing herself in this same mirror, in this room, in this house.

She hadn't been able to stop herself from fantasizing, briefly, about what it would be like to marry Jason Sullivan, how her life would instantly change. She would move into the big brick house, and she would hire a designer from the city to redecorate and some poor girl from town to clean. She would learn to cook, making use of all the heavy pans and casserole dishes Daphne Sullivan had left behind, serving meals in the formal dining room, having babies to fill the bedrooms, getting her nails manicured at the strip mall out on the highway or maybe even a salon in the suburbs with massaging chairs. She would lunch at the Blackwater Country Club, drive an Escalade through town with her hair blown out, wear tasteful outfits ordered from a fancy department store.

That was how it looked when she imagined it, when she filled up the pages in her journal, but she knew it would never happen. She couldn't go back to the Sullivan house now, and even if she could, she wasn't sure if she wanted those things. Even if she swallowed her doubts like a mouthful of gravel and patterned her life after Daphne, becoming the matriarch of the next generation of Sullivans, it would never be more than a game of pretend. No matter what she wore or drove or how she carried herself, she would always be a Pettit underneath. It would show through, her shiny new veneer rubbed off like a cheap finish.

The only way to escape it was to get out of Blackwater, to go places where no one thought they knew who and what she was, places where she had no past. Where she could make herself into anything she wanted, disappear and resurface, coming up clean. The longer she stayed, the deeper she'd be drawn into things she wanted no part of, the knotted threads of her family's misdeeds, her identity an inseparable piece of the whole, all of it sullied.

She wondered if Jason would try very hard to convince her to stay. Surely he understood, as she did, that the very things that made their relationship exciting meant it couldn't last. Its improbable nature, its blistering intensity, all of it transpiring in secret. Small towns liked to keep you in your place, and that extended to Jason, too. She tried to imagine him bidding on pies at the Fourth of July auction, sponsoring the Little League, taking over Sullivan Grain. He'd be miserable in Earl's shoes, would probably chew off his own feet to escape.

Her phone chimed, barely audible over the TV show she'd turned up to drown out the unbearable silence in the house. It was Earl. He'd called her seven times since yesterday, letting it ring until it went to voicemail but not leaving a message. She pressed Decline. Probably he was calling to apologize, though an apology wouldn't fix anything; it wouldn't change the fact that she had scrubbed her lips with a nail-brush until they stung but could still feel the wet intrusion of his mouth, the phantom weight of his body pressing against her every time she lay down on her bed.

Her bitterness toward Earl wasn't the only thing eating away at her. She was mad at herself, because she wouldn't have been in Earl's bedroom when he came home had she not considered—if only for a moment—stealing Daphne's jewelry, and she was angry at her mother for setting her on this course to begin with, encouraging her to take her place at the Sullivans'. She wondered if Earl had ever tried to kiss Missy, and whether Missy had let him. Her mother had worked in Earl's home for years and had never said anything about him acting inappropriately. Surely Missy wouldn't have pushed her to take the job if she thought Earl would lay his hands on her.

She punched the power button on the remote, and the sudden silence unnerved her. The phone rang again and she answered. "Stop calling me," she said, her jaw clenched.

"Wait," he said.

"What do you want?"

"Listen. Just listen."

She clamped her tongue between her teeth, not quite hard enough to draw blood. She would give him five seconds, which was more than he deserved.

"I want to make this right," he said. "I have something for you. I'll bring it by, and we can forget this whole thing."

Forget. As though it were that simple.

"Whatever it is, you can leave it in the shed. I don't want you in my house."

"I want to talk to you in person. It'll only take a minute. Please."

"Fine. I'll meet you outside."

When the call was over, the phone slick in her sweating hand, she realized he hadn't said he was sorry. He had offered her something, but it was still all about him, what he wanted, and what he wanted was for her not to tell.

The tin-roofed tractor shed sat beside the house at the edge of the cornfield, though it hadn't sheltered a tractor in years, not since Paw-paw's John Deere had been sold at auction. It was home now to an abandoned deep freeze, stacks of wood from the dead elm Uncle Raymond had cut down, colonies of field mice nesting in decaying hay bales. A sodium lamp spread a sallow pool of light on the gravel drive, and Earl parked his truck just beyond its reach, probably hoping no one would drive by and see him there. Henley waited by the shed, spiderwebs netting her hair, catching in her lashes. Earl walked up, his boots scraping gravel, and in the slice of lamplight, she saw that his eyes were muddled, saliva crusted at the corner of his mouth. His breath was sharp with menthol and whiskey, as though he'd been suck-ing cough drops to mask the liquor.

Earl's broad hands were empty, and that made her nervous, but they swung loosely at his sides as he shifted on the heels of his boots.

"I picked you," he said, his voice deep and rasped. "Because your mother wanted me to. For the Emily Sullivan Prize." He chuckled harshly, and Henley flinched. "Your essay was fine, but it was no differ-ent from the others. They're always the same. It's like a penance, read-ing those things."

Henley couldn't believe it had never occurred to her that she'd won because of Missy, that her mother had acted so proud of a prize she had rigged. Not that it mattered now. It had been years ago.

"I loved my sister," Earl said. "And I envied her. I was the one—did you know?—I asked her to hide in the hay. I thought it'd be funny to have her jump out and scare Daddy, and she'd do anything to make me laugh. But part of me hoped she might get in trouble. That he'd be mad. He got mad sometimes, if we were goofing around, usually at me. He was strict. I saw him with the pitchfork and I didn't say a word. I kept still like she'd told me, so he wouldn't know we were there. Even when her blood was soaking into his overalls, spilling all over the hay, I didn't move. Her eyes were wide open and she looked at me and blood poured out of her mouth. And then I ran," he said, his voice rising in wonder, like he couldn't believe it himself. "I ran."

Henley felt sick, saliva rising under her tongue. Earl took a fat envelope from his back pocket.

"We didn't understand what was going to happen," he said. "We were just kids. It was an accident. But I knew at the core that I was responsible for a horrible thing that I could never make up for, and all my life I've been filling that same leaky bucket, trying to atone and knowing I'll come up short."

"Why're you telling me this?"

He shrugged. "I wanted you to know that I didn't mean you any harm. It was a misunderstanding on my part. I'm not as good a man as I'd like to be. I drink too much, and I make stupid, shameful mistakes, but I had no ill intentions. I'm sorry, for what it's worth." He held out the envelope and she grasped it, but he didn't let go. She recoiled when his fingers touched hers.

"I'm not trying to send you away—job's still yours if you want it. But I know you were saving up for a trip. That's what your mama said, anyway." He cleared his throat, an uneasy, guttural scrape. The wind shushed through the fields, ghost voices murmuring in the stalks. "Should be enough to get you far away from this place, if that's what you want." The light glowed behind Earl, his face unreadable in the dark. "Sometimes I think about that myself," he said. "What it might be like to leave and never come back."

He sounded weary, like he had no choice in the matter. His silhouette was imposing as ever, but she sensed the weakness in him. It had a smell, like day-old whiskey sweat. The money might have been a pathetic means of assuaging his guilt, but that wouldn't stop her from taking it. She snatched the envelope from his hand and told him to get out, her voice sharp and unwavering. He took a few unsteady steps backward and then turned toward his truck, skirting around the circle of lamplight to walk in the cover of darkness.

CHAPTER 15

SADIE

NOVEMBER

It was rare, living so far out in the country, for anyone to knock at my door unexpectedly, especially at night. I startled at the sound, scraping my chair back and nearly catching Gravy's ear. He didn't stir, and I carefully got up from the kitchen table and crept to the front door, as if my silence mattered. Whoever it was could see me through the glass, illuminated by the living room lamp. I flicked on the porch light, thinking that it might be Hannah.

Crystle blinked at the sudden brightness, her arms crossed over her chest.

We stared at each other. The last time I'd seen her, she'd told me to keep away from her, had nearly shoved me out of her house. Shane's house. I didn't unlock the door.

"We need to talk," she said. "Come on, lemme in."

She was by herself, and I couldn't help being curious about why she had come to see me, what she wanted to talk about. I relented and flipped the latch, and she tromped inside, glancing around. She stood with her hands on her hips in the middle of the room, several inches taller than me, mostly because of her high-heeled boots.

"You know, this is my first time coming here?" she said, taking in the small living room, the green sofa, the woodstove, the funeral lilies. Her gaze caught momentarily on the pie safe, my grandmother's, the one Crystle had found so ugly she'd made Shane keep it hidden in a back room. "I don't think you've ever invited me over."

It was true, but mostly because family get-togethers were always held at Mom's. Crystle had only been to Becca's house once, when Becca had agreed to host a party for Crystle to sell her leggings.

"Can I get you anything?" I asked.

She snorted. "What, you think we're gonna hang out and drink sweet tea? Little late for that. I'm here to thank you for sending that cop over," she said. "Just what I needed, my husband six feet deep, some bitch asking me a bunch of personal shit about my marriage."

"Cop? Detective Kendrick?"

"Don't act like you don't know. She said his family had *concerns*. I figured that meant you."

I was surprised to hear that Kendrick had gone to talk to Crystle after the message I'd left. She must not have gotten any useful information, because she hadn't called me to follow up.

"I didn't accuse you of anything," I said. "We just had questions. Don't tell me you wouldn't do the same for your family."

"You should have talked to me if you had *concerns*."

"I tried, and you kicked me out."

"Listen," she said, her voice going soft. The gentle tone was disconcerting somehow. "My dad had an old hunting dog got caught up in barbed wire out in the woods. Drug himself home a week later, skin ribboned up, infection set in, trailing a fence post behind him. Go to touch him and he'd bite you, even though you're trying to help. That's about how I been feeling since Shane died. Like that dog dragging that fence, trying to survive. I was hurting and you were making it worse. None of this is easy for me. I was trying to stay true to what Shane would have wanted, and he always wanted to protect his family."

She pulled her long hair away from her neck and draped it over her shoulder. It was different since the last time I'd seen her, ironed smooth, the ends bleached a colorless blond.

"I can't do it anymore," she said. "And I'm sorry for that. But it's your own fault."

She let the words hang between us, the house silent except for the hiss of the stove, and I wondered if I had made a mistake in letting her in.

"What are you talking about?"

"The truth. You kept complaining that I wouldn't tell you what happened. I didn't want to talk about it because I knew he wouldn't want you to hear it. He never wanted his mom and sisters to worry about him, think poorly of him. He said when he was growing up, everybody saw him as the bad kid, always getting in trouble, doing stupid stuff. That's how he saw himself, too. He spent his whole adult life trying to show that he was better than everybody thought he was back then. To prove it to himself. That there was good in him. He didn't ever want you to think otherwise. So he hid everything he didn't want you to see. Hid himself from his own family because he was worried about what you'd think. He wouldn't have wanted you to know how he died, but you need to. If you look at his records, talk to his doctor, he'd tell you a heart attack was as likely as anything, and that might make you feel better somehow, but that's not what killed him."

"Then tell me what did."

"What kills everybody around here? He took a little something now and then, when he needed to. He worked hard. On his feet all day long, sometimes double shifts. Flared up his back."

Shane had an old football injury that bothered him from time to time, though he rarely mentioned it. He wasn't one to complain.

"The pain had been bothering him for a while, and he was stressed out, couldn't sleep. He wasn't feeling well. He'd started taking pain pills nearly every night so he could get some rest. I was worried about him, but he didn't want me to say anything. Knew it'd upset your mom. So I let it be. When I came home that night and found him . . . maybe he took one too many. I don't know if he meant to. But that's what happened, and it was too late to do anything."

Her words jumbled in my head, my brain trying to process them and lagging.

"I knew he'd want to spare you and Becca and your mom, so I tossed the bottle and didn't say anything. Figured it'd be easier for you, if you thought it was unavoidable. Spare you the guilt of thinking you could have done something. He was already gone. What did it matter?" She sniffed, shook out her hair. "But you couldn't leave it like that, so you need to know everything."

Everything? It was hard to believe that there was more, that it could get worse.

"There was something weighing on him, more than just bills that needed paying." I remembered the ballooning credit card balances Becca and I had seen in his box of papers, the personal loan he'd taken out, his finances taking a bad turn after Crystle came into his life. "It'd been going on for a while," Crystle continued, "and it didn't occur to me before—not till Roger was found—that maybe what was weighing on him was guilt. That maybe he had something to do with the Calhouns. Because of what happened with Roger and me."

"You were cheating on him," I said. "With his friend." Roger must have been the guy Gorecki was talking about.

She glared at me. "No I wasn't. Roger came on to me when I was drunk; it was a one-time thing. A mistake. He wanted something I didn't, and it pissed him off. He was harassing me and I had to tell

Shane. I'd never seen him mad like that—it scared me. He said he'd deal with it, with Roger. Make sure he'd stay away."

I watched her face as she talked, scanning for signs that she was working up fake tears, trying to manipulate me, but her expression was flat.

"I guess what I'm saying is, do you want that detective coming around asking about Shane? About him and Roger? Wouldn't do a bit of good. Both of them dead. I don't know if he had anything to do with it or not, but something was eating away at him that he didn't tell you and didn't even tell me."

My instinct was pure denial. Even if it had been possible for Shane to kill Roger in a jealous rage, and I wasn't sure that it was, I knew that he would never hurt a child. He couldn't possibly have looked Macey in the eye—a little girl, just like Lily—and pulled the trigger. I was only beginning to uncover the things I didn't know about my brother, but I knew his heart, and I didn't believe that had changed.

"Feel better now that you know?" Crystle said. "I'm guessing you don't. That's on you. Maybe you should have paid more attention when he was alive. Loved him for who he was. I tried to do the right thing. Now leave me be, and let him rest in peace."

Her eyes fixed on mine. I didn't know how much of what she'd said was the truth, but what struck me as sincere was that Shane had felt he couldn't be himself with us, that he couldn't share what was going on in his life. It had hurt to discover how much he'd kept hidden, but it was far more painful to realize that the blame lay with us, that we'd made him feel like he couldn't come to us for help.

I locked the door behind Crystle when she left, turned out the lights, and sat in the dark, stoking the fire. It took Becca several rings to answer when I called, and I wondered if she was avoiding the phone, the possibility of unsettling news we now associated with late-night calls.

"We should have been there for him," Becca said when I finished relaying the conversation with Crystle. I could tell she was crying but trying to do it quietly. Jerry and the boys were probably in bed. "Maybe things would have been different. Maybe none of this would have happened. He was always there for us."

"Do you think there's anything to what she said about Roger?" I asked.

Becca sniffled. "I wouldn't blame him for being upset. I could see him beating the crap out of him—he used to get in fights all the time back in school. Remember when he got in a bar fight down in Alabama and broke some guy's arm? But he couldn't have killed anyone. Could he?" In the background, one of her boys began to wail. "I have to go," Becca said. "We'll talk tomorrow."

I watched the fire burn. When I adjusted a half-green log with the poker, it let out a sound like a muffled scream. I remembered when I was maybe eleven and Shane fourteen, Dad had him pushing against a tree limb while he cut through it with the chain saw. When Dad's blade got close enough to nip Shane's glove, Shane let go and the limb kicked back and hit Dad, who threw down the saw and threatened to beat him bloody.

I didn't mean to, Shane had pleaded. Dad had to have realized that Shane had let go out of instinct, not wanting to lose his fingers.

Spare the rod and spoil the child, Dad said.

That's not how it goes, I said. *It's "Whoever spares the rod hates his son." You already hate him, so what's the point in whipping him?*

Dad had slapped me across the face, an instant tooth-cracking whiplash headache, and Shane had shoved him, muttering for me to run back to the house. He never said what happened, though he walked stiffly for days, and two of his fingers were purple and swollen, surely broken. He didn't go to the doctor. Mom taped the fingers together with a homemade splint and nothing more was said about it.

I hadn't talked back much after that, knowing Shane would end up paying, something Dad had exploited as another means of control. Shane had been protective by nature; he had rushed to defend me without thinking of the consequences. If he truly thought Roger would hurt Crystle, he would have done everything he could to protect his wife. Like Becca, I didn't want to think that he was capable of murder. No one wanted to believe that of someone they loved.

CHAPTER 16

HENLEY
SEPTEMBER

Henley knelt on her bedroom floor and leaned into the window well, inhaling the night air through the screen, the rich, earthy scent of cornfields and the sweetness of fresh-cut hay. She could see the lights on the silos at Sullivan Grain west of town, but she looked beyond that, imagining the world spooling out in the darkness, vast glaciers and snowfields, jagged mountains and frigid seas, places where the sun didn't rise for weeks on end, where her name could be anything, her identity fluid, shaping itself into the open spaces. It was dizzying, all that awaited her outside the farmhouse, beyond Blackwater, but her eyes kept coming back to the lights at Sullivan Grain. Beneath a loose floorboard, tucked under her journal, lay the envelope of Earl's money.

She turned on the radio and crappy nineties music blared through the speakers. Missy must have changed the station at some point to annoy her. She liked to do that sometimes, telling Henley that it was a mother's duty to expose her child to decent music, which in Missy's estimation included Aerosmith, Shania Twain, and her eternal favorite, Fleetwood Mac. Once, when Henley had really pissed her off, Missy had made her listen to Kenny Rogers's *Greatest Hits* on repeat all day. It was ridiculous, and mild in terms of punishment, though it had certainly conveyed the message that she was displeased with Henley's behavior. Missy was never one to ground her or take away privileges like Henley's friends' mothers did. She treated her more like a sister, like they were on the same side despite occasional squabbles. Henley knew she could talk to her mother without judgment, because whatever stupid thing she'd done, Missy had surely done worse. She wanted to talk to her mother now, about what had happened with Earl, but she was alone with her mother's music, and Missy was sitting in the county jail.

She crossed the hall to Missy's room. She'd poked around in there several times since her mother had left, checking to see if she had snuck back for clean clothes when Henley wasn't home, embarrassed to face her daughter. But Missy hadn't come back, and now she couldn't. In her closet, her bright sundresses and halter tops still hung next to her denim jacket, a pile of dirty laundry on the floor. Henley started to shut the closet door, then changed her mind. She stepped on top of the laundry, reaching up to the closet shelf and feeling around for her mother's stash. Missy usually kept some pot on hand, even when she was clean of everything else.

Henley slid the pink music box off the shelf and opened it, the tiny plastic ballerina resurrecting as she lifted the lid. The box had once been Henley's, a birthday gift from Memaw and Pawpaw. Inside, there was a small glass pipe, a lighter, a baggie containing a scattering of stems and seeds, and an empty bottle of OxyContin prescribed three months ago in Ellie Embry's name. Even as Missy had been attending church and chattering optimistically about going back to school, she'd been in touch with Ellie and had been using again. Henley wound up the metal key and the ballerina began to pirouette as the mechanism inside the box produced the tinny notes of "Twinkle, Twinkle Little Star." She shut the lid and hurled the box against the plaster wall.

It would have been so much easier if she could give up on Missy completely, stop caring one way or the other. She'd certainly tried. But even though she was mad at her mother, she still wanted her home. As she knelt to pick up the music box, she saw that the satin insert had popped out. Tucked down in the bottom of the box was a folded square of paper. She took it out and opened it up, spreading it flat on her lap. It took her a moment to understand what she was looking at. A blurry black-and-white skull with a leering face, dark sockets for eyes. Like an X-ray. A sonogram.

The picture was nearly worn through at the folds, as though it had been taken out and put back many times, the soft curve of the skull traced by fingertips until the ink had rubbed off. According to the notations in the upper corner, the sonogram had taken place a few years after Henley was born, and the fetus was estimated to be nearly six months along. Her mother had been gone for various stretches of time, in rehab or jail. Could she have had a baby without Henley knowing? Why wouldn't she have told her? She was already a single mother; it wasn't like she could have suddenly become ashamed.

Her phone buzzed and for a moment she thought that Missy had somehow sensed her discovery and was calling to explain. It wasn't her mother, though; it was Jason. When he'd called the day before, she had told him she'd been busy helping out at her uncles' garage. She hadn't felt like seeing him.

"I miss you," he said. "I haven't seen you in two days."

"I'm really tired," she said. "I think I'm just going to go to bed."

"Are you kidding? It's not that late."

"Jason."

"I could come by just for a little while. I don't mind if you fall asleep."

"No."

He was silent for a moment. "Is something going on? You all right?"

"No. Yeah, I'm fine. I just . . ."

"You're at home?"

"Yeah."

"Stay put," he said. "I'll be right there."

She groaned and got up off the floor. He was coming over whether she wanted him to or not, and she'd have to figure out what to say. That he was smothering her and she needed a break; that his father had kissed her and she had to leave town and it had nothing to do with him; that they should sneak away together tonight and never look back. She couldn't make up her mind. Every time she half convinced herself to push Jason away, he'd show up and draw her back in. She stuffed the sonogram in the pocket of her jeans, restored the music box to its hiding place, and went down to the kitchen to attempt to settle herself while she waited.

She dug around in the cupboard to find Missy's half-full bottle of Captain Morgan and splashed a few inches into a jelly jar. She couldn't find anything to make it go down easier except the unopened bottle of Mad Dog Banana Red that had been in the fridge for so long it was practically a family heirloom. She filled her glass to the rim, leaving a sticky red ring on the counter when she lifted the murky concoction to her lips and chugged. It tasted so bad she chased it with more rum.

Jason embraced her when he came in, rubbed the red stain away from the corners of her mouth with his thumb. "What's going on?" he asked.

"Nothing," she said. "I'm just sick of this place. I need to get out of here, out of this town."

"Hey," he said. "I thought you'd changed your mind about that. Did something happen?"

She shrugged. The alcohol was beginning to work its magic, warming her insides, loosening her tongue. "I'm not working for your dad anymore."

"Why not?"

"I was in his room the other day when he came home," she said. "He tried to kiss me. I pushed him off."

Jason exhaled slowly, jaw twitching and nostrils flaring. "Fucking prick," he muttered. "God, I'm so sorry. He's gonna regret it." He took her hands in his and squeezed them. "You remember how I told you about hitting my dad with a bat that time?"

"Yeah."

"I'd walked in on him and Missy. Dad saw me and went off. I freaked out. I thought maybe he'd hurt her—I couldn't imagine she'd wanted that. I hit him, and that night, after Missy talked to me about it, and told me she was okay, I went into his room and set his bed on fire. I guess part of me thought he should still be faithful to my mom, even though she was gone. Part of me was jealous in some stupid little-kid way, like I didn't want him taking any of Missy's attention away from me."

Henley thought of the black-and-white image of the baby, wondered if it was Earl's. If he knew. She slugged some Mad Dog straight from the bottle and gagged. Why hadn't her mother told her about the nature of her relationship with Earl? Missy had encouraged Henley to take her place at the Sullivan house without mentioning what it was that she did there. Henley remembered Earl saying something about her mother that day in his bedroom, a look of confusion on his face. Had Missy implied to him that Henley would be replacing her in every way?

"I'm gonna go beat the shit out of him right now," Jason said.

"No." She shook her head. "You can't. He'd probably charge you with assault."

"I don't care," he said.

"I do. It's not worth it. He already apologized." She didn't want Jason to confront his father and find out that Earl had paid her off. It was a secret she wanted to keep from him, that she had the means to leave anytime she wanted, that there was no longer anything holding her here.

"I have an idea," she said, her throat burning from the liquor. She wrenched open the door to the cellar and walked down the steps, stopping when her bare feet met the cool dirt floor. She reached out, her fingers spidering into the darkness in search of the beaded chain, and yanked three times before the bulb clicked. Its dull yellow light haloed around her.

Pawpaw's sledgehammer leaned against the hand-hewn workbench, draped with dusty cobwebs. She wiped the scarred metal head with her T-shirt, hefted the sledge, and carried it up the stairs.

"Really?" Jason asked, the corner of his mouth turning up in a smile when she told him. "Of all the things we could do, this is what you want?"

She nodded, her face numb, her head humming.

"All right. It's your party."

They drove to Sullivan Park with the windows down, sledgehammer weighted on the floorboard between them, Henley gripping the handle to keep it from knocking against their knees. No one was around at this lonely hour, the river tarnished black and silver under the waning moon.

Henley climbed out, the hammer scraping the running board, metal on metal, and stood before Emily Sullivan. They were no longer face-to-face, Henley having outgrown her long ago. Emily was so small, much smaller than she remembered. A little girl, her outstretched stone hands holding a trio of abandoned snail shells and a dented bottle cap. She thought of what Earl had said, Emily watching him, wordless, her mouth full of blood. Part of her understood how that must have damaged him, the sorrow that draped over his life like a dark caul, yet it wasn't right that he was using his sister as an excuse for his behavior all these years later, hiding behind her angelic image, invoking the Sullivan family saint.

"I'm sorry," she said, brushing the tips of her fingers over Emily's eternally open eyes as if to close them, like people did for the dead, out of respect, in movies. She cocked the sledgehammer like a baseball bat and swung, the impact working its way back up the handle and shuddering through her arms to her core. She swung harder, dust and debris raining down as cracks erupted, and kept swinging until she'd knocked loose the head.

It felt good. Rage burned through her with each strike, and she smashed the broken pieces into the ground until she was spent.

Back at home, Jason insisted on washing her off in the tub like a child, and she was too tired to resist. He rinsed the grit from her hair, made her drink a glass of water, carried her to bed, kissed the shiny skin on her hands where blisters were beginning to form. He tucked the covers tight as a straitjacket, Memaw's itchy afghan pulled up to her chin, and as soon as he left, she kicked them loose.

She remembered years back when she and Missy had read the Twilight books together, telling her mother she wished she could have a boyfriend like Edward. Missy had snorted. *That all sounds great when you're thirteen and dreaming, but in real life you couldn't go a day with some guy kissing your eyelids and keeping tabs on you before you'd wanna kick him in the balls.*

She wondered what Missy would think of her and Jason together, if that was something she'd ever considered. Had her mother thought about what might happen when she left Henley alone with the Sullivan men in that big house? Was her mother thinking of her at all as she sobered up in jail? She felt around on the floor for her discarded jeans and fished the sonogram from the pocket, squinting at it in the faint moonlight, at this being that was part of her mother, and by extension, her. Was there a child out there somewhere with the Pettits' honey hair and hazel eyes, living a different life with a different name, its destiny unblemished by the preconceptions that would have tainted it in Blackwater? Missy clearly hadn't forgotten about it, but she hadn't told her about it, either, and she must have had her reasons. Henley traced the gray bones with her fingertip, wondering which of them had been luckier.

CHAPTER 17

SADIE

NOVEMBER

I stopped at Casey's for coffee on my way to Leola's, scorching my tongue as I swerved on the gravel road to avoid a possum frozen in the headlights. A light burned in the front window of the farmhouse, a small beacon in the vast darkness of the countryside. It was too dark to see the stone angels that surrounded the house, but I knew they were there, huddled against the wind. The dogs yipped and whined when I knocked on the door but lost interest once Leola opened it.

The living room was noticeably brighter and warmer than it had been the first time I'd visited. Someone had changed the flickering light bulb, dumped the ash bucket, and had the stove burning hot enough to sweat, and I guessed that it had been Charlie. Either that, or Leola had gotten everything in order before he arrived, so he wouldn't worry that she was struggling without him at home, like Mom did when Becca came over.

Charlie ducked into the room right after Leola let me in, chewing on a cookie and wiping crumbs from his mouth. He was pallid and rail thin, rangy enough that he had to mind the low doorframe. He was dressed in a denim jacket with a sheepskin collar and Wranglers. Acne scars peppered his jawline, where a pale, incomplete beard struggled to grow. His eyes were sleepy and shadowed, irises amber as a cat's.

"Hey," he said, offering his hand. "Sadie. Nice to meet you."

Leola patted his arm and adjusted her apron. "I'll let you two talk a minute. I'll be right in the kitchen if you need me."

"Leola told me how close you and Shane were," I said to Charlie. He sucked in his lower lip, nodding. "I thought you might know what was going on in his life recently . . . things I might not know about. Maybe you could help me understand what happened."

"Sure." He hooked his thumbs through his belt loops and studied the worn path on the floor.

"Do you know if he was using drugs, maybe?"

Charlie eyed me warily.

"You can be honest. I'm only asking because we don't know how he died. We're trying to figure that out, but it's difficult because we don't have a lot to go on."

He scratched his jaw and shrugged. "I dunno. He drank, like anybody. Smoked weed. I don't know about anything else."

"Had he been sick?"

"He wasn't feeling great last time I saw him," Charlie said. "But he told me it was just allergies acting up, or a cold coming on."

"How long was that before he died?"

"Maybe a week."

"Your grandma said . . . you don't get along with Crystle."

He made a throat-clearing sound that was almost a laugh. "Yeah. That's fair."

"Why's that?"

"Look, I don't know how good you know her, or what you think of her, but I'm friends with her cousin, so I've known her a long time. She never liked me, right from the start, because I could see through her bullshit. She's a liar, and I'd call her on it," he said. "She didn't want me hanging around Shane when they got together. He tried to make her happy and do what she wanted, but toward the end he saw her for what she was. He wanted out."

"You mean he wanted to leave her? Why?"

"I don't know, exactly, if it was anything in particular. They weren't getting along," he said. "He said he couldn't trust her. I'd been telling him that the whole time."

There was a dull thud, logs shifting in the fire.

"But you're sure he was going to leave her? Did he tell you that?"

"Yeah," Charlie said. "He was trying to figure things out, be smart about it. He'd been putting money aside she didn't know about."

A sharp pain needled through my gut. Her behavior had seemed off even before I knew about her infidelity, about Shane's plans. She might have been angry if she suspected he was leaving and taking what money he had left along with him, worried that he wouldn't be supporting her anymore. Would that be enough, though, that she'd do something drastic to stop him? Maybe Shane had been taking pills like Crystle said, except that he wasn't stressed over a crime he'd committed but over his failing marriage, the secrets he was keeping from his wife as he planned his escape.

"Do you think she knew he wanted to leave?"

"I don't know," he said. "He was gonna tell her, but I don't know if he'd got around to it yet. He wanted to have everything in place first."

Leola came back in with a plate of cookies and held them out to me. They had the same crosshatching on top as the peanut butter cookies my mom used to make. Mom had let Becca and me press the marks in with a fork, until she'd gotten sick of me asking why we only did it for peanut butter and not chocolate chip or molasses. *That's just how it is*, she'd told me. *You ask too many questions for things that don't have answers.*

"I hope Charlie was able to help?" Leola said.

"Yes," I said. "He was. Oh—" I turned back to him. "I wanted to tell you, I found something you made for Shane. I thought you might like to know he'd kept it all these years. It was some sort of craft, made out of paper plates. I can bring it by sometime, if you'd like to have it back."

Charlie cracked a grin, the first time I'd seen his expression lighten. "I remember that," he said. "Granny made me go to Bible camp. Didn't end well."

"Show her what he made for you," Leola said, nudging Charlie. "Go on."

I followed him down the hall to his room, which smelled of wintergreen chewing tobacco and sweaty boots. It was small and tidy, the bed loosely made with a plaid comforter, the desk bare except for a lamp with no shade and a peanut can stuffed with pencils and pens. On a pine shelf above the desk were several pieces of metalwork.

Charlie handed me a dog figurine made from nuts and bolts. "This is one of the first projects we did when I started hanging around his workshop," he said. "And this is what he made for me when I gave him that dumb paper plate thing." I set down the dog and took the heavy metal block with Charlie's name engraved into the shining surface.

"Did he make lots of things like this?" I asked. I knew he was a welder, but I'd never really seen any of his personal projects, the kind of metalwork he did for fun.

"Oh, yeah," Charlie said. "He had all the tools and equipment in his workshop. The coolest thing he made was a rifle—machined it himself. He was real proud of it. Said if the government ever came for his guns, they wouldn't get that one."

That sounded like Shane. His love of guns was one of the few things he hadn't kept from us, apparently.

"He let me try it out. Said he'd make another one sometime for me, show me how to do it. Hadn't got around to it." He picked up the metal block and the dog figurine and carefully placed them back on the shelf, his hand unsteady. I wondered if the rifle had been pawned with all the rest, if it was even legal to sell a homemade gun, though I couldn't imagine that would have stopped Crystle.

When I called Mom from the car to tell her about meeting Charlie, she remembered Shane bringing a friend along one time when he'd come to get some car parts out of her shed. He had been a quiet young man with shaggy hair that kept falling in his face, and boots with the soles coming off. She might not have remembered him at all, except that he'd eaten her boiled cabbage without complaint and asked for seconds, something her own children had never managed to do. She couldn't recall his name, but she felt sure it was Charlie. "Give him the Firebird," she said. "Shane would want it that way."

I drained the cold dregs from my coffee cup on the drive back. Stars had emerged from a scrim of clouds and the moon had risen through the trees, bright enough to cast skeletal shadows over the frozen fields. A northern gust whipped the branches and the shadow fingers skittered along the edge of the road.

I turned over everything Charlie had said, about Crystle being a liar, Shane seeing her for what she was and wanting out. Did she really believe he had something to do with Roger and Macey's murders, or had she only brought that up so Becca and I would stop questioning how Shane had died?

I thought of our brother sealed in his casket, a photo of Crystle wedged beneath his stiff fingers for all eternity, close to his heart. It was possible that the timing of his death—just before he'd planned to leave her—was pure coincidence. It was equally possible that it wasn't.

I had trouble falling asleep when I got home. The wind rattled the windowpanes and crept in through the gaps, billowing the curtain just enough that I kept startling awake, thinking someone was standing there. Shane, perhaps, watching over me or asking for help, haunting me one way or the other.

CHAPTER 18

HENLEY
OCTOBER

A flock of starlings cackled in the trees outside the Pettit Brothers garage. There must have been hundreds of them, moving restlessly from branch to branch, swooping through the leaves. Uncle Denny had once told her that starlings were witches in disguise, that they shed their wings for cloaks in the night, and Raymond had smacked him on the back of the head, knocking his hat in the dirt. She imagined Raymond would do something worse to Earl Sullivan if he found out what Earl had done. She wondered how her mother would react when she told her, whether or not she would look surprised.

Crystle's Jeep was parked in the gravel lot, the top still off though the weather was cooling down. Crystle had always run hot, sleeping with the bedroom window cracked in the winter, even when it snowed. Shane sometimes joked that he made Gravy lie on his feet to keep from getting frostbite, but he didn't mind the cold if it made Crystle happy. She liked the feel of his icy hands. *You know what they say*, Shane had teased, stroking Crystle's flushed cheeks. *Cold hands, warm heart*. Henley wondered if the saying went both ways, if Crystle's sweating flesh meant her heart was stone-cold.

Inside, the garage was quiet and the door to the office was shut, so Henley proceeded to the kitchen area for a Dr Pepper. When the door was closed, it was closed for a reason, and she knew better than to knock. A translucent Walmart bag sat on the counter by the sink, a package of tissues and a box of cough syrup inside. Raymond's allergies always acted up this time of year, aggravated by ragweed and cocklebur and lingering until the first hard frost knocked the pollen down. Junior joked that Memaw had coddled him too much, that he was out weeding the garden and cleaning chicken coops while Raymond stayed indoors, suckling at the teat he'd kicked Junior off of.

Henley drank her Dr Pepper and studied the map on the wall, tracing her fingernail along the blue vein of the Missouri River up into the Dakotas. She heard a noise, and it sounded like someone was coming out of the office, though when she peeked around the corner, there was no one there. As she moved closer, she heard Junior's voice, and Raymond's, and a third she didn't immediately recognize. Crystle wasn't in there, because she was always the loudest in any conversation, and if the men had their voices raised, she'd be yelling right over the top of them. Henley crept up next to the door and listened. She heard the name Calhoun, and she remembered Hannah on the local news, standing in front of Emily's statue in Sullivan Park, pleading to get her daughter back.

She inched as close as she dared, her back flat to the wall. She didn't know Hannah, but she'd seen Roger in the garage now and then. Junior was saying something about Calhoun, and then his voice dropped, and she thought she heard him say Shane's name. The third man interrupted, and this time she knew who it was—Dex, who always got on Junior's last nerve.

The knob turned and she scurried backward. "Hey," she said calmly as Raymond came out of the door. "You wanted to check my tires?"

"Oh. Yeah," he said, shaking his head as if to clear it. "Gotta make sure you still got some decent tread left—especially if you're gonna be travelin'." She hadn't told him that she now had the money to leave whenever she wanted, only that it wouldn't be much longer. He put his arm around her shoulders to lead her outside. "Let's go take a look."

Raymond squatted in the gravel, then stuck his hand in the wheel well and ran his fingers over her rear tire. He moved around the car, checking each one, lifting the windshield wipers and examining the blades.

"Your allergies bothering you?" she asked.

He shook his head. "Nope, not too bad."

Crystle's Jeep started up, Dex at the wheel, gravel spitting out from under the tires. Junior stood in the doorway, watching.

"Everything okay?" Henley asked.

"Sure," Raymond said. "Yeah."

She knew not to ask about her uncles' business. She would certainly never say anything to Junior. But Raymond was softer, and she couldn't help herself.

"I thought I heard Dex say something about Calhoun," she murmured. The starlings shuffled from one tree to another, screeching.

"Yeah," Raymond said, forcing an uncertain smile. "He owed some money when he ran off."

She thought of Dalmire, how he had owed some money, too, how they had joked about the one long bone being all that was left of him. She thought about how she'd never found that joke funny; how Dalmire hadn't been seen in years; how nobody'd come looking for him. You didn't make someone else's business your business, Junior liked to say. Life was easier that way.

Raymond decided he didn't like the looks of her spare tire, so he brought a better one out to put in her trunk, and she rolled the old one into the shop. She stopped in the kitchen to wash her hands before she left. The Walmart bag was gone. As she pumped soap into her palm, she noticed a red ring pooled around the drain, dark as congealed blood. Like the cough syrup had spilled. Even after the water rushed over it, it left a faint stain.

CHAPTER 19

SADIE

NOVEMBER

"Oh, my god," Hannah cried, lurching backward, hands clasped over her mouth. "What is that?"

I peered into the kitchen drawer she'd opened. There were chunks of what looked like human hair, coarse and blond, arranged in a nest. I reached in and extracted the long handle of a basting brush, the kind used for grilling, all the bristles chewed off.

"Disgusting," she said, slamming the drawer with her foot. "Damn mice. Gone for a little while, and they take over."

It had gotten too overwhelming for Hannah out at the farm with her aunt and Chad and his girlfriend, their kids, the vaping, the dismembered dolls. The news vans had moved on. She'd wanted to go back home, to grieve in peace.

"You could get a cat," I said. "A good mouser."

"I don't know," Hannah said, looking around the narrow kitchen. "I don't think I can take care of anything right now. Even a cat that feeds itself."

Her gaze caught on a rustic sign above the sink, white lettering on a barn-wood board: HAPPINESS IS HOMEMADE. Hannah had painted it. She'd done a lot of crafting back when the girls were small. She had made a sign for me and Greg that said THE LOWELL FAMILY, but I'd gone back to my maiden name after the divorce and had thrown the sign away.

"I'll clean up the drawer," I said. "And wash whatever's in there."

She sighed. "Probably need to wash everything."

"Has there been any news?" I asked, checking around for paper towels to pick up the mouse nest.

She leaned against the stove, scraping at a fleck of grit with her thumbnail. "They're interviewing Roger's friends, coworkers. They've already talked to most of them before, so I don't know if they'll find anything they didn't already know. And they questioned me, of course. Asked if I meant it when I said I wished Roger was dead."

"Was it Kendrick?" I asked.

"No. One of the guys. Kendrick's all right. She's about the only one who doesn't look at me like I'm guilty of something. Probably because she and Chad are old friends." She tucked her hair back behind her ears. "I need some air."

I followed her out to the little deck tacked onto the back of the trailer, the wood gray and splintered. Dry prairie grass swayed in the sprawling field beyond the deck, and I thought of the mice creeping through it, seeking warmth and shelter as winter closed in, finding their way through the lattice beneath the trailer.

Hannah looked out over the field, her pale skin nearly translucent, bluish hollows around her eyes and at her temples, the shape of her skull showing through, the natural strawberry tint bleached out of her blond hair so that it no longer matched Macey's. A painted flowerpot balanced on the railing between us. Lily had made one just like it in kindergarten, a Mother's Day gift with thumbprint butterflies. The withered stalk of a long-dead plant poked out of it, cigarette butts stubbed out in the soil.

"How much do you know," I asked, "about that last weekend? When they disappeared?"

She scraped her chapped lips with her fingernail, her face to the wind. "I know he was going to take her fishing. Something she loved and I hated. He wanted to make it fun for her, so she'd want to go. She didn't like his place, out in the sticks, trees all around so it never got light inside. Said it smelled like Granny's old root cellar, dark and damp, wood paneling everywhere, little toadstools growing in the shower. Told me the sheets on her bed were bumpy. She hated that." Hannah cleared her throat, her nose running in the cold. "The carpet was orange, and she'd pretend it was lava, and she'd sleep in her clothes so she didn't have to feel the bumpy sheets. But she liked fishing. The spring peepers were out, and she told me they'd be real loud by the water. She liked to listen to them sing."

Lily loved the peepers, too, the chorus of tiny frogs at the creek announcing that winter was over, that spring had arrived, however brutal and unpredictable it might be.

"She called me Saturday night because there was a bad storm, and the wind was banging all those trees together up against the house so she couldn't sleep. She said it sounded like somebody was pounding on the door. She wanted me to come get her, and I . . ." Hannah squeezed her eyes shut. "I said I couldn't. She called again the next morning, Sunday. Said her dad had bought her a new fishing pole, all her own. The Walmart greeter confirmed it, that old lady who's always there. Said they looked happy when they left the store. They were gonna go out on the river, have a picnic, roast hotdogs. The whole deal. I was glad he was making an effort, though I figured he was doing it as much to spite me as anything. Playing the long game to win her over. Maybe I was wrong. I don't know."

"Was that the last you heard?"

She nodded, her mouth set in a grim line. "He filled up at a gas station near the river later that morning. Some guy thought he saw them fishing later, a man and a little girl with a bright blue pole. He was supposed to take her to school the next day—that was part of the new visitation schedule he'd fought for, so he could get an extra night—and when she didn't show up, the school called him instead of me, and I didn't find out till later, when I went to pick her up and she wasn't there."

A fissure in her cracked lips filled with blood and she reached up to touch it, staring at the red smear on her fingertip. "When they went to check his house, her overnight bag was still in her room. They said he probably left it behind so she wouldn't be recognized—so nobody'd see her wearing the clothes I'd packed for her, or rolling that red ladybug suitcase into some hotel. But now . . . maybe something happened to them at the river. Or when they got back home. Sometime before they would have left for school the next day, but most likely at night." Her mouth twisted bitterly. "Kendrick said disposing of bodies is something best done in the dark."

"Have they found his truck?"

"They're looking for it," she said. "It's about the most common pickup you could have—a white Ford. They're everywhere. They sent a diver into the river back in the spring, in case they ran off the road or something, but Kendrick wants to try again."

"Can I ask you something personal, about Roger?"

She turned to face me. "Yeah."

"Did he ever go out with Crystle?"

"Crystle? I don't know. I didn't exactly keep up with his love life after we split. I didn't care what he did, who he saw, as long as he kept Macey out of it."

"Okay."

"Okay? You asking for a reason?"

"Somebody told me Shane thought Crystle might have been cheating on him. I don't know with who."

"So you think she had an affair with my ex?"

I shook my head. "I don't know what to think. She showed up at my house the other night and told me Shane overdosed, and she didn't know whether or not it was an accident. She implied that he was upset over some things."

"You believe her?" Hannah asked.

"I don't know."

"Nothing surprises me anymore," she said. "I could believe almost anything about anybody. We don't know what we're capable of ourselves, let alone what somebody else might do under certain circumstances. I wouldn't take her at her word, though. From what I know of her, she's all drama. Might've come over to stir shit up just for attention because she was bored."

"Yeah. Maybe."

"I wonder if Kendrick's talked to her, if she and Roger hung out. She's always saying, you never know where a lead'll come from. Somebody somewhere knows something."

I headed straight to Mom's house from Hannah's, not bothering to call first. It was rare these days for her not to be home, though I wouldn't have minded if she was gone.

"Oh," she said, her hand going up to touch her uncombed hair. "I wasn't expecting anybody." She wore an old-fashioned housecoat with snaps down the front, the wide pockets bulging with tissues. *Judge Judy* was on TV and the volume was blaring.

"Sorry to pop in on you," I said. "I was wondering if you still have my old prom dress in a box somewhere. I wanted to show it to Lily." A look of tired resignation crossed her face, and I felt a twinge of guilt. I knew she kept the formal dresses she'd sewn, the costumes, Shane's first communion jacket, all of it, and she knew it, too—but she didn't know where she'd put them, which closet, which unmarked box. I was counting on her having to dig.

"Let me check," she said.

She disappeared down the hall and I scanned the room. Shane's drawing wasn't by her recliner or on the table just inside the door where she stacked the mail. I turned down the hall and nearly bumped into her.

"Gimme a minute," she said, opening the door to the basement. "I think I might have put it downstairs."

She shut the door behind her, probably not wanting me to see the mess she was cultivating down there, lest I threaten an intervention like on *Hoarders*. I slipped into her bedroom. The walls were sallow with nicotine stains, the duvet pocked with burn holes from years of Dad smoking in bed every night while reading Louis L'Amour novels. Mom had talked about painting the walls, sewing a new duvet, driving out to Walmart to look for a good price on sheets, though years had passed since Dad died, and the room still looked exactly the same. A pile of paint chips gathered dust on the dresser, all various shades of blue, and I could hear her declaring the colors too bright, too dark, too similar, the thought of making a decision about such a small change enough to paralyze her.

I checked the dresser drawer where she kept a cache of old birthday cards from her mother beneath a tangle of shriveled nylons and flesh-colored underwear, and then the jewelry box where she stored her antique cameo, her agate worry stone, and a scattering of our baby teeth. No luck. The nightstand was crowded with wadded-up tissues, a forty-year-old clock radio that no longer told time, and a precarious stack of Dad's paperback Westerns, as though she still worried, even after he was dead, that she'd get smacked for moving them. The piece of paper with Shane's drawing wasn't there, or in the nightstand drawer, or tucked into the Bible that lay inside. I hurried back to the living room as I heard Mom's footfalls on the stairs.

The shimmering taffeta dress hung over her arm like a lifeless mermaid. Teal, Becca's favorite color. Becca's dress. "This one?" She held it up, the fabric intricately wrinkled from being stuffed in a box, the musty scent it had acquired over the years unlikely ever to come out.

"Yes," I said, forcing a smile. "Perfect." It was a small thing, to not remember the color of a dress, which daughter preferred coral to teal all those years ago, though it wasn't like her to forget. I watched her face for any sign that she knew what I was up to, that she'd brought the wrong dress up to see what I would say, but there was no deceit in her eyes. She looked tired, as tired as I'd ever seen her.

I couldn't bring myself to ask her where she'd put the paper, to tell her why I needed to see it. I wanted to be wrong and maybe I was, the shapes uncertain depending on the angle and shadow and the way the lead had smudged into the grooves, but for a moment, when I had tilted the paper toward the light, the letters appeared to form a word: *Calhouns.* Plural, as in Roger and Macey. I hadn't thought much of it at the time, before I'd talked to Crystle and Hannah, but now I couldn't help wondering what else he had written on the page with such a firm hand, and who he had written it to.

CHAPTER 20

HENLEY
OCTOBER

The Cutler County Jail was a plain limestone building next to the courthouse, surrounded by white-limbed sycamores with broad canopies, each yellowing leaf larger than Henley's hand. Missy wore black-and-white stripes like an old-fashioned jailbird, her dark blond hair limp and oily, skin blotched and flaking. She seemed to have aged at an accelerated rate during the weeks she'd been gone, undergoing a perverse metamorphosis from diaphanous butterfly to faded moth.

They sat across from each other at a wobbly table with one gimpy leg.

"Hey, baby, I missed you so much," she said. She was gaunt, a skeleton shrink-wrapped with skin.

"Me, too, Mama." She smiled at Missy, wanting to cry. She hated seeing her mother like this, unwell, not yet herself, but sober enough to be aware of what she'd done. She wondered how Ellie was faring, if her outlook would change at all while she sat in jail, her tan fading and her fractured skull knitting itself back together.

"So glad you came to see me. What're you up to?"

"I'm gonna be leaving," she said. "I think it's time. You don't need me when you're in here, and I can't stick around doing nothing. There's no reason not to go."

Missy winced, but she made herself nod and to her credit didn't spill any tears.

"I just wanted to let you know."

Missy cracked a fake smile. "Tell me where you're going," she said. "I want to hear all about it. I want to be able to picture you there when you're gone."

Henley knew, despite everything, that her mother loved her. She conjured a storybook image for her of a place they'd never been. Mile-high mountains thick with snow like fine sparkling dust, the sky painfully blue. The sun cresting a ridge, igniting the valleys in diamond glints, rich people swooshing down the slopes, throwing out money with abandon, drunkenly overtipping people like Henley who cleaned up after them and served them pricey drinks. And after that, on to Alaska for the summer, spying whales, climbing glaciers, the sea lit by the midnight sun.

"You'll come back and see me," Missy said. "Right? When I'm outta here?"

"Sure," she said. "Hey, Mama, I want to talk to you about something. About you and Earl."

"Earl?" Her lip twitched when she said his name.

"I found the picture in the music box."

Missy looked stricken. She tugged at her greasy hair.

"That baby was Earl's, wasn't it?"

Missy dug her thumb into a gash on the tabletop. Her nails were gnawed to the quick and rimmed with dried blood.

"Tell me."

She nodded, finally, her dry lips pressing together.

"Did you ever tell him?"

"Of course."

"Where's the baby now?"

"Out behind the tractor shed," Missy said, "with all of Memaw's roses looking out over the fields." Her gaze drifted from ceiling to floor like she was watching a spider descend from a thread. "Lost it not long after they took that picture. Worst day of my life. They knew something was wrong. Wasn't meant to be. Never was able to have another one after that."

She didn't know whether all of that was true, but "tractor shed" had rolled out of Missy's mouth so easily that Henley had to consider it might be. "Did you want to keep it?"

"More than anything," Missy whispered.

"Did Earl?"

She shrugged. "It was a hard time for him," Missy said. "Daphne'd been gone a couple years. Jason was struggling, both of them were. Earl promised to take care of me, whatever I decided. And he did. From then on. I always had a job, always had a paycheck, even when I wasn't really working." She looked up at Henley, one eye missing its lashes, as though she'd pinched them all out.

"Were you working for Earl when you got pregnant with me?"

"Yeah." It came out as a breath, the ghost of a word, her head nodding like she had a palsy.

"*Mama.*" Henley's mind ricocheted from one horror to the next like a pinball smacking targets in a machine. Earl. *Jason.* Saliva pooled in her mouth, sweat beading her scalp and neck and tracing down between her breasts.

Her mother's eyes lost their faraway haze and snapped into focus. "He's not your daddy. Is that what you came here to ask me?" She let out a sharp barking laugh. "I was just a stupid kid, screwing around. Not unlike yourself. Hell, I was seventeen. I had a *lot* of boyfriends back then."

"I know, Mama, everybody knows."

"Earl was faithful to his wife," she said, sucking at a fresh well of blood along her ragged thumbnail. "Didn't so much as look at me till I was of age and she was bones in her grave."

Henley studied her face, unconvinced.

"They have those spit tests, now, if you don't believe me," Missy said. "You can get one from the goddamn Walmart. Not that it matters. Just garbage for a bunch of old biddies to gossip about. Earl's a good man."

Henley was done listening to her mother defend him. "Do you know what happened when I was at the Sullivans' the other day?"

Missy's head swiveled back and forth.

"Earl and I had a talk in his bedroom," she said, her voice going low. "And then he tried to kiss me. He fell over and landed on top of me on his bed."

Missy's mouth opened, but no sounds came out.

"He was drunk, and he seemed to think I *wanted* it. Why would he think that? He said you were just fine with the idea of me taking over for you. Did you mean more than cleaning, Mama? Were you gonna tell me?" Henley leaned forward, gripping the edge of the table. "Did you worry what was gonna happen to me in that house after you left?"

"No! Earl and me—" She gestured wildly with her hands, trying to form the thought she couldn't articulate. "He wouldn't do that. He's not like that. It must've been a mistake."

"You don't believe me?"

"Oh, baby." Her eyes glossed with tears. "I'm sorry. I never meant for anything like that to happen, I swear. I just wanted you to have a job, to be taken care of. He's not in his right mind, sometimes, when he drinks. If I ever thought . . ." Her face buckled and Henley didn't doubt that Missy felt bad about what had happened, but she couldn't help wondering if some of Missy's tears were due to the fact that she'd so easily been replaced as the object of Earl's attentions.

"All right, Mama."

"No. You need to understand, Henley," Missy said, her face twisted up, her lashless eye seeping tears. "I was a single mother, living with my parents, no hope of ever doing anything better than cleaning somebody else's house. I thought if I had Earl's baby, that'd change things. He'd marry me, you and I'd move into the big house, you'd be one of those kids that took horseback riding lessons and ballet. That was my one shot to give you a better life, and I took it. I did it for you. I know I haven't been the best mom, but I did everything I could. I'm sorry it didn't work out like I hoped it would."

Henley didn't buy Missy's claim that she'd done it all for her—her mother had wanted a different life for herself as much as she'd wanted it for Henley. Earl had supported Missy for years, and none of what he'd given her had been spent on horseback riding lessons or ballet or whatever else Missy claimed she'd wanted for her daughter. She felt a swell of pity for her mother—that her greatest aspiration was to trick Earl Sullivan into marrying her. Henley was embarrassed that she'd had her own daydreams about marrying Jason, but she had enough sense, at least, to know it was a fantasy, that she could find her own way out of the life she was stuck in.

"How did it go with your mom?" Jason asked.

She'd barely left the jail when he called, like he'd estimated exactly how long she'd be there. She felt slightly queasy talking to him after the things Missy had told her. "It was fine," she said. "I was mostly just there to say goodbye."

"How's she doing?"

"Looks like a stray cat that got put down but didn't die," she said. "But she's coming back to herself. She'll get there. I hope."

"Did you tell her about us?"

She hesitated, wondering which answer he'd prefer, and whether she should lie. "No," she said.

"She might feel better knowing I'm going with you—that you won't be alone."

Henley hadn't told him that she was going by herself. It was easier to let him believe she was doing what he wanted than to have to talk through it again. The boyfriends she'd had before Jason had been fairly taciturn, more interested in riding four-wheelers or making out than dissecting the nuances of their relationship. She never imagined she'd grow so weary of talking about her feelings. She and Charlie had largely avoided discussing the sometimes complicated nature of their relationship, calling themselves best friends and leaving it at that.

She'd been thinking of Charlie a lot lately, wishing she could talk to him about everything that was going on, but they hadn't spoken much since Labor Day weekend, when he found out that she was seeing Jason. She missed him terribly. Jason had suggested several times, under the pretense of joking, that her best friend had abandoned her, to the point that it felt true. Jason was always with her, pushing everyone else out of the way, making her feel that he was all she needed, that he was the only one who truly cared.

His attention was by turns exhilarating and overwhelming, his desire to know every intimate detail of her life before they met, of each hour they spent apart. As though he could somehow possess her through an encyclopedic knowledge of her heart. But she was a Pettit, not prone to laying herself bare, and she took quiet pleasure in her secrets, their dark spiraled passages like the unseen whorls inside a shell. The plans she'd been making. The things Missy had told her at the jail. The way she thought of Charlie, still, how she stirred when she smelled smoke on the river, like the night they'd first kissed. All of it locked away in places Jason couldn't reach, if she didn't let him. She had to keep making room for herself inside. She needed to stretch out, push back, because if she didn't, Jason would spill into everything, swallow her up like a flood, consuming all the light and space and air, leaving room for nothing else.

CHAPTER 21

SADIE

NOVEMBER

After confirming that Greg would drop Lily off at my house the night before Thanksgiving, I asked him how the diet was going—my nonconfrontational way of determining whether he and Heidi had gone back to stocking their pantry with normal food. He reminded me that it was not a diet and then rambled on about how it had given him unprecedented clarity and focus, to the point that he sounded like he'd entered an altered state. It reminded me of the time he'd dropped acid in college and stayed up all night talking about his teeth, how the inside of his mouth was a cathedral, a stadium, filled with rows and rows of teeth, more teeth than there were tombstones in Arlington Cemetery, and he had just never realized it before. *I never knew what a negative impact sugar/dairy/legumes had on my mind and body!*

It occurred to me that much of my time with Greg had been spent listening to him talk about himself. He'd always had plenty to say and seemed confident that other people wanted to hear it. I was glad— genuinely—that he'd found someone he was happy with, someone who enjoyed listening to his blather but also had no qualms telling him when to shut up. I'd recently realized, as I thought about how well he and Heidi complemented each other, that I was completely over the divorce. It had taken a long time to grind my anger down to a fine powder of irritation and a little while longer to brush the last of the dust away, but I had managed it. I hadn't been angry that Greg had met Heidi while we were still married, that the spark between them, though not acted upon, had likely precipitated our already inevitable divorce. And it wasn't that I'd wanted to stay with Greg—I hadn't. I'd been upset that things hadn't turned out the way I'd wanted. I'd thought my life would follow a trajectory more like Heidi's—a flourishing career, a happy marriage, a big house in the suburbs—and while I'd blamed Greg for part of that, I knew it was mostly my own fault. I'd been too passive, let him push me into things. I'd given up on myself, on what I wanted, too easily.

I was looking forward to the long weekend with Lily. After work on Wednesday, I met up with Theo at the clinic to buy some of the dog food Gravy seemed to hate the least, based on the samples we'd tried.

"Hey," he said. "I'm gonna go next door and grab a quick bite before I head out of town, if you'd like to join me."

I didn't even think before agreeing. I was starving, and the Dairy Barn would always win out over a Lean Cuisine or the frozen pizza Lily would undoubtedly ask me to make when Greg dropped her off later. The parking lot was nearly empty, and I figured most people were probably either scurrying around Walmart for last-minute groceries or on the road to someplace else.

We ordered at the counter and took a booth overlooking the highway, the plate-glass window shuddering as a semi hurtled by. "Where are you headed for Thanksgiving?" I asked, shrugging my arms out of my coat.

"My parents', in the city. And I'll get to spend some time with my girls."

"You have daughters?"

"Yeah." He swiped through the photos on his phone and handed it to me. Two girls with long wavy hair, their mouths wide with laughter, surrounded by a blur of frolicking dogs. The girls looked nearly identical, except that one had braces. "Liv and Stella. They're fourteen and fifteen."

"They're lovely," I said. "My daughter's eleven. Are those beagles?"

"They are. We foster for a rescue group. Lots of hunting dogs get dumped around here when they can't or won't hunt. So far the girls have talked me into adopting a three-legged redbone and a pointer that's half blind. If they had their way, we'd have at least twenty dogs by now."

The server came by with my Oreo concrete, ice cream dripping down the sides of the cup.

"Looks good," he said. "Now I wish I'd ordered dessert instead of dinner."

"Want to try a bite?" I asked. "I haven't touched it yet."

He shook his head, looking amused, and I felt silly for offering. Maybe it was a mom thing—I was so used to Lily eating off my plate, stealing the last cookie I'd wanted for myself, drinking from my glass because my tea supposedly tasted better than hers, even though it was exactly the same.

"So, Gravy's eating better?"

"A little," I said, digging Oreo chunks out of my ice cream with a long plastic spoon. "He's been sleeping a lot, but it's nice just having him around. Lily loves him. And the house doesn't feel quite so empty when she's gone."

He nodded. "I know what you mean."

"Lil always wanted a dog," I said, "but my ex didn't like animals in the house. Nothing with fur, anyway."

"Really?" Theo laughed. "Gotta wonder about people like that."

His food arrived, and he sprinkled pepper all over his fries. "Hey, can I ask you something personal?"

"I guess."

"What are you doing in Shade Tree? Seems like most people get out, if they can, if they're not here to farm. I expected you to end up someplace else."

"I didn't think I'd end up here either," I said. "I was pretty determined not to. Things change, though. I wanted to be near my family when I had Lily." It had been almost like an animal instinct, the desire to return, to bring my baby back home. I wondered now if the feeling would have passed, like so many of the intense directives of pregnancy —the midnight craving for candied ginger and Velveeta cheese, the frenetic scrubbing of every household surface when nesting kicked in. Maybe, if I'd ignored my homesickness, we would have stayed in the city and everything would have turned out differently.

"So you came back. And you stayed."

"Yeah. I'd rather be near the city than in it, I guess. Shade Tree's quiet. Familiar. I like my job. I'm not sure I'll stay forever, though. I don't really like Lily having to go back and forth. It'd be easier if Greg and I lived in the same place."

"That part's hard," Theo said. "It was the only thing that made me hesitant to take the opening here, even though I'd always wanted some land, room to spread out. My ex and I are good friends, though, thank goodness. Makes everything easier when it comes to the girls."

I wiped my mouth and pushed the melting remains of the concrete away. "Yeah. Greg's a good dad. I can put up with all the rest."

Theo put down his burger. "I don't know how it's been for you," he said, "but it seems like being divorced in a small town like this is tricky. You'd think it would be easier to meet people, but it hasn't worked out that way. It's hard to even make friends. My kids finally convinced me to sign up for online dating. Have you tried that yet?"

"No." I had looked, scrolling through the pictures without signing up, dreading the thought of filling out my profile, summing up my life in one pathetic paragraph: This is who I am. This is what I want. *Single mom of an anxious preteen. I bake a good pie but hate making dinner. Looking for someone who likes to watch* Dateline *and take tediously slow walks with my incontinent dog.*

One of the younger girls at work had informed me that dating worked differently now. It was standard procedure for men to text pictures of their genitals. I couldn't imagine the horror of Lily playing *Minecraft* on my phone and having a strategically angled photo of some stranger's penis pop up on the screen.

"There are a lot of crazy people out there," Theo said. "And sometimes you don't figure it out until you meet them in person, when you're stuck at dinner with someone who seems really interested in your job and then you realize it's only because she's after animal tranquilizers."

"Animal tranquilizers?"

"Yeah. She was looking to get high on ketamine. Thought I could hook her up."

"Maybe you're on the wrong site," I said. "My friend from work tried to get me to sign up for Cougar Date." I rolled my eyes.

Theo chuckled. "Huh. I might be too old for that one." He tapped his knuckles on the table. "Chemistry's hard to find online. It's hard to find, period."

"Tell that to my sister," I said. "She's been trying to set me up with random guys who I have nothing in common with. It's like she doesn't think single people can be happy."

He was looking at me, and I had the uncomfortable thought that Becca had somehow set up this very encounter. It wasn't likely—even she had her limits—though I remembered her asking, after Gravy's first appointment, if the vet was single. I'd thought about dating again, though it wasn't one of my top priorities, certainly not lately. I felt like I needed to plot out my immediate future first, decide if I should move closer to Greg or go back to school, and I couldn't figure out any of that when so much was still unresolved with Shane. Theo was attractive and kind, and I liked being around him, though maybe that was only because he knew the old me, the old Shane, because there were things I didn't have to explain. I could be myself with him.

"Maybe we could get the girls together sometime soon, when they're all in town," he said. "Liv and Stella don't really have any friends to hang out with when they're here. We could take the dogs on a walk."

"I'd love that," I said, something loosening inside me as the words came out. The response had come automatically, before my brain could phrase it in a more neutral way, something along the lines of "that would be fun for the kids" or, at the very least, replacing "love" with a less enthusiastic word. The same thing had happened when he'd asked me to join him for dinner—I'd said yes without thinking. Maybe Theo just had that effect on people. On me.

He nodded, smiling at me in a way that no one had in a while. Heat prickled my chest, even though we'd only vaguely agreed to walk dogs at an unspecified time in the future, which wasn't even necessarily a precursor to an actual date. "Great," he said. "I'd love it, too."

I had to speed a little to get home before Greg arrived to drop off Lily. I knew he'd be testy if I was late, and he was already driving in holiday traffic.

I called Leola as I drove, telling her that Mom wanted Charlie to have Shane's Firebird. "We can have it towed to your house," I said. "We don't have any keys. He could get new ones made, though."

Leola put the phone aside to holler for Charlie, who was home for the weekend, and then he got on the line. "Thank you," he said. "For the car. That means a lot to me."

"He'd want you to have it."

"Hey," he said. "You don't have to get it towed—I've got a key."

"You do?"

"Yeah. He loaned me a key ring so I could get into his place and borrow tools. I'm pretty sure the Firebird's spare key is on there. So I can pick it up this weekend."

I looked forward to seeing his face when he came to get the car, and Mom's relief when the Firebird would no longer be haunting her outside her window.

I turned into the driveway ten minutes after Greg had said he'd be there, but I didn't see his car. I hurried into the house to switch on the porch light and nearly tripped over Lily's duffel bag by the front door. It was bright pink, with emojis all over it, a birthday gift she'd picked out from Justice the year before and had probably now outgrown. I hadn't expected Greg to take off before I got home, leaving Lily alone, but maybe he'd been in a rush. He and Heidi and the baby were getting ready to leave for Florida, to spend the holiday with Heidi's family.

"Lily?" I called. There was no answer. The house was dark. "Lily!" I yelled. I moved toward the stairs, thinking she might have gone up to her room, and froze. The sheer curtains in the front window were moving, ever so lightly. I hadn't noticed at first, but standing still, I could feel it. A cold breeze pushed in from the back of the house, snaking into my jacket and chilling me. I crossed the living room to get to the kitchen, where the sliding door gapped open by several inches. Gravy wasn't under the table, where he'd taken to napping, and my breath eased. Maybe Lily had taken him out. The sliding door could be stubborn, difficult to close all the way once you had it open.

I flicked on the light and stepped out into the yard, expecting to see them, but no one was there. The light illuminated a stretch of brown grass, dead leaves cartwheeling in the wind, a tennis ball that Gravy never even bothered to smell. Lily wouldn't go far from the house in the dark, unless Gravy had wandered and she'd gone to fetch him.

"Lily!" I hollered, stepping to the edge of the light. I dialed Greg, straining to see into the darkness as the phone rang.

"Hey," Greg said, "you home yet?"

"Did you drop Lily off? Her bag's here and I can't find her."

"She's with me. We got there a little early. You weren't there, and she was starving, so we went to get her something to eat. Didn't mean to worry you."

"Oh, thank god." My legs wobbled as I backed up to the house. Lily was okay.

"Everything all right?"

"Yeah," I said. "I just . . . the back door was open, and I thought . . . I don't know. Maybe Lily opened it when she brought her bag in?"

"No. I was with her."

"Did you see Gravy?"

"No, but I didn't look."

"Maybe I didn't close the door all the way and he pushed it open somehow to get outside."

"That doesn't sound likely. Do you think someone broke into the house?"

I looked toward the dark kitchen. If anyone was inside, they knew I was here. They would have heard me calling for Lily, talking to Greg on the phone.

"I don't know," I said.

"Why don't you call the police to check it out, just in case. We'll be there shortly, but I can't stay. And if someone did break in, you and Lily probably shouldn't stay either. Maybe you should go to your sister's."

I waited outside for Greg and Lily, calling around the yard for Gravy, even though it was pointless, since he couldn't hear. The deputy who showed up was Robby Frazier, whom I'd known since Head Start, when we were three or four years old, and I did feel much safer once he'd stomped his hefty uniformed frame through every room and confirmed that whoever had broken in was gone. The sliding door had been jimmied, and Robby, his face red with exertion, sawed off a piece of two-by-four he found in the garage and stuck it in the track to keep that from happening again.

Robby said break-ins out in the country were common these days, unlike when we were growing up and no one on a farm locked their doors. "Druggies," he said disdainfully. They targeted the elderly, the sick, homes where someone had recently died—places they were likely to find prescription pills. They looked for money, too, or things they could pawn, though it didn't appear that anything had been stolen, which made Robby think that it might have just been juvenile delinquents messing around. I wondered if maybe Crystle was somehow responsible, if she'd do something like that just to scare me.

I couldn't quite tell if anything was out of place, and it was unsettling knowing that someone could have rifled through our things and then carefully put it all back as it was before. I was ready to start making calls and launch a search party for Gravy when Lily and Greg arrived, and Lily located him, wedged against the wall beneath the pie safe, dead asleep. She poured a little pile of Gravy Train on the floor near his head, for when he woke up, and then sprawled on the couch to watch A Charlie Brown Thanksgiving. Lily complained that she was hungry again, another growth spurt no doubt on the horizon, so I fixed her favorite snack, Totino's frozen pizza, the pepperoni cut into tiny cubes.

We'd have Thanksgiving dinner at Mom's house the next day because that's what we always did, though it wouldn't be the same without Shane. I took Gravy out one last time to pee, sticking close to the house, Lily training a flashlight on me from the porch, as though worried I'd disappear into the darkness if she lost sight of me.

She didn't want to be alone in her room, so she crawled onto my bed, stealing my favorite feather pillow and curling up on top of the covers in her smiling-sloth nightgown, falling asleep effortlessly.

Sleep didn't come as easily for me. I thought about what Robby had said, his angry tone when he talked about addicts breaking into houses, committing crimes. The year before, I'd met a recovering addict, a waifish young woman named Allie who'd been referred to social services. She'd been caught stealing from her church's collection plate so she could buy fentanyl lozenges. Her family ran the Hallmark store in Blackwater, and they'd poured everything they had into treating her addiction. Her mother quit working to be with her around the clock, and they'd tried every kind of therapy and rehab program available, but Allie would always relapse. She was sweet and soft-spoken and smelled of lavender and bergamot, essential oils meant to aid her recovery. Her slender wrists were encased in bracelets made of crystals and other healing stones. She had recently returned from a therapeutic program out west where addicts communed with wolves, and hadn't yet told her parents that it had failed to cure her.

A wolf can go for weeks without eating, Allie had said, *but they can't live like that forever. After a famine, they'll feast. Gorge themselves. If there's livestock around, they'll kill it. People hate them for it, but they're only following their instincts. They're not bad, they're misunderstood. Like me. I don't want to hurt anyone,* she said. *I'm just surviving. I can hold off for a while, stay clean, but the hunger comes back, and when it does I'm ravenous.*

I saw her obituary in the paper months later. It detailed her many talents and interests. She had played the piano at her church and gone on a mission trip with the youth group. She had been beloved by many, survived by a long list of friends and relatives. The final paragraph revealed that she had died of an overdose at home while her mother made a quick run to the gas station for a gallon of milk. I admired her

parents' honesty, their desire to shine light on the struggle, to let people know that it could happen to anyone.

Plenty of people in Cutler County had contemptuous or even hos-
tile attitudes toward addicts, questioning why taxpayer money was
being spent on Narcan and emergency services to save people who
were willingly taking drugs that could kill them. Maybe Shane had
assumed we felt that way, too. He had kept his problems hidden, not
wanting us to know, unable to ask us for help.

I lay as still as I could, listening to the faint whisper of Lily's breath,
the wind siphoning through keyholes, the furnace brooding below. I
was drifting near sleep when a sharp tapping sound jolted me awake. I
was paralyzed, trying to imagine who or what might come out of the
woods at this hour, wanting in, when the sound came again: *tap*, *tap*,
tap, *tap*, from somewhere inside the house. My pulse surged, and I
leapt up to crack the bedroom door, my chest burning with held
breath. I heard rustling, Gravy sniffing around in the darkness, his
nails clicking on the hardwood, *tap tap tap*, as he wandered through
the house, looking for something he wouldn't find. He finally came to
rest at the foot of the stairs, a deaf and ineffective sentry.

CHAPTER 22

HENLEY
OCTOBER

Henley had first set foot in the Ray-Lynne Funeral Chapel in Blackwater when she was four years old. Memaw's brother Herb had died of pneumonia, and when Henley had come up to the casket, she'd poked his cheek and found it disturbingly cold and unyielding, like overcooked pudding. *That's not him!* she'd cried. Great Uncle Herb had always fancied himself a magician, sometimes using sleight of hand to cheat at poker, other times to pull nickels out of Henley's ear. It had to be a trick; Great Uncle Herb had fooled them all, placing a dummy in the casket, and she fully expected him to come out from behind a curtain and yell *Voilà!*

Now, seeing Shane laid out in a silver casket in the viewing parlor, his head on a satin pillow, her breath left her body, eking out through her closing throat. She knew that it was really him, that he was truly gone. He didn't look like real death now, though, not like he had the other night, when his body lay cooling on the floor. Somehow this artificial version was worse, a selfish attempt to make the dead palatable to the living. His eyes were shut, his jaw cleanly shaved, Gravy's claw marks covered with makeup, lips and cheeks just pink enough to hide the pallor without appearing garish. She tried not to think about the draining of blood, the stitching and stuffing that had gone on behind the scenes, like the making of a human scarecrow. She pressed her knuckles against her eyelids to push back a fresh bout of stinging tears.

She hadn't wanted to come. She feared that the things she knew would be visible on her face, that anyone who looked at her would be able to tell.

Pettits knew how to turn out for funerals, though, and it would have been odd if she hadn't shown up. The extended clan filled the chapel, including Beauforts and Copelands and a few of the Rudds, along with Crystle's friends, Shane's kin, and a few of his coworkers. Charlie wasn't coming, and that was one small relief, because she wasn't sure she could have held herself together with him there. Shane had meant the world to him, and she couldn't have lied to Charlie's face. She circulated among her relatives, trying to blend into the herd, though it was impossible to act normal when her skin felt like it was crawling with electric ants.

The Pettits migrated between the spread of food in the adjoining lounge and the open space at the back of the parlor, talking, laughing, eating. Junior rooted himself in the corner, holding a plate of Lit'l Smokies drenched in oily red sauce, spearing them two at a time with a toothpick. He nodded as Henley walked by, his eyes locked on hers as he murmured to Big Boy about getting into the workshop and moving out Shane's tools. Henley kept walking, her spine prickling.

She recognized Shane's family right away, though she'd seen them only once, at the wedding the year before, and had never actually met them. Several rows of folding chairs had been set up facing the casket, and the Kellers huddled quietly in the very front, the only people seated. Shane's mother had hair the dull gray of galvanized tin, hacked unevenly at the nape of the neck like she'd cut it herself. Henley imagined her reaching over her shoulder with the scissors, not bothering to glance in the mirror, not caring much how it turned out. Shane had rarely talked about his mother, though Henley had gathered from overheard stories of his delinquent youth that Mrs. Keller was a practical woman who'd been rightly frustrated by her son's antics and was both surprised and intensely proud of how he'd turned out—the high school diploma, the lack of a criminal record, the steady job. Shane's sisters sat on either side of her, and if she remembered right, Sadie was the one with straight shoulder-length hair and Becca wore hers longer, the ends curled. She'd seen their children playing in the gravel parking lot with one of the husbands, and she didn't blame them for not wanting to be inside.

The women's faces were wet and raw. She watched them as they studied the photos they had pinned to a felt board and followed, on a loop, a slideshow of Shane's life: a swaddled baby in his grandfather's arms; in a suit with high-water pants, taking his first communion; digging in the dirt, a huge grin revealing gaps in his teeth; standing on a woodpile in a snowstorm with a black, wolfish dog; a senior class picture against a backdrop of fake trees, hair neatly combed to the side. It was strange to see his entire life unfold over and over, a life she knew relatively little about except for the end and what bits he'd spent with the Pettits. As she watched Shane's family react to the images on the screen, their grief commingled with hers, forming something new, something denser, thornier, harder to bear. Her stomach cramped.

One particular photo jarred her every time it popped up on the screen—Shane sunburned on the riverbank, the day of his wedding— and on the third go-around of the slideshow, she realized why. She'd seen it before, not the picture itself, but the image, framed in the view-finder of a disposable camera that had been set out for the wedding reception. She'd snapped the picture, at Shane's request, because he wanted evidence of his clean, unwrinkled white shirt before they started eating barbecue and drinking in earnest. He'd already thrown back shots of Johnnie, Jack, and Jim, which had left a few amber spots along the collar, but she didn't tell him that his shirt was no longer pristine. His eyes were a vivid blue against his reddened skin, his grin goofy and blissful. She remembered the joke he had told her just before she took the shot, one of his dumbest yet. *Hey, Henley, why did the foot smile? Because it was toe happy!*

That's why it felt like he was looking at her, and her alone, in the crowded viewing room. She had captured a brief moment they had shared, just the two of them, before the families arrived and the sun dipped into the river and Crystle got so drunk she vomited on the skirt of her mermaid wedding gown. Shane stared at her, again and again, the last picture before the screen flashed black and he reappeared as a swaddled infant. The easy smile. Earnest eyes the color of a jay's wing. She could hear his voice in her head, clear despite the din in the funeral home, the words he'd spoken as he handed her the camera that day. *Hey, Henley, can you help me?*

Crystle sauntered into the room, the crowd parting for her, and took up residence by the casket, leaning against it like she was bellying up to a bar. She wore a black lace tunic over a black tank and leggings, her hair freshly highlighted and styled in long waves, iridescent blush sparkling along her cheekbones. A small audience gathered around her, and she started into the story of the day Shane died, her voice loud enough that it cut through the crowd and Henley could hear her from the back of the room. Henley noticed that Shane's sister Sadie had tilted her head to the side, like an attentive bird, her interest pricked by something Crystle had said.

Crystle was bemoaning how unfortunate it was that she hadn't been home when Shane died. On a normal day, she would have been there, but she had stopped to see her cousin—Henley. Shane had been texting Crystle that morning, she said, about how much he loved her. He hadn't been feeling well, but he hadn't said anything about it that day. He probably hadn't wanted to worry her; he was thoughtful like that.

"Henley." Crystle waved her forward and she reluctantly obeyed, keeping her back to Shane's family. The stabbing sensation in her stomach grew sharper with each step, as though her flesh might split open, spilling her guts out onto the floor.

"I set my phone down somewhere," Crystle said. "Go get it for me."

Henley found the phone in the bathroom, balanced on the toilet paper holder. She locked the door and turned on the faucet, not terribly surprised to discover that Crystle was still using the most common and ill-advised security code, 1-2-3-4. She scrolled through the texts until she found Shane's. Most of them were pedestrian, Crystle telling him to get her a bottle of Bloody Mary mix on the way home from work, complaining that Gravy had pissed on the floor and she wasn't going to clean it up, Shane responding each time with one letter, *K.* They hadn't texted at all the day he died until late that afternoon, when Crystle sent *Love you babe* out of the blue. He had responded with *Love you more*, the brief exchange uncharacteristic compared to all the ones that had come before, like maybe Crystle had sent it herself, but Henley couldn't be sure what had happened that afternoon, before it got dark, before she'd gotten there.

Squeezing through the crowd, Henley spotted her cousin Trina, her scarlet hair unmissable, her massive studded purse known to be as well stocked as any Walgreens pharmacy. While Henley wasn't one for pills, she quietly purchased a single Xanax and swallowed it with a swig of Trina's Pepsi.

Back in the viewing room, as she handed Crystle her phone and turned to leave, one of Shane's sisters caught her eye. Sadie, the one who had been listening to Crystle's story so intently. Henley ducked her head and walked faster, away from the continued unspooling of Shane's life, the bleak vacuum of the Kellers' sorrow, and out the door, the pain in her belly radiating through her chest to the base of her skull.

The night air brought cool relief from the suffocating atmosphere of the funeral home. The leaves were still on the trees, the grass still growing, but summer was gone, its lingering overtures stale and depressing as darkness crept in ever earlier. She couldn't leave town now—it wouldn't look right—but in a couple weeks' time, Raymond assured her, she could be on the road. He wanted it that way, in fact, for her to cut ties and get far away from Blackwater for a while, no forwarding address, so that if things started coming apart, she wouldn't get caught up in it.

She'd started searching online for places to stay, youth hostels and campgrounds and tiny rooms illegally sublet in other people's apartments, ferreting out job openings for pet sitters and dishwashers and maids, all of it less daunting with Earl Sullivan's money tucked away beneath her floor. She suspected it wasn't possible to escape the growing dread in her gut no matter how far she ran, but her plan was the only thing drawing focus away from it, and she wished for the mountains to fill her head and blot out thoughts of Shane, of Earl, of Jason. There was already plenty of snow in the Rockies, and she imagined herself sinking into a frozen drift, being cleansed by the wind, the ice, the bitter transformative cold.

CHAPTER 23

SADIE

NOVEMBER

Though she had mostly stopped cooking after Dad passed away, Mom usually made exceptions on holidays, resigned to laboring over our favorite yeast rolls, sage stuffing, and German potato salad made with bacon grease. She couldn't bring herself to go through the motions now, and after she'd announced that we'd be eating canned ham and Pillsbury biscuits from the Dollar General, Becca had decided that we would take over the Thanksgiving feast. Becca arrived early to put the turkey in, and Lily and I worked on pies at the kitchen table: pumpkin, apple, old-fashioned buttermilk, and Shane's favorite, sour cherry, which Becca had requested last minute, sending Jerry and the boys to Walmart for frozen fruit, knowing they wouldn't likely have fresh.

Mom sat in her recliner, eyes drooping shut while the Macy's parade played on TV. I'd found the piece of paper from Shane's house. She'd hung his drawings on the wall above the television, including the sketch of Gravy. She'd trimmed away the part I'd wanted to see, the part with the writing, to fit it in a tiny frame.

I'd only brought three pie pans, so I brushed the flour off my hands and dug through Mom's cabinets to find one of hers. I unearthed the green jadeite one with the fluted edges, a wedding present to her and Dad from one of her aunts. As I wiped it off with my apron, I felt something stuck to the underside. I flipped it over and took it to show Becca.

"Look," I said. "I guess Mom figured she'd never make another pie."

A note was taped to the bottom, her careful cursive neat enough to belong in a manual, declaring that the dish would go to me when she died. Grandma had done the same thing when she'd found out she had liver cancer, attaching labels to the bottoms of her most-loved possessions in lieu of a will, notes we didn't find until after she died. She had left me the cream pitcher shaped like a cat, which we'd always used to pour milk on our oatmeal when we stayed with her. Shane had gotten the pie safe, which I would come to covet; I hadn't yet fallen in love with baking when Grandma died.

Becca and I had joked about crawling around on the floor at Mom's, peeking under the rolltop desk and waterfall vanity to see which one of us would get what, not knowing whether Mom would bother to label anything and not wanting to consider what it meant if she already had. No matter how practical and necessary it might be, it was uncomfortable to imagine her alone in the house, distancing herself from her possessions, preparing for death.

Becca drew in a breath and sighed. "I wonder if she did this before or after Shane."

I buried the dish back in the cupboard and found a plain tin pan to use instead, one with no memories attached, an unsentimental object that wouldn't get passed down to anyone.

Charlie showed up to get the Firebird just before we started in on dessert. When I opened the door, I spied Leola waiting in the truck and waved them both in for pie. Leola resisted at first, on the grounds that she hadn't dressed up or brought anything, but relented when I told her that Mom had been wanting to meet her. The house felt warm and full when we all sat down together, extra chairs squeezed in, Becca's boys sitting on her and Jerry's laps, Gravy asleep beneath the table.

The Burdetts fit right in. Becca quizzed Charlie with the zeal of a nosy mother, asking about school, his favorite classes, his dorm, his future plans, barely giving him time to chew. After a tentative start, speaking gingerly about Shane, Leola talked about the loss of her own son, and Mom slowly began to open up to her, staring at her plate as she spoke, and then, as she grew more comfortable, meeting Leola's empathetic gaze. It was good for Mom to have someone to talk to, not just someone who knew Shane, but someone who knew how it felt to lose a child. I couldn't help thinking what it would have been like if we'd been able to get together, Leola and Charlie and all of us, when Shane was still alive. It made me hurt for Hannah, too, who'd refused my offer to join us and was spending the holiday alone.

When Becca finally eased up on her interrogation long enough for Charlie to finish his plate, I went outside with him to see if he could get the Firebird started. Together, we peeled back the tarp and admired the silver car.

"I remember the first time I saw it," Charlie said. "When I smashed the taillights. Boy, was he pissed. Figured I was in for a beating." He shook his head. "Never thought it'd be mine."

He swung open the heavy door and settled into the driver's seat. The key turned, and the engine grumbled and roared. "He took good care of it," Charlie said, gripping the steering wheel.

"How much gas have you got?"

"Nearly a quarter tank."

"Let's go fill it up. My treat. So you'll have enough to get back to school."

He drove extra slow at first, like I imagined he did when Leola was with him, but couldn't help himself once we reached the highway. He bore down on the accelerator, grinning as the car leapt forward. I clicked on the radio. It was tuned to a classic rock station from the city and grainy with static. The barren fields slipped by, and I imagined Shane driving to work in this car, along this same highway, then remembered him saying he never commuted in the Firebird because it burned through too much gas. I wished that he'd had more time to enjoy it, that he'd driven it every day. Maybe he would've, had he known what was coming.

"This'd make him happy," I said. "You, with his car, out on the open road." We crested a low hill and Led Zeppelin screeched through the speakers, the reception suddenly clear, at least until we dipped back down.

"Hey, Charlie, did Shane ever talk about Roger Calhoun?"

"That guy they found?" He shrugged. "I don't know. Not to me. Why?"

"They were friends, or used to be, anyway. Crystle mentioned him. I just wondered."

He shot me a sidelong glance. "Henley'd probably know. She was around him more than I was lately."

"Henley?"

"Crystle's cousin. Good friend of mine. She's not like the rest of 'em."

The rest of them. The Pettits, I assumed. I wondered if she was the girl I'd seen at Shane's funeral, the one who'd looked at me, made eye contact, if briefly. The only one of the Pettits who genuinely appeared to be grieving.

"Do you think maybe she'd talk to me?"

"I don't know," he said. "She might. I can give you her number. Just watch what you say. She's close to her family, but she always liked Shane."

Charlie and Leola headed home as daylight faded, Leola not wanting to drive after dark. Mom sank into her recliner, exhausted from socializing, and we settled the kids on the couch with popcorn to watch *The Wizard of Oz*. When Becca and Shane and I were growing up, it had been on TV every year around Thanksgiving, and Becca found comfort in tradition, prodding us to keep nostalgic rituals alive, still making Grandma Keller's coconut-covered lamb cake every Easter, though no one in our generation even liked to eat it. I might have shrugged at the Dollar General Thanksgiving menu, but Becca had been horrified, as though one missed tradition might have dire consequences for our family. And maybe she was right. Shane and I had always been lazy in that regard, relying on her to remember elderly relatives' birthdays, to know which rose bushes or recipes had been passed down from whom, to take pictures at gatherings and send copies to everyone. I wondered, if something happened to Becca, whether the family would fall apart—no *Wizard of Oz*, no sage stuffing, nothing to hold us together anymore.

I excused myself to run a plate of leftovers to Hannah. I stopped at home first, to grab some of Gravy's food in case he got hungry for dinner. He hadn't touched the turkey broth I'd given him at lunch.

I'd stowed all of his things in the pie safe after I'd brought it home from Shane's—bags and cans of food, the treats he wouldn't eat, the toys he wouldn't play with, the blankets he'd chew up but not lie on. I remembered how the cabinet had caught Crystle's eye when she'd come over. She'd probably been shocked to see something she'd considered too hideous for her own home prominently displayed in mine. I unlatched the doors with the punched-tin panels and opened them up. Everything was in its place. I hadn't even thought to check after the break-in, knowing there was nothing valuable inside. When Grandma had left the cabinet to Shane, she'd probably pictured him getting married, his wife placing fresh pies on the shelves, never guessing how things would turn out, her favorite piece of furniture now serving as storage for a dog. Eventually, Mom's green pie plate would end up inside. Both she and Grandma would be gone and this would be my inheritance, everyday things they had used and loved, the bittersweet notes they'd left behind.

I wondered if Grandma's note to Shane was still there, where we'd found it. I wanted to read it again, to see her familiar handwriting. I yanked at the stubborn lower drawer and worked it back and forth until I was able to remove it, then flipped it over, dumping out the spare leash and the printouts Theo had given me about Gravy's various ailments.

There was the note card that Grandma had attached, the edges brown with age. *For Shane, who always tried to get the pie before it cooled.* I noticed that someone had pressed shiny new pieces of packing tape over it, and I doubted that Shane, who wasn't terribly sentimental, had done that to preserve it. As I ran my fingers over it, I felt the slight protrusion of something underneath. My pulse quickened. I picked at the tape until I could get my fingernails under one end and peel it back, carefully removing Grandma's note. Beneath it lay a folded piece of paper, and when I opened it up, a small silver key fell to the floor. The paper was similar to the piece Mom had taken from Shane's notepad, with the sketch of Gravy, the block letters appearing to match the indentations I had seen. The full message was unmistakable, etched firmly in black ink: *This is the gun that killed the Calhouns.*

I mouthed the words, whispered them in the silent house, weighed them on my tongue. A sharp pain burned in the center of my chest, like an axe splitting my sternum, making it hard to breathe. I had to face what this might mean. At the very least, Shane had intimate knowledge of the murders. At worst, he had committed them. Either way, he had hidden the evidence and left more questions than answers. Why had they been killed? Where was the gun? If he wasn't responsible, why hadn't he gone to the police?

Once, when I was about thirteen, Dad had taken Shane and me into the woods to fell a deer. We needed the meat. The washer was broken, and Becca had stayed at the house with Mom to wring out the laundry by hand and hang it near the stove. Our clothes turned stiff when they dried that way and smelled of smoke.

Dad left us at the top of a rise and headed down the draw to check for tracks. Shane had carefully raised the gun to his shoulder, following Dad with his scope. He had a fading bruise the color of a Golden Delicious apple on his cheek.

What do you see? I asked, looking out over a landscape of dead leaves. *Any deer?*

I could do it, he murmured. *I could pull the trigger and it'd all be over.*

Shane?

I could shoot him. It'd look like a hunting accident.

It wouldn't. You're too good a shot. They'd take you away.

He kept his breath slow and measured, one eye squinted, but his finger slipped away from the trigger.

I could do it, I said.

No you can't. The tension in his shoulders fell away and he lowered the rifle, keeping it firmly in his grip. *If it's anyone, it'll be me.*

Maybe Shane had gone after Roger to protect his wife, like she'd said. Maybe something had gone wrong. I held the key in my palm, ticked the notches with my fingernail. It didn't belong to one of his gun safes, which had digital locks and were sealed with large pins like a bank vault. Crystle had already cleared those out, anyway. It could be for a gun case, something portable, though there was nothing to indicate where it might be.

Shane hadn't been the best at thinking things through—not the version of him that I knew—but he'd clearly done this for a reason. He knew I loved the pie safe. He'd chosen to hide the note and key in the one piece of furniture that Crystle had hated, knowing she wouldn't want to keep it for herself, that it was the most likely of his possessions to find its way back to his family. He had trusted us to find this. He had wanted us to know the truth, whatever it was. But it also seemed, in a way, that he was planning for his death, like Grandma or Mom when they hid their notes—an odd thing to do at thirty-six. Maybe he had taken his own life, as Crystle had implied. Either that, or he'd feared that something was going to happen to him.

I left the plate of food at Hannah's door and texted her as I drove away. I couldn't face her, knowing what I knew. She'd want me to turn the note over to Kendrick, and what else could I do? No one could give me the answers I needed. Shane was gone, and I didn't trust Crystle to tell the truth. I pulled into a dark field, turned off my lights, and dialed the number Charlie had given me for Henley Pettit. It was a last resort, because I didn't know if I could trust her, either. The phone rang and rang, but Henley didn't pick up.

CHAPTER 24

HENLEY

NOVEMBER

Junior had been agitated all day. There was a lot of chatter on the police scanner, and he'd taken a six-pack into the office and shut the door. Henley didn't dare knock to tell him goodbye. He knew she was leaving and wasn't particularly pleased about it. It made things more complicated for him, given what she knew, that she wouldn't be in range of his watchful eye. Warnings weren't necessary; she understood what was expected of her and had witnessed his skill in carrying out threats, hunting people down.

Raymond topped off the Skylark's oil and antifreeze and rechecked the tire pressure, warning Henley not to keep all her cash in one place when she was traveling, in case she got mugged at a rest stop or someone broke into her car. Then he decided she should avoid rest stops altogether now that it was getting dark, only stopping someplace well lit, like a Casey's, where the restrooms were indoors. He looked forlorn when she drove away, his frown lines cutting deep, but he told her everything would be fine, to get away from Blackwater and disappear for a while or more. He hugged her and she pressed her face against his flannel collar, inhaling the familiar sweat-and-tobacco scent and telling him not to worry.

She purposely waited until the last minute to text Jason, who was furious as expected but quickly honed the edge of his anger into a conciliatory tone, begging her to come talk it over. Finally, when she refused, he backed off, asking her to at least come say goodbye in person, that she owed him that much.

She relented, once he assured her that Earl wasn't home, and drove her Buick into the Sullivans' driveway for the last time, parking by the barn.

Jason greeted her at the door, his eyes rimmed red, and took her hand to lead her up to his room.

"I'm gonna miss you so much," he said, snaking his arms around her waist.

"I'll miss you, too," she said, though she wasn't entirely sure that she would. While she'd felt as bored and isolated as Jason when they'd first gotten together, she'd come to realize that he was desperately lonely in a way that she wasn't, and she was excited at the prospect of being on her own.

"Why does it have to be tonight?" he asked. "Can't you at least wait until morning? Stay with me. Just one night."

"I can't," she said, knowing he only wanted more time to sway her, to convince her to stay. He was good at that. It wouldn't work this time.

"Why not?"

"There's just a lot going on. I feel like I can't breathe here. Like if I don't get out now, this place'll swallow me up and I'll never leave. I already told everyone I'm going. I said goodbye."

She couldn't bear to wake up to another day in this town. If she started driving now, she'd be in Colorado by sunrise, in time to see the first rays hit the peaks, the snow lit up like flames. Fire and ice. At least, that was how she imagined it.

"I'll come with you, then."

She shook her head and took a step back, already thinking of working her way out the door.

"We talked about it. I can take the jewelry—Dad probably wouldn't even notice it was gone."

"I can't do that. I can't let *you* do that."

"But you need money," he said. "I know you don't have enough. You said so."

She pressed her fingers to her lips, as though that might keep the secret in. "Earl called me," she said. "After what happened. He called and he wouldn't quit calling, and he wanted to pay me off and I let him."

His jaw twitched, muscles tightening in his neck and down his arms.

"Jason. I'm going, and I'm going alone. It's something I need to do."

He shook his head, the anger draining away, hurt taking its place. She remembered how she had felt in the beginning, before his attention had overwhelmed her—there had been something real between them. She might not have loved Jason, exactly, but she had come close, and she knew he had felt it, too.

"I'm not saying I won't be back, but I have to clear my head for a while. You understand, don't you?"

"There's nothing left for me here if you're gone," he said. He looked bereft, almost childlike, tears filling his eyes, and she thought of his mother dying and leaving him behind. Missy had taken Daphne's place, but she'd never been terribly reliable, her attention likely focused on Earl, and now Henley was leaving, too. It wasn't her job to stay and make up for everyone who'd abandoned him, but she felt a stab of guilt nonetheless. She still cared about him.

He seemed to sense her hesitation and drew her into his arms, holding her to his chest. He kissed her neck, her lips, tenderly and then insistently. The familiar warmth began to spread through her body, though when he went to bend her back onto the bed, the memory of Earl lurched into her mind. Her reaction was swift and visceral. She shoved him away from her, but his hands locked onto her biceps, his strong fingers curling all the way around. His teeth gritted together.

"I thought you loved me."

"What did you think was gonna happen?" she snapped, thrashing out of his grip. "Did you think we'd get married and be the king and queen of Blackwater and wait for your dad to die so we could live off his money? In this house? In this room? It was never gonna work."

"I wanted us to be together. I thought that's what you wanted, too."

"Grow up and stop being such a fucking idiot! You don't even know me."

She turned to walk out, and he thrust her onto the bed in a rage, pinning her down before she could move. "*I know you better than anyone!*" he roared, spit flying in her face.

His hands were at her throat, choking out anything she might have said in return. She was owl-eyed and jerking, tears spilling down into her hair, clawing and kicking and pleading wordlessly as he held her tighter and tighter and tighter, his heart a bellows feeding a fire, his insides filling with molten ore that burned through the love and the pain and then finally, finally, began to cool.

She was limp, her eyes partly closed, and he didn't think that she was breathing. He scrambled backward, flinging the blanket over her so he didn't have to see her, and then he stood in the middle of the room, scrubbing his face with his palms, not knowing what he'd done, or what to do.

He turned on the stereo, pushing the volume and the bass high enough to throb in his chest like a second heartbeat, drowning out everything so he could think. He tried not to imagine Henley's body cooling and stiffening on the bed, the scent of death absorbing into the bedding. He didn't want to have to look at her, or touch her, but he knew he had to move her out of his room, out of the house before his father came home. If everyone thought she'd left town, no one would be looking for her, no one would know she was missing. He could drive into Kansas City, dump her at Kaw Point, near the West Bottoms where the Kansas River spilled into the Missouri. Make it appear that something had happened to her on the road, a random crime, a vulnerable country girl slain in the city.

He tucked the blanket around her and carried her out to her car. As he readjusted her so he could open the door, one of her arms slid down and swung loosely, and his stomach lurched, tears and anger welling up all over again. He set her on the floorboard in the back, where she wouldn't be seen, found the keys still in the ignition, and headed toward town to get on the highway. Halfway there, he started to feel light-headed, like he couldn't breathe, and realized the heat was on high. He rolled down his window and sucked in the sharp night air. When he switched off the heat, he noticed the gas gauge was low— too low to get him into the city without stopping somewhere. He crushed the brake pedal, and the car shimmied. He pounded his fist on the steering wheel.

If he got gas, he might end up on camera with Henley's car. There'd be a timeline. Would he be able to get back before Earl got home? And how would he get home if he dumped the Skylark? If he was going to drive it back, was there even any point in taking her body somewhere else?

He swung the car around on the empty road and drove until he reached the next gravel turnoff, following it to the private lane that marked the Gundersons' old farmstead, where they had gone swimming that summer, where the current flowed wide and deep. He cut the lights and passed through the screen of trees that lent privacy from the road, parking on the hill above the river. The water was black and fairly smooth, reflecting a fingernail moon.

Jason closed his eyes for the worst part, reaching back to snag the blanket that covered her and tugging it free. Then he shifted the car into neutral and pushed until it gained enough momentum to roll down and drop off the bank. When the current caught it, it began to turn and drift. He waited near the crest of the hill while it floundered, slowly filling; then it finally bucked and began to sink.

His muscles burned as he ran back home, cutting through the fields and edging ditches slick with dead leaves. It felt good to run with purpose, the cold air searing his throat, his body finding a powerful and familiar rhythm from his days of intense training, back when he was the town's star athlete and Earl was briefly proud of him.

His mind began to clear as he neared the house. He wondered if Henley had told anyone about her encounter with Earl. She hadn't spoken much lately to Missy or Charlie. Even if she hadn't mentioned it, though, there'd be proof—the calls Earl had made to her would show up on phone records. The money he'd given Henley must still be in her car, at the bottom of the river, waiting to be found. It would be best, of course, if she wasn't found at all, but if she was, it might not look good for Earl.

He couldn't bring himself to lie on his bed where Henley's body had lain, so he stretched out on the floor, sleepless, until dawn.

A small part of him thought that it hadn't happened. He imagined Henley driving, the sunrise in her rearview mirror as she sang along with the radio, a habit she and Missy shared, though when Henley sang, it was more of a whisper, like she was telling a secret, her lips softly mouthing the words. Her lips, lightly parted, were the last thing he'd seen before he'd shrouded her with the blanket.

He took a long shower, tried and failed to eat an energy bar, which chalked up his mouth and made him gag, and waited for Earl to leave, driving in to work right behind him. His dad sat ramrod straight in the driver's seat of his truck, his hands always positioned carefully at ten and two, the farm report most likely droning on the radio. Earl obeyed the speed limit and came to a complete stop at each intersection, waving other vehicles to go ahead even though it wasn't their turn, always doing his damnedest to appear as a model citizen.

Jason mulled the idea of blackmailing him, telling Earl to give him his trust fund and cut him loose. He could threaten to tell everyone that Earl had killed Henley. If that didn't work, he'd promise to destroy the one thing his father might care about more than his personal reputation: Sullivan Grain. Earl lived in fear of an explosion at the grain elevator, like the infamous tragedies at Continental or DeBruce, the kind that took over the newspapers and courtrooms and tore communities apart. After Emily, he didn't want to be responsible for any more dead bodies. Each death at the elevator over the years had sent him spiraling down into a whiskey bottle. He maintained an impeccable safety record, doing whatever was necessary to avoid negative publicity and paint himself as the savior of the town.

Earl had always wanted to be the good guy, despite his obvious flaws. *Do good things*, Earl had told him, *day in, day out, without fail. Make good choices, do good things, and you become a good person.* As though it was a choice to be made, like his actions could somehow shape his character instead of the other way around. Like Jason could do it if he just tried hard enough, no matter what he felt on the inside. Earl couldn't accept what Jason inherently understood—that a person's nature, like an animal's, couldn't be changed.

CHAPTER 25

SADIE

NOVEMBER

"We have to give it to Kendrick," Becca said, staring at the note. We huddled on her front porch in the dark, a lighted inflatable Santa looming over us, fan whooshing to keep it aloft. Icicle lights hung down from the gutters, flapping in the wind. I'd waited until Sunday night to talk to Becca, after Lily had gone home. I'd known what she would say, and I knew she was right, though it didn't make the thought of walking into the police station any easier.

"What if they just assume he's guilty?" I said.

"That doesn't matter," she said. "It's what he wanted us to do. Why else would he have left it for us to find?"

"Then why didn't he do it himself? He could have sent it straight to the police, gone there in person."

"I don't know. But he wanted to be sure it would come out eventually."

Through the front window, colored lights blinked on Becca's Christmas tree, illuminating all the glittery handprint ornaments Colton and Logan had made in their short lives. Becca and Jerry and the boys always went out to cut their tree the day after Thanksgiving, without fail. It was something she and Shane and I had done growing up, sawing down an unwieldy cedar from our own land, dragging it home through the fields. The cedars were usually too fat and rarely stood up well on their own, so we'd have to anchor them to the wall.

"He may have made some mistakes," Becca said. "But he was a good person. He was always helping people. Whatever he did, whatever went wrong—once he realized the mess he was in, he must have tried to fix it, to do the right thing."

I remembered what Theo had said about the prank that had gotten Shane in trouble back in school. How Shane had confessed without ratting Theo out. How he'd set off the firecrackers in the first place to get back at someone who'd hurt his friend, and accepted the punishment he had coming.

"I still don't think he could have killed a child," Becca said.

"Not on purpose."

"What do you mean?"

"I don't think he could have shot Macey, either. He couldn't have looked at her and pulled the trigger. But what if it was an accident?"

I'd been thinking about what Hannah had said, about the recent change to Roger's visitation, how he'd fought for that extra night. If someone had thought he was taking Macey home Sunday night instead of Monday morning, they might have come after him not realizing she was there. I'd assumed that anyone who cared about Macey or had qualms about shooting a child wasn't likely to have committed the murders, but now I wasn't so sure.

———

I kept Shane's note folded in my coat pocket as I drove to work. Three days in a row, I parked downtown near the courthouse and walked straight past the police station, intending to stop and unable to convince my body to comply. When I got home from work on the third day, I found a beautiful handmade card from Hannah in the mailbox. A bright red cardinal adorned the front, and on the inside, in embellished script, she thanked me for bringing her a plate at Thanksgiving and told me she was grateful for our friendship. I was glad to see that she had gotten out her craft supplies, and I was touched by the effort she'd put into the card, though her gesture made me feel extra guilty for not telling her about Shane's note.

The next morning, the sun shrugged off a veil of clouds as I exited my car, one of the few times I'd seen it unobscured in recent days, and the light angled between the buildings to shine in my eyes. I told myself it was a sign, that today was the day I would give the note to Kendrick, that I would feel better once I had done so.

I heard shouting as I passed the post office and looked up the sidewalk to see a slope-shouldered man in oil-stained coveralls throwing his arms up, hollering at Detective Kendrick, who stood firm in the face of his ranting.

"I'm telling you, I know who did this."

"And I'm telling you to calm down and come inside so we can talk. I promise we will do our jobs, we will look into it, and we will find out what happened."

"You don't arrest him now, he'll run." He gestured toward the street, and I saw his silver beard in profile, a thick mass of steel wool.

"I can't just arrest someone without any proof, any reason," Kendrick said.

"I told you, they were seeing each other. There was something going on between 'em."

"We will look into that, Mr. Pettit. These things take time. We are taking every tip seriously, and we are investigating."

He moved closer, towering over her like a posturing grizzly, and then he stomped off across the street, got into a pickup, and slammed the door.

Kendrick watched him go, hands on her narrow hips, catching sight of me as I was about to pass by. She nodded hello, her jaw clamped tight, and I nodded back and kept walking.

When I got to work, Rhonda, the administrative assistant who was married to Brody Flynn from the dispatcher's office, hovered in the break room making coffee, breathless, her face pink and dewy like she'd worked up a sweat holding in a secret. It burst out of her before I could grab my coffee mug. "Did you hear about the car they found in the river?"

"No."

Rhonda nodded vigorously. "Found it yesterday, and they drug it out early this morning. It was Henley Pettit's."

Charlie's friend. Crystle's cousin, the one who liked Shane.

"They were looking for Roger Calhoun's truck and found her Skylark instead. They didn't find the body," Rhonda said, barely pausing for breath, "but they found some of her things. I guess her family thought she'd left town, didn't know she was missing."

My stomach twisted, knotting itself. I wondered if she'd already been gone when I'd tried to call her, if the phone didn't pick up because it was lost underwater.

"This county, I swear." Rhonda shook her head mournfully. "It's all the drugs. Just keeps getting worse and worse. We need to get prayer back in schools before it's too late."

Prayer clearly wasn't enough, considering the staggering number of churches in Cutler County, but I didn't say anything as I filled my mug and backed away.

I sloshed coffee on my desk in a rush to set it down so I could text

Hannah and ask if she was free to meet up that evening. I didn't know if what had happened to Henley Pettit had anything to do with what had happened to Shane, but I didn't want to hold on to the note any longer. I'd give it to Kendrick in the morning, and I'd tell Hannah about it first. It had been selfish to wait.

She didn't text back until I was leaving work, telling me I could join her and Chad at the Barred Owl. I asked if I could stop by and see her before she went out instead, but she replied that it was too late—they were already there for happy hour. I had to drive all the way home first, to let Gravy out, and while I was there, I changed out of my work clothes into jeans and boots. I hadn't been to a bar in a long time, and I didn't plan on staying long or having much to drink.

The Barred Owl was out on the highway, a country bar, the kind with a mechanical bull and peanut shells on the floor. Happy hour was ending when I got there, the early crowd filing out as the night crowd began to arrive, snippets of an old Rascal Flatts song blaring out the door each time it swung open. I found Hannah and Chad in a booth near the restrooms with a near-empty pitcher of Bloody Mary beer and four shot glasses upturned on the table between them. Chad emptied the last of the pitcher into a plastic cup and pushed it toward me.

"Sit by me," Hannah said, her voice syrupy. "And look out for that guy!" She wiggled her fingers at Chad. "He doesn't have an alibi. Watching TV by yourself doesn't count." She started an old grade-school chant. "U-G-L-Y, you ain't got no alibi!"

I remembered her saying that Chad had offered to take care of Roger for her. I glanced at him and he laughed.

"Nothing to see here," he said. "She went to talk to Kendrick today. Got her a little worked up."

Hannah hugged my neck when I slid in next to her, her hair smelling of onion rings and hair spray. I worried she'd had too much to drink, though Chad didn't seem concerned. She wore a peach halter top and glittery eyeliner, her hair styled in tousled waves. Seeing her like that took me back to the night of her accident, before everything changed. She'd stopped by my house to return the stuffed Barney doll Lily had left in her car. She was dressed up, on her way out for a drink. *Hey, why don't you come with me?* she'd said. *Greg can watch Lily for a couple hours, can't he?*

I had wanted to go, to carve out a space for our tentative friendship, to talk about grown-up things without filtering our conversation for tiny ears. I'd been hesitant, though, to ask Greg to watch his own daughter. He'd been working long hours, and he was tired, and I knew he would try to make me feel selfish for wanting to go out and enjoy myself.

A young guy in a stars-and-stripes cowboy hat strutted past our table and Hannah whistled at him, admiring his tight Wranglers. "God bless America!" she hollered. Two women at the bar glared in our direction, whispering, scowls contorting their heavily made-up faces, like Hannah had no business going out, getting drunk, flirting with random men. I wondered how much time had to pass before she would be allowed to do normal things. Could the mother of a murdered child ever go out and enjoy herself again? Hannah was undoubtedly mourning, but everyone needed a break at some point, the grace to smile or laugh, or why carry on living?

"I gotta go to the bathroom," she said, climbing over my lap before I could scoot out of the booth. "Can you grab some more drinks?"

"Sure," I said. Chad and I watched her stagger toward the restroom, the ladies at the bar tracking her every move. "Is she okay?" I asked.

"Yeah," he said, rubbing his hand over his red beard. "She hasn't even had that much to drink, she's just a lightweight these days. Really needed a night to relax, let loose. She's stretched so thin you can see through her."

"Do you know what she wants to drink?"

"I'll come with you," he said. "I think we need some shots."

I didn't think Hannah needed any more shots, and I didn't want any, either. The place was filling up, the music painfully loud, people shouting over it. It was starting to look like I'd have to find a better time to talk to Hannah.

Chad ordered Alabama Slammers and a pitcher of Bud at the bar, and on the way back to the table I bumped into someone, literally, spilling beer onto her boots.

"I'm so sorry," I said, looking up to see who I was apologizing to. Detective Kendrick looked back at me, her mouth set in a tight smile. She had lipstick on, a dramatic brick red, and wore a silky burgundy top and jeans, her hair swept back in a ponytail. I wished that I had put slightly more effort into fixing myself up to go out. At least brushed my hair.

"Lacey!" Chad stepped up, threw his free arm around her shoulders. Kendrick smiled a real smile, and I realized I'd never seen so much of her teeth. Her hand lingered at Chad's waist after he let go. "You know Sadie Keller? She's a friend of Hannah's."

She nodded, her eyes on him, not bothering to glance at me. "Yes, I do."

I felt someone brush against my elbow and turned to see Theo. "Hey," he said, looking genuinely happy to see me. "How are you?" He shook hands with Chad and introduced himself. It didn't occur to me, until he explained to Lacey how he knew me, that they had come to the bar together.

"One thing I love about small towns," he said. "I think everyone I know is here."

"Yeah," I said. "It's great."

"Hey, why don't you come sit with us?" Theo offered.

I was about to say that I should check on Hannah, but Chad beat me to it.

"Sure, I'll be back in a minute," he said, handing me my shot, downing one himself, and threading into the crowd to take the last one to Hannah.

I followed Theo and Kendrick to their table and sat down opposite them. I hadn't wanted a shot, but it seemed like a good idea given the circumstances. I tipped it back, cringing as the Southern Comfort seared its way down my throat.

"So," I said, trying to think of a topic of conversation that wouldn't be too personal or awkward. "I heard about the car."

"Yeah." Kendrick nodded. She seemed to be looking past me, over my shoulder. "And you heard me talking to Pettit this morning, I imagine."

"That was a little tense."

She shrugged. "He was upset."

"Was he asking you to arrest someone?"

She rolled her head to the side, cracking her neck. "Well, he said Henley'd started working for the Sullivans not too long ago, and she'd been hanging around with Jason. Claimed they were romantically involved, but I haven't been able to confirm it. No one's so much as seen them in the same vicinity, aside from the Pettits, apparently. Earl couldn't even say for sure whether Jason had ever been in the house when she was over there cleaning."

"Are there other suspects?" I said. "Are you allowed to say?"

"We haven't named any suspects," Kendrick said evenly. "We don't even know yet that a crime was committed. We haven't found a body."

"But her car was in the river," I said. "In what scenario does her car end up in the river if there wasn't a crime?"

"She could have driven it there herself. You can't jump to conclusions every time something looks strange, when you don't have all the facts." She gave me a pointed look, and I knew she was making a dig about Shane. She still thought I was crazy. I wondered what it would be like to grab her ponytail and throw her down on the floor, filthy with peanut shells and who knew what else. I'd never been in a fight before and was sure she'd have no trouble beating me.

Kendrick took a napkin from the table and dabbed at her boots. I'd forgotten about spilling beer on her.

"Let me get you some wet paper towels."

"That's all right," she said. "I'm gonna go clean these up in the bathroom."

"I'm really sorry about that," I said, but she'd already left the table.

Theo leaned forward. "I wouldn't take it personally," he said. "She's pretty stressed from work, as you can imagine."

"It's fine."

"We're . . . uh . . . not here together," he said. "Not *together* to-gether, anyway. We're friends."

"Okay," I said. "You don't have to explain anything to me."

"Just wanted to let you know," he said, smiling. "In the interest of transparency."

I unstacked the plastic cups that had come with the pitcher. "Do you want some of this beer? I'm not sure when Chad's coming back."

"No thanks," he said. "So how did you two meet?"

"Cougar Date," I said.

"Oh." He nodded politely. "Seems like a nice guy."

"I guess," I said. "If you like doing shots and vaping."

"First date?"

I laughed. "Did you think I was serious? We're not on a date. He's my friend's cousin," I said. "I came to see her, he was here. Your ket-amine story scared me away from online dating."

He flushed slightly, grinning. "Good. I hoped it would. Narrow down the competition."

My face warmed from the shot or from the way Theo was looking at me, and I almost forgot what I was doing there, that I hadn't come to the bar to have a good time.

I spotted Hannah then, waving her arms like she was signaling a plane. I waved back and she motioned for me to join her.

"I need to check on my friend," I said, getting up. "Catch you later?"

"Yeah," he said. "I hope so."

Through the crowd, I thought I saw Chad standing near Kendrick, over by the restrooms, but I couldn't tell whether they were talking to each other. When I got to Hannah, she took my hand in hers and led me to the mostly empty dance floor, clasping her arms around my neck like you would at a junior high dance.

"I'm glad you came," she said. "Nobody else'll dance with me." She rested her head on my shoulder and swayed to the music. I could feel people staring. "Remember those little dance parties we used to have with Macey and Lily back in preschool? Put on that Kidz Bop CD, and they would go to town." She sighed. "Those were good times. I wish we could go back."

"Hannah, I need to ask you something."

She stopped swaying, her arms falling away from my neck. Her eyes were half closed, glitter smeared beneath them.

"When Roger's visitation schedule changed, so he could get that extra night, who knew about that besides you?"

"I don't know."

"Did your family know?"

"I don't know. Maybe. Listen." She leaned in close. "Kendrick told me something today." Her breath tickled my neck, making the little hairs stand up. More than a few people were watching us, some disdainful, others curious. She put her lips to my ear so I could hear her over the music, her words vibrating against my skin.

"She said Roger might have been killed over a *debt*. See, he deposited a chunk of cash in his account a while back, money he borrowed to pay for lawyers and court fees—divorce and custody aren't cheap, not when you're fighting. He quit his second job so he could have Macey on weekends, and then he didn't have the money to pay the loan back. Kendrick thinks whoever gave him that money might have killed him." She swayed off-balance and I reached out to steady her.

"Cotton Eye Joe" blared out of the speakers and more people moved onto the dance floor, but they gave us a wide berth.

"What do you think of that?" Hannah said. "My baby's dead because of the divorce—because I wanted her all to myself. If I'd known . . . I would have rather let Roger have her all the time, just to know she was alive, that she was there. It comes back to me every time, no matter what happened, no matter how I figure it. I'm her mother. The one who was supposed to protect her. And I failed. I have to live with that."

She pulled back, hands on my shoulders, her eyes unfocused. "Let's get another round."

It took all four of us working as a team to convince Hannah to leave when the bar began to close. Chad and I were in charge of bribing and cajoling. Theo carried her purse and escorted her out the door with the gentle manner of someone accustomed to dealing with squirming animals. Kendrick, who'd had nothing to drink but club soda, insisted on driving both Chad and Hannah home.

I climbed into my car and closed my eyes, leaning back in the seat, thinking I'd rest for a while until I was sure I was sober enough to drive. Theo had offered to follow me to make sure I got home safely, and I'd accepted at first, but by the time we got Hannah buckled into Kendrick's car, I'd started to worry that things might turn awkward when he got to my house. I didn't know whether he'd want to come in or whether I should invite him, so I told him I could get home fine on my own. I regretted it after he left and considered calling to tell him I'd changed my mind again, but I couldn't bring myself to do it.

I'd almost drifted off when an urgent rapping vibrated the window glass. I twitched, instantly alert, and nearly screamed as a face appeared.

"It's me," Charlie said. He was alone in the dark, hunched over so we could see each other eye to eye.

I took a deep, steadying breath and rolled down the window. I wasn't sure how he'd known where to find me, though it wouldn't have taken much luck or effort. The Barred Owl was the only place open this time of night, and my car was parked in view of the highway.

"Hey," I said. "Is everything all right?"

"Here." He shoved a book at me. It was a journal bound in purple fabric, the pages edged with silver. "It's hers," he said. "Look."

Inside the front cover, a name inscribed in marker: Henley Pettit. I flipped through the pages, crowded with the fat bubble script of a teenage girl.

"Henley's? Where'd you get it?"

Charlie shrugged, looking out toward the road, back to the bar, a neon Budweiser sign glowing in the window.

"You can tell me," I said.

"From her bedroom," he mumbled. "I went to her house. I knew where she hid it."

"Charlie? Why are you giving this to me?"

He shook his head. "She wrote about him. Jason Sullivan. It's proof she was seeing him." Blood rushed to his face, flushing his skin. "I was gonna show it to that cop. Raymond said she didn't believe him."

"Is there something in here that incriminates Jason?"

"No," he said. "But there's something you need to see."

He reached out and spread the journal open to a page marked with a ribbon. I stared at it until Shane's name emerged from the frantic crush of letters.

"She was there," Charlie said. "The night he died."

CHAPTER 26

HENLEY

OCTOBER

Henley pulled her journal from under the floorboard in her closet, where she still liked to keep it even though Missy wasn't around to try to read it. Flipping back through the pages, Henley noticed that she wrote in it mostly when Missy was using or gone, a habit formed years ago when her mother was in rehab and a counselor had told Henley it would help to write out her thoughts and feelings. She only did it at first because the counselor had made her, but she'd found it was useful in those times she couldn't, or didn't want to, talk to Missy or Charlie or anyone else. She definitely couldn't talk to Charlie now, not about this.

She wished that Missy were here, though she knew that her mother wouldn't be any help. Missy wasn't good at dealing with trouble; she'd go in one of two directions: fall apart or run and hide. Henley wanted to run now, before the sun climbed up over the east field and spilled light over everything. But Junior, seeing it on her face, had clamped his hands on her shoulders, his green eyes sharp and steady. *Go home*, he'd said. *Stay put.*

Even now, in her room with the door locked, her breath came shallow. Her stomach tensed so tightly she hunched forward, wanting to get it all out, purge what she knew like a gush of vomit and be rid of it. She rolled the point of her pen in circles to get the ink going, the night replaying in her mind.

Crystle had called while she was studying the map of Idaho in Pawpaw's atlas, tracing a route to the Seven Devils Mountains in Hells Canyon Wilderness. The peaks had names like the Goblin, She Devil, Black Imp.

You at home? Crystle asked.

Yeah.

You been anywhere or seen anybody in the last couple hours?

No. Why?

Get over here now. I need you for something.

When she got to Shane and Crystle's place, the last strip of purple light on the horizon went dark, like a blade slicing down, the first evening star gleaming high above the house. Crystle was pacing manically on the front porch, her spike-heeled boots scritching on the concrete.

"We were at your place," she said, "if anyone asks. You came back to the house with me. We walked in together." She yanked up the bottom of Henley's shirt and stuffed something into her jeans pocket, a small plastic container. "Hold on to that for me and don't fucking open it."

"What's going on?" Henley said.

Crystle led her in the front door, and Shane was lying on the floor in the living room, on his back, next to his recliner. Henley might have thought he was asleep, his eyes and mouth cracked open, if it weren't for Gravy scratching at him, whining. A shudder went through her, and she felt dizzy, like she might puke. There was a puddle of piss on the carpet at Gravy's feet. He clawed Shane's face, and Crystle screamed and kicked the dog in the rear, shoving him away with her boot, but he only moved around to Shane's other side and resumed his scratching. Henley wondered how long Shane had been lying there like that, how long Gravy had been urging him to get up.

Junior burst in then and instantly lit into Crystle.

"Why's she here?"

"You said I needed somebody to—" Crystle hollered.

"Not her!" he interrupted. "Jesus. Henley, get that dog outta here."

Henley tried to grab Gravy, who snapped his teeth, but she managed to grasp the back of his collar and pull him out the front door just as Dex was coming in.

She stood on the porch, watching Gravy sniff around the yard, her heartbeat filling her throat, pulsing red behind her eyes. Goosebumps ridged her arms as the night chill set in, but she barely noticed the cold.

Crystle was yelling inside, Dex trying to shush her.

"You said not to let him call anybody, and I didn't," she said, half sobbing. "I took his phone while he was puking, and when he came back in here, he fell down."

"What are you bawlin' for?" Junior scolded. "You knew what was comin'."

"I know!" she screeched. "But you didn't have to watch it happen. You didn't have to sit here and fucking *wait*."

"How long you think it woulda took your idiot brother's way, antifreeze in his cough syrup? One spoon at a time, just enough to make him sick? What if he went to the hospital, what do you think would've happened then, to all of us?"

"It's all right," Dex said. "It's done. Had to be. He was too worked up over Calhoun."

Calhoun. Henley could still picture Hannah crying on the news, begging her ex-husband to bring their little girl home. She didn't know Macey, had never seen her in the flesh, only her large eyes and bashful smile on the MISSING posters around town.

"We need to find the rifle," Junior said. "He's got to have it hid somewhere, and we don't need loose ends."

"It's not here," Crystle said. "I've checked all his hidey-holes."

"You got anything you need to deal with before you make the call?" Dex asked. "You got your story straight?"

"I cleaned up," she said. "They're not gonna poke around, are they? They'll just take him and go?"

"I'll do a quick sweep," Dex said. "Don't want 'em catching sight of something stupid like a bag of dope and making a fuss."

"I'll talk to Henley," Junior growled. "Now that you done dragged her into it."

Henley backed away from the door, and when Junior opened it, Gravy wormed his way back inside. She clenched her jaw, teeth on the verge of chattering.

"Listen," Junior said. "You need to stick around town long enough for this to run its course. You were at your place with Crystle, you both came over here, walked in, and found him cold. That's it. Don't offer it up if nobody asks."

Fear cinched her throat tight, and her head throbbed with questions her tongue refused to form. She could only nod when Junior told her to go home.

Raymond's truck pulled up as she neared her car, and he climbed out, his face grim. "You all right?" he asked.

Her head jittered side to side, and Raymond wrapped an arm around her, the warm flannel soft against her chilled skin.

"What happened to Calhoun?" she asked, her voice wobbling.

"He's gone," Raymond said.

"Did Shane kill him?"

Raymond sighed. "Don't matter now," he muttered.

"What about the girl?"

"Nobody wanted that," Raymond said. She felt his lungs filling and emptying as she folded herself against his chest, his breath making ghostly plumes in the night air. "She wasn't supposed to be there."

She looked back at what she had written, gray light seeping into the room, her hand stiff from clenching the pen. It felt like she had been staring at the page for hours, yet she had only managed three lines.

I have never seen a dead body like that before, one that was not made ready for me to see, and now I can't unsee it. Crystle told me to say we were together when Shane died but we weren't. He was dead when I got there and she said she watched him die.

The rest of the story coiled like a tension spring inside her, stretched tight between her heart and lungs, constricting each heartbeat, every breath.

CHAPTER 27

SADIE

DECEMBER

"Where did you get this?" Kendrick asked, holding the diary in front of my face like I hadn't yet seen it, like I wasn't the one who'd just handed it to her. She was back to her regular clothes, her lips coated with Carmex, her demeanor about the same as it had been at the bar the night before when I'd spilled beer on her. She'd told me to come in immediately when I called, had ushered me into her office and shut the door, waving me to the chair with the duct-taped armrest and immediately launching into interrogation mode.

"A friend of Henley's gave it to me. Charlie Burdett."

"And how did he come to have it?"

"He said he knew where she kept it. He asked me to give it to you."

I waited while she read the pages I'd flagged, her face betraying nothing as her eyes scanned back and forth. She looked up at me when she finished.

"Is that enough?" I asked. "To bring him in?" I knew Charlie was hoping for more than that, though when I'd read the passages for myself I'd been surprised not to find a more troublesome picture of Jason. If anything, Henley's account of their relationship was flush with the thrill of new love and intimacy—I had to stop reading at one point because it felt uncomfortably voyeuristic, things she wouldn't have wanted anyone to see—though I knew she might have only written about the good parts, that love didn't preclude violence, that the lack of fear didn't mean that no threat lurked there. Abuse often stayed hidden, especially when inflicted by those closest to us. Kendrick surely knew that, too.

She shrugged. "It's enough to establish the relationship. Enough that it makes sense to talk to him."

She set the book on her desk.

"So let's talk about Shane. Where's the note?"

I took it from my pocket and handed it over, along with the key. I had made a copy for Kendrick, keeping the original attached to my keychain.

"So this was in with the belongings you took from his house?"

I nodded.

"But you don't know where the gun is that he's talking about."

"Crystle sold all the guns, as far as I know. Right after he died. Somebody said they got hauled to the pawn shop."

Kendrick picked up a pen and tapped it against her lips. "Did your brother have an alibi for the night the Calhouns went missing? It would have been a Sunday, April twenty-third, the week after Easter."

"I don't know," I said. "I could look at the calendar, maybe. Go back through my texts." I hadn't known Shane's schedule, if he had a Sunday routine.

"I think he loaned Roger some money. He'd taken cash out a while ago, at the same time Roger hired a new lawyer to try to get his custody agreement changed. The amount Roger paid was close to the amount Shane took out of the bank. Then later on, around the time of the murders, Shane was in some financial straits, as you know. Bills coming due, not enough to cover them."

She had looked into his finances after all, after I told her what Becca and I had found in his boxes of paperwork.

"You also mentioned hearing from one of his coworkers that Crystle'd had an affair," she continued. "This alleged affair was apparently with someone they both knew, and it is starting to look like that person was Roger. Imagine if you loaned your friend some money and then something made you think he was messing around with your wife. It might make you pretty angry."

It took a moment to grasp what was happening. She had followed all the leads I had given her, though instead of casting suspicion on Crystle—that she might have done something to Shane—it was being used against him. She was focusing on motives for him to kill the Calhouns and ignoring the rest.

"Did you read what Henley wrote about Crystle?" I asked. "The part about watching him die? Even if he did this—*if*—". The words choked off, my throat threatening to close up.

There was a slight softening in Kendrick's eyes, a hint of compassion, or possibly pity. I'd seen the same look the night before when she was dealing with Hannah. "I promise you that we will look at everything."

"What about Chad?" I blurted. "I know you're friends, but Hannah told me he offered once to take Roger out. And when I talked to him, before Roger's body was found, he said, 'Roger always was a waste of flesh,' almost like he knew he was dead. Hannah said he didn't have an alibi for that night."

Kendrick mashed her lips together and exhaled sharply through her nose. "Chad had nothing to do with it."

"You said you'd look at everything."

"I will. And I have. He was with me."

"Then why did Hannah say he didn't have an alibi?"

"Because he has two small children with his longtime girlfriend, and it wasn't necessary for her to know he was with someone else overnight."

"You and Chad." I thought back to the night before at the Barred Owl, how Kendrick had lit up when he hugged her, her offer to drive him home. They seemed like complete opposites, never mind the fact that he was in a relationship with someone else. Even Kendrick, with her rigid demeanor and love of rules, was able to loosen up and go out to a bar and unapologetically enjoy herself. Why couldn't I do the same?

"Pick your jaw back up," she said. "I don't let my personal life get in the way of my job. Missy Pettit is sitting in jail right now, and we're going to see if there's anything she'd like to share." Kendrick picked up the phone and waved me out. "I'll be in touch," she said, pushing the door shut behind me.

I could hear Leola's dogs bouncing up and down on the other side of the door as I waited for her to answer. Low clouds had moved in, and the air smelled like snow. The garden spinners whipped around so fast they blurred.

Leola appeared in her housecoat, sagging nylons, and loafers, her hair flat on one side as though she'd been napping on it. She invited me in and I told her I couldn't stay long.

"I wanted to ask about Charlie," I said. "See if he's doing all right. I saw him last night, and he was pretty upset about his friend Henley."

Her chin wobbled, dentures clacking as she worried them back and forth. "More than friends," she said. "She was special to him."

"They were dating?"

"Can't say for sure," she said. "He wouldn't have told me that. But they were awfully close. I thought they might end up together some-day."

The dogs whined at her feet, but Leola didn't seem to hear them. "I hate to see him like this," she said. "He's hurting and angry, and I can't blame him. He doesn't want to talk to his granny about any of it. Shane was always the one he went to, when he wanted to talk."

The wind buffeted the house, rattling the windows, and I was re-minded of something Hannah had said. How it had stormed so hard the night before Macey and Roger were killed. "Leola—you remember telling me how Shane brought you the lantern, after the storm? Was that back in the spring?"

"It was," she said. "The lily of the valley was blooming."

"Was it a Sunday, do you think?"

She looked up at me, her eyes rheumy. "Could have been. He was off work."

"How long did he stay?"

"Quite a while. He helped me clear a downed tree out of the yard— chopped it up for firewood, stacked it by the porch to season. I made him stay for supper. We had cured ham and the last jar of the Red Hot cinnamon applesauce I'd canned in the fall. I remember because the fridge was out and most things went bad, but I wouldn't let him leave without feeding him first. Chopping wood's hungry work."

"Do you know what time he left?"

She eyed me quizzically, blinking. "No, but I'm sure it was dark. He was tuckered out, his back giving him a bit of trouble. I felt bad about that, that he'd aggravated it helping me. He was ready to go home and sleep."

It wasn't an alibi, exactly, that he'd spent the day helping an elderly woman, but he was worn out, his back hurting, and he had to be at work in the suburbs early the next morning. It didn't seem like an ideal time to commit a double murder and carry two bodies out into the woods. If he'd killed the Calhouns after leaving Leola's, driven all the way back to the conservation area to dump the bodies, and then disposed of the truck, that could have taken most of the night. It might not be enough to convince Kendrick that he was innocent, but it opened a window of possibility for me.

Hannah was waiting on my porch in the dark when I got home, wearing only a T-shirt and jeans, her skin icy to the touch. I was worried that she'd been drinking or worse, but she was perfectly lucid.

"I couldn't wait to tell you," she said, squeezing my hands. "Kendrick's got something. They talked to some friend of the Pettits sitting in jail for armed robbery, and she offered information about a murder. They were trying to see if she knew anything about Roger and Macey, but it was something else entirely."

Her cheeks were flushed, her eyes bright. She looked different somehow, more alive. More like herself.

"That's great," I said. "But how does that help?"

"She claimed she saw a human bone belonging to someone named Dalmire out on the Pettits' property. They couldn't find any missing persons reports under that name, but there was a Dalmire who used to live around here, and he hasn't been seen in several years. Should be good enough for a warrant to search the salvage yard. It's what Kendrick's been waiting for."

Hannah gave me a quick hug, her arms tight around my rib cage, her tears wetting my cheek.

CHAPTER 28

HENLEY

DECEMBER

E arl had spent the better part of the day talking to his lawyers, discussing his options without telling them why he was fooling around with the trust. His own son had been making threats, demanding that Earl release the money that he wasn't meant to get until his twenty-fifth birthday, and Earl wasn't sure he'd be ready for it even then. He didn't understand what Jason was doing at first. The sudden outburst of crazed demands and accusations made Earl think the boy was suffering a mental break, that he needed help. Then it became clear that Jason was extorting him, his volatility pushing Earl to consider acquiescing, imagining the relief he'd feel if he gave him what he wanted and set him out of the house. His son had said some things that were deeply unsettling, and Earl had been grateful when he got home from signing all the papers at the lawyer's office that Jason was in his room with the door shut, that there was time to pour himself a drink before going up to talk to him.

Now the furnace eased off and the big house was quiet save for the sleet clicking against the picture windows. A glass of whiskey sat half finished on the table. Earl clutched the phone to his ear, though the person on the other end had hung up. He couldn't seem to unbend his arm, to move his feet. He'd been given a heads-up, a courtesy not everyone received, and he wasn't sure what to do with it.

He had thought, when he met Daphne, that he had finally been forgiven for Emily. His wife had been beautiful and selfless, a rare combination in his experience, and she loved him, despite and possibly because of what had happened to his sister, and how it had shaped him. When they'd married, he had no desire to touch any other woman. Then when Daphne got sick, he knew it had been a cruel joke, a brief respite. His wife had taken care of everything in the home, doted on Jason, granted Earl room to believe he was worthy of a normal life—all of which made it more difficult when he was left alone with a troubled little boy. Consumed by his own grief, he'd struggled to comfort his son properly. He should have spent more time with him before Daphne had died, then maybe things would have been different, though Earl knew it was possible that Jason had always been that way and he just hadn't noticed, that Daphne had smoothed Jason's edges as she had smoothed everything else in Earl's world.

He'd tried to straighten Jason out, to instill values by raising him in the same way he'd been raised by his own father—telling himself that hard work ironed out moral wrinkles. Wear somebody out on the farm and they'd develop respect for themselves, a sense of purpose and accomplishment. They'd learn that no one is too good for honest work, be it shoveling manure or harvesting grain, and as a bonus, they'd be too tired to make trouble. But Jason was stubborn and Earl hadn't been able to break him enough to reform him. His flaws had leaned toward unfixable.

All of this was punishment for Earl's failings. For the women. The liquor. For Emily. For thinking he'd been forgiven. Whatever crimes Jason had committed fell on him, too, because he had failed to fix him. Still, he loved his son. And now the police were coming to take him in for questioning, and there were decisions to make.

Earl was jolted by a knock at the door, a series of powerful thuds, like an axe driving down into a log. Were they already here? He didn't want to open the door but knew that he would. He straightened his spine, drew his shoulders back, and turned the knob. Charlie Burdett stood in the dark gap.

He hadn't seen Charlie much since he was a boy, since his father had suffocated in a silo at Sullivan Grain and was buried in the fine walnut casket Earl had paid for. Earl never forgot anyone who died on his watch, nor failed to feel a wash of guilt when he saw their families around town. There was a scholarship fund for the children of the fallen, which was helping Charlie go to technical school. The Burdetts were still on the company's Christmas card list, and Earl personally signed each card by hand. *Dear Leola and Charlie*, he had written, *may you have a blessed holiday season.*

Charlie's face was pale and wind-bitten in the glare of the porch light. He hoisted a shotgun and Earl stared dumbly.

"Drop the phone," Charlie said. "We gotta talk."

The phone slipped from Earl's fingers and clattered to the floor. "Charlie," he murmured, his arms hanging heavily at his sides. "What is this?"

Charlie ignored his question, gesturing with the barrel. "Come on outside."

The wind slipped stealthily into Earl's pressed shirt and stiff blue jeans, eliciting an involuntary shudder. Charlie urged him to the edge of the porch, where Raymond Pettit materialized from the darkness, sleeves rolled up on his thick, tattooed forearms, head down like a charging bull. He pushed past them and into the house.

Charlie forced Earl forward, the shotgun prodding between Earl's shoulder blades every time he slipped on the light glaze that filmed the walkway. When they reached the grain bin behind the barn, Earl turned to face him, the frigid wind hitting the back of his throat and making him gasp.

"My son."

"Start climbing," Charlie said, nodding toward the metal staircase that spiraled around the massive silo.

"What if I don't."

Charlie aimed the shotgun at his groin. "I shoot you and watch you bleed out."

"Are you sure you want to do that?"

Charlie shook his head, and Earl sensed a slight softening in the boy's demeanor, a reluctance beneath the bluster. "I don't want to. I'm just keeping you out of the way."

"You want money?" Earl said. He hadn't planned to bargain, but it was an old habit when cornered.

Charlie grabbed his shoulder and shoved him onto the stairs. They were slick, and he gripped the handrail, ascending into the darkness. When he reached the narrow platform at the top, the wind hurling grains of ice, he could see the lights of town, the outline of his kingdom. Down below, away from the main house, the wooden shack his grandfather had erected when the Sullivans pushed down roots in Cutler County.

His family had spent generations building their small-town empire, fortifying it with good deeds and hard work, yet it was the same for everyone when the wolf was at the door wanting in. You had to hope that you were ready, that what you had built was sufficient to withstand the threat. That was the lesson his father had taught him: be strong, be good, be prepared. But a big brick house was worthless if the wolf was already inside, his own son the one baring his teeth, threatening to bring the walls down on top of them.

Charlie was right behind him, wedging himself against the rail to steady himself from the hungry gale and block Earl from reaching the stairs.

"What did he do to her?" Charlie said, his features pinched against the wind. "To Henley."

Charlie had come for Jason, not for him, though it made little difference. Earl closed his eyes, a weight pressing on his chest. He remembered the look on Henley's face after he'd drunkenly tried to kiss her and she'd struck her head on the bedpost. The shame that had burned through him like an electrical current. He thought of all the times he'd protected his son when he shouldn't have. Times he'd felt something coming, like the pressure drop before a storm, and hadn't known how to stop it. Vigilance was exhausting. Over the years, Jason had started fires, gotten into fights, been expelled from a private school for stalking a fellow student. His attitude had seemed to improve over the summer, though, and Earl had thought his son was making progress. He grew lax, didn't realize he was involved with Henley until it was too late.

The wind screeched through the metal staircase, and Charlie leaned closer. "Where is she?" he asked. "Did he kill her, like Raymond said?"

Charlie's voice wavered and threatened to break, the gun forgotten, dangling at his side. The boy's eyes were watering from the cold, or he was crying, and Earl knew he could push past him if he wanted, that Charlie wouldn't hurt him. His own face was wet and stinging from the sleet. He imagined Henley weighted down in the freezing river, buried in a silo full of grain. He thought of Emily, blood spilling out of her mouth, onto the hay. He looked down and couldn't see the ground. He wondered what was happening in the house, what was happening to Jason.

"Tell me," Charlie sobbed.

"I don't know," Earl said finally. He didn't. And he didn't want to.

The bucket was empty and would never be filled. He'd been a fool to think otherwise. Snowflakes spun down, fat and wet, plastering his shirt to his skin. "The police are coming," he said. "Forget about whatever's going on down there, forget about me. It'll all play out. You should leave while you can. No one has to know you were here."

CHAPTER 29

SADIE
DECEMBER

I t had been dark for what felt like hours, everyone else in the office gone home while I stayed to finish up some paperwork. In the empty parking lot outside the break-room window, the gooseneck lamp illuminated a curtain of wintry drizzle drifting down. I was debating eating an expired yogurt that I'd found in the back of the office fridge when Leola called, her voice shrill and frantic.

"I'm worried about Charlie."

"What's going on?"

"He got a phone call and lit outta here, and I'm scared he's going after the Sullivan boy. I don't want him to ruin everything he's worked so hard for, everything Shane did for him. And I don't know who else to call."

"Did you try Earl?" I asked.

"Yes. I tried the number he's got listed, and he didn't answer. Maybe you can talk sense into Charlie, Sadie, before he does something he can't undo. He might listen to you."

I thought of Shane and all the fights he'd gotten into and wondered, if he were here, whether he'd talk Charlie out of doing serious damage to Jason Sullivan or take a swing at Jason himself. If Charlie was determined to do something, I doubted that he'd listen to me any more than he'd listen to Leola, but I promised her I would try. I dialed his number, though of course he didn't pick up, and I found myself driving out of town as fast as I dared on the slick roads, my car sliding sideways for an agonizing moment as I neared a low-water bridge, tires catching on the narrow gravel shoulder just in time to correct course and avoid dropping into the creek bed. I regretted my suspicion, inherited from my mother, that the mechanic was always trying to dupe me into buying new tires before I really needed them. I tried not to think about the lack of tread as freezing mist veiled the car and ice clogged the wipers and spread across the road in dark patches that were all but invisible.

Everyone knew where the Sullivans lived, though I'd been inside the big brick house only once, for a holiday party Earl had thrown for Sullivan Grain employees and their families back when Daphne was still alive. Mom had sewn red pleated skirts for me and Becca to wear, and Dad had given Shane strict instructions not to touch anything. The house had seemed like something out of a fairy tale at the time, the grand columns wrapped in twinkling lights, rising up from the empty fields like a mirage that might disappear if you looked away.

The mist was turning to snow as I rounded the curve of the Sullivans' driveway. It coated the fields in a soft white dust. I was relieved not to see anyone in the circle drive out front, until my headlights glanced off Shane's Firebird parked beside the barn. I drove up next to it, skidding dangerously close, but didn't see anyone inside, so I pulled up to the house and got out. One of the double front doors hung open, the wind dragging it nearly shut and then slamming it against the wall.

I climbed the porch steps, which were edged with ice, and eased into the house. "Hello?" I called. "Mr. Sullivan?" A cellphone lay on the floor in the entry, the screen splintered, but there was no sign of anyone. I knelt to pick up the phone and saw, on the polished wood floor, a single drop of blood. I ran to the staircase, calling for Charlie, but the house was silent. I went back outside to check Shane's car, hollering Charlie's name, and finally heard a faint reply.

"Sadie."

His voice wisped down from above, and I looked up into the falling snow, scanning the barn and the silo, where I spotted Charlie's pale face in the dark. I broke for the staircase and bounded up as fast as I could, circling higher and higher, my hands clutching the frozen rail. The snow thickened, falling in clumps, swirling down to melt on my face and wet my hair.

When I reached the platform, breathless, Charlie was alone.

"What are you doing up here?"

"I was with Earl. Raymond went in the house after Jason. I think he took off."

"Raymond Pettit? Where's Earl now?"

Charlie shook his head, dazed. He was shaking. "I just wanted him to tell me what happened to her."

He turned to face me, and I saw the shotgun held loosely at his side. My stomach lurched.

"You shot him?"

"No—I just wanted to scare him," Charlie said. "It's not loaded." He was sobbing now, his shoulders heaving up and down.

"Charlie! Did he fall?"

He wiped his face with his coat sleeve. "He closed his eyes," Charlie said. "Like he was praying. And then he went over the rail."

"Did you call 911?"

"He said they were already coming," Charlie mumbled. "That they're on the way."

"Come on." I grabbed his sleeve and dragged him down the stairs, leaving him at the bottom while I circled the silo to find Earl. Halfway around, I nearly tripped over him. Earl was splayed on the frozen ground, unmoving, and the snow was working to shroud his body. Grateful that it was too dark to get a good look at him, I knelt by his side and tried to find a pulse with half-numb fingers, but couldn't. My hand came away dripping blood and I scrubbed it in the snow until my skin stung. I still didn't hear sirens, so I called for an ambulance myself, told them Earl Sullivan was unresponsive, hung up as they started asking questions.

I ran back to Charlie, who clung to the railing, half dazed, the gun at his feet. I picked it up. "Do you have a blanket in your car? Something to cover him."

"Uh . . . yeah. I think so."

We hurried back to the Firebird. Charlie unlocked the trunk and pulled out the old tarp that lined the bottom, handing it to me. As I laid his shotgun down in the trunk, something caught my eye. A small lock, embedded in the floor. Looking closer in the faint light, I saw the outline of a panel. The tarp slid to the ground, my hands shaking. I hesitated, thinking of Earl, but there was nothing to be done for him aside from covering his body. That could wait.

I took out my keychain and grasped the key Shane had hidden in the pie safe. It slid into the lock and turned, and I lifted the metal panel. Shane had fabricated a shallow storage compartment, presumably when he'd rebuilt the car, and inside it lay a rifle. My heart felt as though it was being squeezed in an unrelenting fist.

"Is that the one he made?" I asked Charlie.

"Yeah," he said, his voice hitching.

"Listen to me," I said, folding the key into his palm. "Get out of here now, as fast as you can. Take the back way, away from town. Tomorrow you need to turn this gun in to the police. Don't touch it. Tell them where you found it, in Shane's car. That's all. Nothing else. Don't say anything about tonight. You weren't here. I'll take care of this."

He stared, mute and trembling.

"Tell Leola you changed your mind and didn't come here. You just went for a drive and headed back when the weather turned bad. Understand?"

He nodded.

"Go."

I watched him leave. The snow came down in sheets, swept by the wind, working quickly enough, I hoped, to mask his tracks. I didn't know for sure that Charlie was telling the truth, that Earl had leapt to his death, but I had made the decision in an instant: to believe him, to protect him, to give him a chance, like Shane would have done. Once I'd mapped out the lie, it was too late to turn back.

Sirens screamed from the direction of town, lights flashing against the snow, and I ran to meet them, waving my arms to direct them to the silo. Later, Kendrick or one of the others would ask why I was here, how I had come across Earl. I would tell them the truth, that Leola had asked me to look for Charlie, that I'd gotten worried when I found the door open and no one at home, had followed tracks to the silo. Called for the ambulance. I didn't know what had happened to Jason.

My teeth began to chatter, my hair stiffening as it froze. I wondered if it was only by chance that Shane had given the car keys to Charlie, knowing the Firebird would go to Mom, hoping the note and the key to the gun box would find their way to me. Drawing us together, his disparate families. It couldn't have been an accident. He must have known something was coming, that he might not survive, and he wanted us to discover the truth, whatever it was. He had given Charlie the key, trusting him like he trusted his own blood. The one person he should have trusted most of all had no part in it. Crystle. His wife.

CHAPTER 30

HENLEY

NOVEMBER

The sky was clear, the moon extravagantly large and mottled with bruises, a wolf moon or blood moon or some such thing, she couldn't recall. It appeared, from her spot on the riverbank, to be just out of reach, balanced atop a skeletal crown of cottonwoods. Her throat burned, her breath was ragged. The bitter cold knifed through her, paring away the pain and exhaustion and fear. It cut down to the bone, revealing with sharp clarity that the only thing she truly wanted was to live. To keep breathing, to feel the crushed weeds digging into her back, the solid earth beneath her.

She had awoken in the car, roused by the creak of the door hinge but too disoriented to understand what was happening. She'd gasped when the blanket that had been covering her was whisked away, not sure whether she should lie still or try to run, and then the door slammed shut and she was alone. Her breath was too loud, her throat on fire. The door stayed shut and she decided that running was better than waiting, even if she wouldn't get very far, because she already knew what he would do if she waited. She pushed herself up from the floorboard, staying low in case he was right outside, wanting to see where she was, what she could run to. Jason had left the driver's side window partly open, and she could see the stars, feel the night air shushing in, clearing her head. For a moment, she didn't even realize that the car had begun to roll. She didn't have to think about what that meant. The knowledge was innate and incontrovertible, that anything she was moving toward wasn't something she would likely come back from.

Panic lit up inside her as the car gained momentum and she understood. There were only so many hills like this in Blackwater, and one common thing they sloped down to. She scrambled to get into the front seat, to reach the brake. The nose of the car pitched forward over the riverbank and she tumbled into the dash, rolling back as the rear of the car slammed down. Fear pinned her to the seat as frigid water rushed in. She felt around for the window crank as the river sluiced up to her neck and the Skylark began to sink, and then she took a breath and closed her eyes. In the darkness, she could hear the muted gurgle of water filling the empty spaces, air bubbles escaping to the surface.

She remembered the sweltering summer day when Jason had taken her to the bottom of the river, crushing her against his chest until she surrendered and went still. She forced herself to focus. Her lungs were already burning, but she'd had enough air to reach the surface that day in July, and she could do it again.

She thought only of the most urgent and immediate obstacle; the hardest part was pulling herself through the window as the car sucked her downward, and then the hardest part was navigating blindly through the freezing current as her body numbed, and then the hard-

est part was trying to surface undetected—in case he was watching—
when she was desperate for air.

She failed at the last part, thrashing out of the water choking and
gasping, but either the river had carried her downstream or Jason had
already fled.

She climbed the bank and lay at the river's edge, watching the
moon float up from the trees, and after some time the stars came into
focus, the rush of wind and the distant scream of coyotes replacing the
ringing in her ears. It hurt to swallow. She rolled onto her side, winc-
ing as she realized that her hair had frozen to the ground, and pulled
herself up.

Her head whirled at first, and she stood still, choking down shallow
breaths, until she could make her way to the crest of the hill to get her
bearings. The lights of Sullivan Grain winked in the distance, a more
useful guide than the stars. There was no one around, her phone lost
in the river, but she knew which direction led home. She clamped her
jaw shut to stop her teeth from chattering and set off through the fields.

When she got to the farmhouse, she drank from the kitchen faucet and
slid down to the floor, shaking. She struggled to peel off her damp
clothing with half-numb hands and then curled up near the radiator in
her underwear, exhausted. She wanted to sleep for days and days, dig
through Missy's bathroom drawer for a pill that would knock her out
and make her forget. She closed her eyes and willed her mind to drift,
but she thought of Jason's hands at her throat, and the fear she had
staved off as she'd stumbled through the fields crashed down on her in
an unrelenting torrent, and she scrambled through the dark house to
lock the doors.

She had no phone and no car, no way to reach anyone unless she
went back out into the night and walked toward town. She could hole
up and wait for dawn, but what then? Would the police believe that

Jason Sullivan had tried to kill her? What if they didn't arrest him right away? What if he'd taken off and they couldn't find him and she had to go to sleep every night knowing he was out there somewhere, that he might come back for her? Her uncles would try to keep her safe, but they had their own mess to deal with right now and needed to lie low.

Her entire body was beginning to ache. Henley rubbed her thawing hands together, the friction painful but necessary, and climbed the dark staircase to her room, which she'd said goodbye to hours before. She layered on warm leggings, a thick sweater, and an old parka from the back of Missy's closet, a stocking cap to hide her hair.

Her family thought she'd left town. Jason thought she was dead. Earl's money was mostly at the bottom of the river, stowed in the Skylark's glove box, though Raymond had warned her not to keep all her cash in one place when she was traveling. She dug into the pocket of her discarded jeans and found the small zippered pouch and the hundred-dollar bills she'd folded inside. It would be enough to get away, to disappear. She would cut through the north field to the truck stop on the highway. Ellie Embry had told her once that if she ever had to hitchhike, female truckers could be counted on to give a girl a ride, and they weren't near as likely to kill you. Most of what came out of Ellie's mouth was bullshit, but Henley hoped this once she was right.

CHAPTER 31

SADIE
DECEMBER

"They found it," Hannah said, her voice wavering over the phone. "They found the truck at the salvage yard. Part of it, anyway. It was burnt, half crushed, but they think it's Roger's."

I wasn't quite sure what to say. I was happy for her, that her wait might soon be over, though I wasn't sure what it would mean for Shane. I didn't know how I'd face Hannah if he was the one who had taken her child away.

"Do you want me to come over?" I offered.

She hesitated. "My mom and dad are here with me."

"Oh. Good," I said. I was glad that her parents were there to support her and hoped it was a sign that their relationship could be mended. They'd largely shut her out when she was struggling with her addiction, and I knew how much that had hurt her. "Just wanted to make sure you weren't alone."

I didn't want to be alone, either, waiting. Gravy was with me, but I was worried about him. He had stopped eating, and not even Gravy Train could get him to do more than twitch his nose and sigh. I'd called Theo, who warned that it could be the beginning of the end, and he promised to come over after work, to see if there was anything he could do to help.

I wasn't ready to give up. I dug through the pie safe, taking out all the remaining food to see if there was anything Gravy might find appetizing. As I pulled the cans out, I spied an unfamiliar container at the back of the shelf that I knew hadn't been there before. I took it out, a sleek metal canister with engraving across the front. DREAM BIG, HENLEY, it read. CONGRATS FROM CRYSTLE AND SHANE.

I could feel the blood squeezing through my heart, in one chamber and out another, my heartbeat vibrating my rib cage.

It had been a gift for an important occasion—graduation, I suspected. Shane must have made it himself, and as I turned it over in my hands, admiring the craftsmanship, I heard something rattle inside.

I removed the lid and tilted the cylinder, and a pill bottle slid into my hand. The prescription was made out to Shane. The label said Percocet, which he had taken when his back was acting up, and several tablets were nestled inside.

I thought of Henley at the funeral, her eyes catching mine for a brief moment, a flickering connection. I imagined her jimmying the sliding glass door the night before Thanksgiving, slipping into the house, and leaving the canister for me in a place she thought I would find it, but not before she left town. Henley had wanted to help, to do what she could to make things right for Shane.

I pictured him working in his shop, cutting her name into the metal, placing cash inside, maybe, or a rolled-up check, something ephemeral, the package itself the real gift, the part that would last, a keepsake that would survive them both.

I grabbed my things and rushed out the door to see Kendrick, calling Becca on the way to come sit with Gravy.

They're counterfeit, Kendrick said, when the test came back. *Laced with fentanyl. A single pill could have been enough to kill him, and if he believed he was taking his regular Percocet, he might have taken more than one.* Someone had switched out the pills, someone close to Shane. The Pettits had long been suspected of involvement in the local drug trade, according to Kendrick, though there had never been any firm evidence against them, no informant willing to utter the Pettit name.

It took one of their own to turn on them. Dex, Crystle, and Junior said nothing when Kendrick questioned them, and they were caught off guard when Raymond decided to talk. He might have done it to ease his conscience, or maybe because he was already in custody for the attempted murder of Jason Sullivan. The police had called Earl on the night he died, telling him that his son was a suspect in Henley's murder and they were coming out to see him. Raymond had gotten there first and taken Jason down to the river, where he beat him barehanded to the verge of death, leaving him in the snow to die, his body half in the frigid water. He was pulled over later with Jason's blood freckled across his face and beard, his shirt soaked through, hands stained red. He never said anything about Charlie being at the Sullivans' that night.

Jason was still alive, in the hospital in Kansas City, the fingers on one hand lost to frostbite, a section of skull removed to ease swelling in the brain. They didn't know if he would wake up, but he wouldn't likely be the same person if he did. Sympathy for him was in short supply, while all of Cutler County grieved the loss of Earl and blamed his son for driving him to his death.

With Raymond's cooperation and the mangled truck and the fentanyl pills looming over them, the Pettits talked, one after the other, each one trying to scurry out from under the shadow of blame, eager to shove someone else in their place. Junior wasn't willing to protect Dex, claiming his idiot nephew had brought the pickup to him and he hadn't wanted to help, hadn't wanted any part in it, but the vehicle was empty by then, the Calhouns already gone, he didn't know where. Dex ripped out the seats and burned them and Junior crushed the truck.

Dex caved next, pointing his finger at Crystle. The way he told it, Crystle went to collect Shane's money from Roger, because Shane was too much of a pussy to do it. Roger cussed her out and shoved her off the porch, claiming his daughter was with him for the weekend, that it'd have to wait. She took Dex with her the next night, and Shane's rifle, waiting for Roger to come home after dropping off Macey. They came out of the darkness, approaching Roger's truck in the driveway and spooking him. He said he didn't have the money, that the lawyer was bleeding him dry and he wasn't near done, and then he saw the gun and asked Crystle what the hell she was doing, calling her a string of foul names, a bitch, a liar, a whore.

Dex's and Crystle's stories diverged from there. Crystle said Roger got out of the truck and she raised the weapon in self-defense, while Dex said she aimed the rifle before he came out after her. Crystle wasn't one to let a man talk shit about her, according to Dex, and from what I knew of her now, it wouldn't have surprised me if she'd shot Roger for that reason alone. I wondered whether Crystle had lied about the nature of her affair with Roger—if she had been the one pursuing him, and he'd shut it down because of his friendship with Shane. That could have fueled her anger, put more pressure on her trigger finger. Roger wasn't around to ask, and Crystle wasn't likely to tell the truth. Dex claimed that Roger had hollered, as he exited the truck, that Macey was asleep in the back, but Crystle said she didn't hear him.

Raymond had filled in the rest. Shane had grown suspicious that they knew something about the Calhouns' murders, and Dex let it slip that Shane's gun had killed them. Shane couldn't live with that; it was eating away at him. He wanted Crystle to turn herself in. Junior considered him a liability and tried to keep him in line, suggesting that since his gun had been used in the murder, it would be easy to pin the crime on him. He'd made credible threats against our family, promising that if Shane tried to go to the police, we'd all be dead before he left the station.

So he had hidden the gun, left his note and key. In case something happened to him. He'd been trying to find a way out of the mess he was in without anyone else getting hurt, but the Pettits got impatient and decided the only way to be sure he'd keep quiet was to kill him.

In the end, just as Becca had said, Shane had tried to do the right thing. We'd never given him enough credit, and that guilt would stay with us, that he hadn't felt he could open up to us, turn to us for help. He'd wanted to protect his family, as he had always done. Kendrick arranged to have his body exhumed for testing, though the results wouldn't change what we already knew. That we'd lost him too soon, that nothing would bring him back.

Lily was home for the weekend, and we headed out into the woods behind the house with Gravy to cut a Christmas tree. It had warmed up a bit, reminding me of the freak eighty-degree day twenty Decembers ago when Shane and Becca and I had gone out in shorts and T-shirts to fetch a cedar. We'd come back itchy and sweating to find Dad home early from work, something that normally put us all on edge, but he was in an uncharacteristically good mood. Earl Sullivan had given everyone a Christmas ham and a bonus to celebrate the end of a hard year. Dad had brought home cold Cokes from the gas station and a beer for himself, and the five of us sat in the grass, Shane cracking jokes about the tree, which was too fat to fit in the door, all of us laughing. I didn't remember the gifts we got that year, which were surely not impressive, but I remembered the smell of the cedar, the heat of the sun on my winter skin, the way it felt to have my family all together. It had been hard for me to let go and enjoy the fleeting moments of Dad's kindness, unable to put aside all the terrible things he'd done, but Shane had managed it effortlessly. Out of all of us, he'd always had the most generous heart.

Lily and Gravy and I tromped together through the melting muck in the back field, Gravy wearing one of Lil's old turtleneck sweaters with the sleeves cut off. As usual, he had perked up with Lily there. He was acting almost frisky, bouncing in the mud on his stubby front legs, making us laugh. He would need a good bath.

Theo had stopped by after work earlier in the week to check on Gravy. I told him I had dinner in the oven and asked if he wanted to stay, and when he said yes, I had to explain that dinner was caramel apple pie, because I didn't like to cook anything but dessert. Dinner led to after-dinner drinks (the last of the margarita pouches from Walmart) and then we ended up on the couch watching *Dateline*. A near-perfect first date, in my opinion, and it had happened so naturally that it was hard to remember what I'd been so afraid of. We had made plans to get together with Lily and his girls over the holiday break. We'd take them to the square in Shade Tree to see the annual concert and light display and walk the dogs if Gravy was feeling up to it. Theo had run new blood work at Gravy's last office visit and gently informed me that the results were worse than expected. Gravy's kidneys wouldn't hold out much longer. He explained the signs to watch for and told me to call him at any hour if we needed him. Despite his deteriorating condition, Gravy seemed to have regained some of his hearing, a sign, Theo said, that he was coming out of mourning. He had started to look up whenever we said his name, or Shane's. Becca, of course, framed it as a miracle.

With a new year approaching and the old one coming to an end, Mom had become obsessed with getting rid of things. She'd reached the tipping point, she said, where you stop accumulating and start to let go. She didn't want to leave behind a house full of possessions like her own parents had done, for someone else to sort through. She was paring down Shane's things, too, tossing papers, clothes, anything that didn't remind her of who he was, the Shane we knew. She kept his drawings, his work jacket with PERFECT ATTENDANCE 2016 embroidered beneath the power company logo. I couldn't bring myself to throw out the old letters from the friends he'd lost touch with, the craft Charlie had made. I would keep these reminders of my brother's life, the things he loved, evidence of his impact in this world, because I couldn't bear to let him disappear. One day, maybe Lily would sort through my belongings and find these treasures and remember him, too.

While I knew Charlie wouldn't forget my brother, it made me sad to think of Shane not having children to pass down his stories, to carry his resemblance. I hadn't thought of Lily as some hedge against oblivion, a way to live on past death, but I was grateful to the point of guilt that I had her.

Hannah was taking things day by day, going to meetings, working part-time at a nail salon, rebuilding her fractured relationship with her parents. They'd been deeply hurt and disappointed by her when she was using, and Hannah had been bitter at their lack of support, but Macey's death had reminded the three of them how much they loved and needed one another. Theo had helped me find Hannah a rescue cat, an enormous ragged-eared tom with a knack for mousing who liked to sleep on her chest, a purring weight across her heart.

Hannah's grief counselor had suggested she take up crafting again, and Hannah had dragged me along, in the name of therapy, to a place in a strip mall where you painted while drinking wine. Hannah had painted the serenity prayer for me, the words embellished with flowers and butterflies: *God, grant me the serenity to accept the things I cannot change, courage to change the things I can, and wisdom to know the difference.*

I had attempted to paint a snowman, which seemed within my limited abilities—I had none of Shane's artistic talent—but its face came out all wrong and Hannah had nearly choked herself laughing at it, claiming it looked like something out of a horror film. It was good for me, she said, to loosen up and try new things, even if I failed sometimes.

Amid the recent turmoil, Hannah and I had crossed the threshold into genuine friendship. We understood each other, had fun together. I'd forgotten how good it felt to open up and let someone in, how necessary human connection was to our survival. Hannah had shown me that it was okay to enjoy myself even if life hadn't turned out the way I'd thought it would—that we had to go on living in the face of grief and loss and disappointment, accepting moments of peace and happiness when they came. It was hard for her, sometimes, when Lily was around. Seeing us together, mother and daughter, watching my child grow up, something Macey would never do.

We were all making adjustments as we came to terms with death, painfully aware that time was winding down for us all, some more quickly than others. I'd decided for the time being to remain in Shade Tree, close to Mom and Leola if they needed me, though while Lily was staying with Greg during the week, I'd start taking night classes toward my law degree. I wanted to make the most of whatever life I had left, and in the present moment, there wasn't much I would change. I would still be walking through the woods with Lily, watching my brother's dog roll in the mud, smiling at a sweet text from Theo. Shane's absence was a hole that couldn't be filled, but his death had brought Theo and Charlie and Leola into my life, and I was grateful for that. I thought of my brother, how we had drifted apart, all the time we'd lost, but there was nothing to be done about the past. I would do my best to embrace each day as an unfolding mystery with a thousand possible endings, reminding myself each night before I closed my eyes, Gravy snoring at the foot of the stairs, that while the days at times feel endless, nothing is guaranteed—that this dog might yet outlive me.

CHAPTER 32

HENLEY

JANUARY

H enley wasn't terribly surprised that Ellie Embry had opened her half-rotten mouth and regurgitated every single thing she knew about the Pettits. She was more surprised to learn that the cops had found Dalmire's bone, and that it wasn't even human. Maybe it was only a story, made up by Uncle Denny, like the one about starlings turning into witches at night, something to scare the kids, keep them in line. Perhaps Dalmire had escaped Blackwater much as she had, born again through a bitter baptism with a new name, living undetected on the margins. Or maybe Dalmire really had ended up in a hog trough but had left no bones behind. She didn't dwell on it.

The mountain town had a vacation feel, even though she was often at work. It wasn't hard to blend in with all the others who flocked there for the skiing or the seasonal jobs. She'd stayed in a youth hostel at first, where she bought a fake ID, claiming she wanted it to get into bars and using it instead to get a job. She'd dyed her hair brown in a gas station bathroom and gotten a girl at the hostel to cut it so it angled down just beneath her jaw, not that anyone was looking for her, and not that anyone here knew what a Pettit looked like, anyway. No one outside of Blackwater would see her hazel eyes and freckles and sturdy hips and equate them with trouble.

On a rare day off, like today, she'd snowshoe on the mountain. It had taken a while to acclimate to the altitude. She'd been warned about the thin air, and at first it was hard to breathe, but now she'd push herself to the limits of her endurance, feeling dizzy and weightless and free.

This new life was a gift Jason had unintentionally given her. The name on her license was Emily, a reminder of the strength and courage of Emily Sullivan, of how lucky Henley was to leave Blackwater. She didn't have to be a Pettit anymore. Her family thought she was dead. She wouldn't have to testify against them or be held accountable for what she knew, and Junior wouldn't be sending anyone after her.

She missed her mother, and Raymond, and kept up with them as best she could through the news and online gossip. She knew that Earl was dead, that she didn't have to worry about Jason anymore, that he would live out what was left of his life in a hospital or nursing home, unable to hurt anyone. If he somehow made a miraculous recovery he would be penniless from medical bills and have to settle for a public defender if charged with her murder. She wondered if she should have found a way to let Raymond know she'd survived, if that would have kept him from doing what he'd done, though knowing her uncle, it likely wouldn't have made a difference. He had a softer heart than his brothers but had no trouble punishing those he felt deserved it. He'd told her to disappear, to not look back, and maybe some part of him imagined that she'd made it out, that she had listened, that she was alive despite her silence.

Henley had worried how her mother would grieve her loss, if it might cause a relapse, though from what she could tell secondhand, Missy was holding up better than expected. She'd watched her own memorial, which someone had filmed and posted online. The Pettits and Beauforts and Rudds and other assorted relatives crowded into the farmhouse, Missy doing her best to be in charge. There were Dr Peppers and boxes of cream horns from Why Not Donuts spread out on the kitchen table.

Missy wore a bright new dress, and while she looked frail as a damaged butterfly, a faint hope lit her eyes. Henley knew from her mother's oversharing Facebook page that Missy was enrolled in outpatient rehab and had Earl Sullivan's personal attorney working to get her charges dismissed. Earl had willed most of his estate to the Sullivan charitable trust, signing papers to cut Jason out entirely just before his death and leaving a generous gift to his longtime housekeeper, fulfilling his promise to take care of Missy all the way to the grave. To the relief of the entire town, Earl had arrangements in place for Sullivan Grain to continue operations without him, running much as it had before, a portion of profits funneling into the trust that fed back into Blackwater. There would still be a Little League, a summer jobs program for disadvantaged teens, an Emily Sullivan Memorial Essay Contest, a city fireworks display on the Fourth of July. The Sullivan legacy would live on.

Missy led everyone out into the backyard, standing under the clothesline where Memaw used to hang the wash, next to the tractor shed, where Missy's dreams of being a Sullivan lay buried.

"Thank you for coming today," she said. The words squeaked out, barely audible, and she cleared her throat and started again.

"Thank you for coming today to honor Henley. Having her was the one smart thing I ever did, as you well know. We didn't have much at times, but Henley was always rich in family." The elders nodded, one of the Beauforts calling out, "Amen."

"Henley loved this farm," she continued. "She had roots here going back generations, and a piece of her will always be here with us. But I can't bury my girl and I think the good Lord made it that way. She wouldn't have wanted that. She didn't want to be pinned down to a piece of soil, marked with a stone."

"Praise Jesus." Heads nodded, hands raised heavenward.

"Fly where you want, baby," Missy said, her voice breaking as she flung her arms wide. "Your spirit's free. We'll see you on the other side."

Henley's chest ached as she watched the screen. Her mother had loved her intensely, despite everything, and she'd always carry that love inside her, a vital organ, a second heart.

A hymn started up, but Missy didn't join in. Henley understood if she wasn't quite ready for singing. There was so much to grieve and regret and repent, and in the moment, her mother appeared barely able to hold herself steady, keep her knees from bending toward the ground.

The shorn fields were desolate and empty, the lonely farmhouse exposed to the cruel winter wind, but Henley knew that in the spring the corn would grow, as it always did, that somehow Missy would find the strength to carry on. She was a Pettit, after all.

The hardest to leave behind was Charlie. It felt unbearable to stay silent when there was so much she wanted to say. She wanted to apologize for not telling him what had happened to Shane; to explain how everything had gone so terribly wrong; to let him know that she had held back her feelings for him only because she feared he would anchor her to the place she wanted to escape. She fantasized about showing up on his doorstep, taking a chance rather than leaving it up to fate. Maybe he'd be glad to see her, and maybe he wouldn't. Maybe she'd send him a postcard from a town she was passing through, to let him know that she was out there somewhere, thinking of him. A picture of the mountains, no name, no address, just the words *I miss you*, or maybe *I'm sorry*.

There was much to be sorry for. She understood what Earl had meant about filling a leaky bucket, trying to make up for the wrong he'd done and knowing he'd always come up short. It was impossible to atone for her family's sins, for the Calhouns or for Shane. She could only hope that she'd given the Kellers some closure when she left the pills for Sadie, the prescription bottle that Crystle had hastily stuffed into the pocket of her jeans the night Shane died.

She hoped that Shane had found peace, too. She wished there was more she could have done, that she could have stopped it somehow, and that would always haunt her. She thought of Shane looking at her through the other side of the viewfinder as she took his photo on his wedding day, the tiny stains on his clean white shirt, the river glittering behind him, his easy smile, his jay-blue eyes. His jokes would pop into her head at odd times.

Hey, Henley, what comes suddenly and never leaves?

A bad date, she'd said. Shane had cleared his throat and covered his mouth, trying not to laugh.

Death, he said. *The answer is death.*

She'd argued with him. Memaw had lingered for months as the cancer ate away at her; it wasn't sudden at all. They could feel it coming, like footsteps down a long hallway, striding ever closer. She wondered now if Shane had felt it coming for him, too.

That's dying, he'd said. *It's a process. We're all dying, all the time. Death flips a switch, just like that.* He'd snapped his fingers. *It all goes dark.*

She paused at an overlook to peer through the trees. The sky was deep sapphire blue, a saturated shade rarely seen in low-lying Kansas, the mountains that much closer to the edge of the sky. It was bright here, brighter than it ever got back home, the sun on the snow almost blinding. When summer came, she'd head farther north, as far as she could go, where ice veiled the peaks year round and the sun shined all day, never setting, so bright that every cell in her body would feel vividly, achingly alive. So bright that the darkness couldn't catch her, even when she closed her eyes.

ACKNOWLEDGMENTS

I couldn't get by without the support of my family. Hugs and gratitude to the McHughs, Runges, Berners, Gilpins, and Gipsons, and especially my mom, my brothers and sisters, Barb and Bill, and Piper, Harper, and Brent.

Thank you to Jill, Jen, Ann, Nina, and Allison for all things Beastie. Jill has many superpowers, including a knack for showing up at Starbucks when she is needed most, and I couldn't be more grateful to have her as my sister in crime.

Heartfelt thanks to the friends who support me in so many ways, including Elizabeth Anderson, Hilary Sorio, Angie Sloop, Nicole Coates, Sally Mackey, Liz Lea, Adonica Coleman, and Martha McKim. Thank you to Amy Engel for the thoughtful writing discussions. Many thanks to Jason Vinyard and Dave Abbott for offering their expertise, and a special shout-out to the awesome Kamella Neeley, who drove all the way from Arkansas to my reading in Oxford, where we struck up a friendship over books.

A huge thank-you to everyone at Spiegel & Grau and Penguin Random House. I am lucky to work with such talented people, including Beth Pearson, Amy Ryan, Maria Braeckel, Allyson Lord, and many others. I'm especially grateful to Annie Chagnot and my brilliant editor Cindy Spiegel. Eternal thanks to my agent, Sally Wofford-Girand, and to Judith Murray in the U.K.

As always, thank you to all the readers, writers, librarians, booksellers, bloggers, and everyone else out there supporting authors and sharing a love of books.

THE WOLF WANTS IN

LAURA McHUGH

A BOOK CLUB GUIDE

WHERE THE DARKNESS COMES FROM

LAURA McHUGH

(Reprinted with permission from Powells.com)

When I made my way through the local book club circuit after the publication of my first novel, *The Weight of Blood*, one topic came up again and again. People would remark that I seemed so normal, so *nice*—they were surprised that a pleasant Midwestern mom would write about such dark and disturbing crimes. I didn't have an easy answer prepared for the question that would inevitably arise: *Where does the darkness in your writing come from?* I would smile, and shrug, and drink more wine.

I used to think it was simply my nature, that the darkness was innate, but that's not quite true. My earliest writings were as innocuous as any other child's, though that wouldn't last long. As the youngest of eight children, I wasn't sheltered. By age five I'd seen horror films and centerfolds, knew the words to my brothers' favorite Black Sabbath songs. I already had secrets of my own. People think of the youngest child as coddled, but in a large, struggling family, it often means you're unsupervised or forgotten, that things might happen to you without anyone noticing.

When I was seven, my father, a Type A workaholic who smoked Swisher Sweets nonstop, had a heart attack and flatlined. He was resuscitated with a memory of a tranquil field, a voice telling him that it wasn't his time. He decided to make a drastic change, to quit his job and retreat to the countryside. We moved from Iowa, where we'd been surrounded by friends and extended family, to the Ozark Mountains, where we lived in a remote and rough-hewn house in the woods between the East Wind commune and the compound of extremist group the Covenant, the Sword, and the Arm of the Lord. A woman from the commune jogged past us, topless, as we waited for the school bus. When we met our nearest neighbor, an elderly widow, she warned, "If you see a grave in the woods, keep walking." I learned that scorpions can crawl up the covers and into your bed. That tarantulas migrate in the fall, lurking in the trees and crossing roads in unsettling hordes. I didn't know it at the time, but I was gathering material for what would one day be my first novel.

In this vast and ominous wilderness, my world narrowed. We were miles from anything resembling a town, my only companions two teenage siblings restless for escape. Our father did not believe in leisure or idleness. During any spare moment of daylight, we were put to work hauling wood, weeding the enormous vegetable garden, and picking rocks, a chore as dreary as it was endless. I was in second grade and felt like I'd joined a chain gang.

We were poor, desperately so. My father opened a shoe repair shop but had trouble carving out a living in a community wary of outsiders. He made barters when he could, repairing sewing machines at the commune in exchange for rabbits. Dad had a volatile temper, and the slow country life did nothing to calm him. He would make me get down on my knees every day and tie his shoes. He expected our absolute obedience, and earned it through fear. I tried to be small and quiet, to draw no attention to myself, to disappear.

The only work my mother could find was a live-in position cooking and cleaning for an elderly woman on weekends, and without her tempering presence in the house, we grew feral. I couldn't sleep at night; my mind and body tensed in a constant state of alert. My brother and I shared an unfinished basement bedroom with one tiny window near the rafters. Spiders congregated above my bunk. When it rained, water seeped in through the cracked concrete floor, and the blood-red carpet remnant at the center of the room floated and grew toadstools.

I longed to be anywhere else, and I found my escape in stories. I wasn't picky. I devoured stacks of my mother's old *True Story* magazines and Nancy Drew mysteries with brittle brown pages. I read the classics my older siblings brought home from school, *Ethan Frome* and *Animal Farm* and *Of Mice and Men*. There was no library in town, so when school closed for the summer, there were no more books. The black-and-white TV, with its three channels, was my savior. While my dad was at work, I'd lose myself in *Little House on the Prairie* and *Scooby-Doo* and *The Facts of Life*. When the TV was struck by lightning, we couldn't afford to replace it. I felt empty, scraped bare. When my children, with their iPads and pool memberships and overflowing bookshelves, say they are bored, I tell them about that summer, how my sister and I spent an entire afternoon watching a dung beetle as it tried and failed to roll a ball of manure over the threshold of our house like a humble backwoods Sisyphus.

I had an abyss of time, and nothing to fill it but my own mind. In the long, dull hours of hauling rocks and clearing brush, I imagined other people's lives. I made up stories, sometimes about girls like me, girls who wanted something different from what they had but didn't know how to get it. They struggled against the same obstacles, but I made them braver than me, stronger, more resourceful. These stories were dark, but there were hints of hope, moments of levity—the bits of light that keep darkness from consuming you, in real life and on the page.

When I was in junior high, my mother read a story I turned in for an assignment. It was about a girl who killed her father with a chainsaw while they were out cutting wood. Mom asked where I got such awful ideas. I wondered where I could have gotten ideas of any other kind. I'd spent countless hours covered in sweat and sawdust, had watched my dad lurch into the house roaring like a bear, drenched in blood, after the chainsaw kicked back and tore open his throat. What other sort of story would I write?

My novels revolve around crimes, but at the heart, I'm always focused on the characters and their families—the lives they scrape out in unseen corners, the sacrifices they make for each other, the things they do to survive. There are pieces of myself in each book. I've been inspired by real crimes in the rural communities where I grew up, and The Wolf Wants In was especially personal, inspired by the unresolved death of my brother. I've been asked if writing about disturbing things takes a toll, if it depresses me, makes me fearful. Writing doesn't take me to dark places. It brings relief, bleeding out the darkness like leeches, making room for more light to seep in.

My mother hasn't disowned me over any of my stories. She told me that she'd pledged long ago not to get angry if I published things she didn't like; she always knew I'd be a writer. In return, I make sure to tell people that none of the bad mothers in my novels are based on her. She is the one who taught me the importance of books. When I complain about my childhood, she says that it gave me something to write about.

Recently I asked my mom what had happened to a mean old goat we had in the Ozarks. She reminded me that we had kept him tethered with a boat anchor so he could roam but not get far, and then one day he was gone, anchor and all, so she assumed someone had stolen him.

"Don't you think it's more likely," I said, "that he made it to the woods, the anchor got stuck, he starved to death or was eaten by coyotes, and some hunter will find a skeleton chained to an anchor in the middle of nowhere and wonder what the hell happened?"

She asked how I could think such a terrible thing. I smiled. I didn't tell her my other, worse, ideas. (No one liked that goat; I wasn't convinced that his demise was an accident.) I knew her question was rhetorical, that she didn't want a reply, so I didn't say it out loud: *What else would you expect from me?*

QUESTIONS AND TOPICS FOR DISCUSSION

1. Siblings Becca, Shane, and Sadie grew up in an abusive home. How did this shape them and their relationships with one another, and how did it affect their lives and relationships as adults, even after their father had passed away?

2. After Shane's death, Becca and Sadie learn that their brother had been keeping secrets from them, including financial and marital problems, but also good things, such as his relationships with Charlie and Leola. Why do you think he kept so much hidden from his family? How did Sadie answer that question and make peace with it in the end? Have you ever discovered something surprising after the passing of a loved one?

3. Addiction touches many of the characters in the small town of Blackwater, either directly or indirectly. Hannah struggles with prescription painkillers; Henley grows up with an addicted mother in a family of drug dealers; Sadie witnesses the fallout of the epidemic in

her job as a social worker. In what ways both obvious and unexpected does the opioid epidemic impact families and entire communities?

4. Haunted by the tragic death of his sister, Emily, and the loss of his young wife, Earl Sullivan tries to be a good person and sometimes fails. How did Emily's death impact Earl? Was there anything he could have done to prevent his son's crimes? Do you think his failures outweighed his good intentions? In the end, what drove him to take his own life?

5. When Henley gets involved with Jason Sullivan, she has no idea that the relationship will become abusive. Did her situation make her more vulnerable to Jason's controlling nature, or would anyone have been susceptible to his manipulations? What tactics did he use to gain control? What were some of the early warning signs that Henley missed or disregarded?

6. Sadie and Hannah are unlikely friends. What draws them together before and after Hannah's daughter's disappearance? How does Hannah's addiction affect their friendship? How do they help each other heal?

7. With some amount of closure in Shane's case, Sadie seems to accept the fleeting nature of life, stating, "This dog might yet outlive me." Determined to make the most of the time she has, she opens herself up to new dreams and new relationships, including a romance with Theo, Shane's childhood friend and Gravy's veterinarian. What role did Shane's dog, Gravy, play in helping Sadie and her family navigate life without Shane and come to terms with his death? How is Sadie's relationship with Theo different from her relationship with her ex-husband, Greg? Do you foresee a happy ending for her?

8. At the end of the novel, Henley has left everything behind and started a new life, just as she'd always dreamed, though she brings one piece of Blackwater with her: Her new name is Emily, after Emily Sullivan. What significance did Emily have in Henley's life? Do you think Henley will truly be able to escape her family and her past? How will Missy and Charlie move forward without her? How do you think Shane would have felt about Henley's efforts to give closure to his family?

9. What was your interpretation of the title *The Wolf Wants In*? Did its meaning change for you over the course of the book?

LAURA MCHUGH is the internationally bestselling author of the novels *The Weight of Blood*, winner of an International Thriller Writers Award, a Silver Falchion Award for best first novel, and the Missouri Author Award, and *Arrowood*, an International Thriller Writers Award finalist for best novel. Her short story "Endgame" was nominated for a Pushcart Prize in 2019. McHugh lives in Missouri with her husband and daughters.

Facebook.com/lauramchughauthor
Twitter: @LauraSMcHugh
Instagram: @lauramchughauthor

RANDOM HOUSE BOOK CLUB

Because Stories Are Better Shared

Discover

Exciting new books that spark conversation every week.

Connect

With authors on tour—or in your living room. (Request an Author Chat for your book club!)

Discuss

Stories that move you with fellow book lovers on Facebook, on Goodreads, or at in-person meet-ups.

Enhance

Your reading experience with discussion prompts, digital book club kits, and more, available on our website.

Join our online book club community!

📘 🅖 randomhousebookclub.com

Random House Book Club ™

Because Stories Are Better Shared

RANDOM HOUSE